Joanna couldn't stop staring at him.

He was big, wide-shouldered, long-legged and narrow-hipped, and well over six feet tall. But it wasn't the perfection of his body that held Joanna spellbound. It was his rugged, masculine face. Straight, jet-black hair that touched his collar at the back of his neck had blown down across his forehead, escaping his Stetson. Over his left eye, he wore a black patch. And the look he was giving her unnerved her.

"Can you help me?" she asked him.

He dismounted his horse slowly, crossed his arms over his chest and inspected Joanna from head to toe. And when he stepped toward her, she stepped back....

Dear Reader,

We've got six drop-dead-gorgeous and utterly irresistible heroes for you this month, starting with Marilyn Pappano's latest contribution to our HEARTBREAKERS program. Dillon Boone, in *Survive the Night,* is a man on the run—right into Ashley Benedict's arms. The only problem is, will they survive long enough to fulfill their promises of forever?

Our ROMANTIC TRADITIONS title is Judith Duncan's *Driven to Distraction,* a sexy take on the younger man/older woman theme. I promise you that Tony Parnelli will drive right into your heart. *A Cowboy's Heart,* Doreen Roberts' newest, features a one-time rodeo rider who's just come face-to-face with a woman—and a secret—from his past. Kay David's *Baby of the Bride* is a marriage-of-convenience story with an adorable little girl at its center—and a groom you'll fall for in a big, bad way. *Blackwood's Woman,* by Beverly Barton, is the last in her miniseries, THE PROTECTORS. And in J.T. Blackwood she's created yet another hero to remember. Finally, Margaret Watson returns with her second book, *An Honorable Man.* Watch as hero Luke McKinley is forced to confront the one woman he would like never to see again—the one woman who is fated to be his.

Enjoy them all, and come back next month for more great romantic reading—here in Silhouette Intimate Moments.

Yours,

Leslie Wainger
Senior Editor and Editorial Coordinator

Please address questions and book requests to:
Silhouette Reader Service
U.S.: 3010 Walden Ave., P.O. Box 1325, Buffalo, NY 14269
Canadian: P.O. Box 609, Fort Erie, Ont. L2A 5X3

BLACKWOOD'S WOMAN

BEVERLY BARTON

Silhouette®

INTIMATE™ MOMENTS®

Published by Silhouette Books

America's Publisher of Contemporary Romance

SILHOUETTE BOOKS

ISBN 0-373-07707-6

BLACKWOOD'S WOMAN

Printed in U.S.A.

BEVERLY BARTON

has been in love with romance since her grandfather gave her an illustrated copy of *Beauty and the Beast*. An avid reader since childhood, she began writing at the age of nine and wrote short stories, poetry, plays and novels through high school and college. After marriage to her own "hero" and the births of her daughter and son, she chose to be a full-time homemaker, a.k.a. wife, mother, friend and volunteer.

When she returned to writing, she joined Romance Writers of America and helped found the Heart of Dixie chapter in Alabama. Since the release of her first Silhouette book in 1990, she has won the Georgia Romance Writers' Maggie Award, the National Readers' Choice Award and has been an RWA RITA finalist. Beverly considers writing romance books a real labor of love. Her stories come straight from the heart, and she hopes that all the strong and varied emotions she invests in her books will be felt by everyone who reads them.

To three loyal, caring and supportive friends,
Edwina Bressette, Gail Froelich and Sheila Hargett.
This love story is for each of you, for very special and
completely individual reasons.

Prologue

Trinidad, New Mexico
September 1925

*We met in our special place today and made love for the
last time. Tomorrow Ernest, the boys and I will leave New
Mexico and return to Virginia, and I will never see Benjamin Greymountain again. No, that isn't quite true, for I will
see Benjamin through my precious memories until the day
I die. We cannot be together, and yet we shall never truly be
apart.*

*I had not experienced passion and real love until I met
Benjamin. I would give my life to save his, but I cannot stay
with him. I have given him my heart forever, but I cannot
share my life with him.*

*He brought two rings with him. They are beautiful, intri-
cately carved silver bands, each embedded with three small
turquoise stones to represent the two of us and the child we
can never have together. When he placed my ring upon my
finger, I wept. He brushed away my tears and told me that*

*he loved me. Then I placed his ring upon his finger and we
pledged ourselves to each other for all eternity.*

*If only there weren't so many obstacles standing in the
way of our happiness. No, I must not dwell on what could
have been if our lives and the world around us were different. I must be thankful to have known such love, to have
experienced such ecstasy.*

*For as long as I live—indeed, for as long as my soul ex-
ists—I shall love Benjamin Greymountain, and know that
my love is returned in equal measure.*

Joanna couldn't bear to read another word. She closed
her great-grandmother's diary, tied the worn leather volume with the yellowed ribbon and laid the book inside her
suitcase.

For the past six months, ever since she had returned to live
in her parents' home and discovered the diary in Annabelle
Beaumont's old trunk in the attic, Joanna had found sol-
ace in her ancestress's tragic love story.

In a world gone mad around her, Joanna had lost the
ability to believe in love; and she could not imagine ever
finding joy and passion in sex.

She had to admit that the months of therapy had helped,
but nothing could ever erase the nightmarish memories of
that fiendish face or the feel of those bruising hands. Even
knowing that she and the three other women who'd bravely
testified had put their attacker in prison for the rest of his
life could never erase the past nor undo the pain. His punishment did not end their punishment. What he had done to
them, and to others, had irrevocably changed their lives
forever. Had changed Joanna's life forever....

Her fiancé had deserted her, her overprotective mother
treated her as if she were dying, and she had resigned from
her job at the museum, unable to cope with being around
people every day. People who whispered behind her back.

But she knew she could not go on forever in this state of
recovery. She was young and healthy, with the rest of her life
ahead of her. And she had decided that she did not want to
stay in Richmond where everyone knew what had hap-

pened to her, where her mother smothered her with attention, where she might run into her ex-fiancé and his new girlfriend. She'd made up her mind weeks ago, but had told her mother only today.

She, Joanna Beaumont, was moving to Trinidad, New Mexico, to find a new life, to paint the land and the people her great-grandmother had found so fascinating, and to dream of finding a man who would love her the way Benjamin Greymountain had loved Annabelle. A tender, sensitive and gentle man.

Joanna lifted from her suitcase a small leather pouch that had been tied to the diary she'd found in Annabelle's trunk. She loosened the drawstring, turned the pouch upside down and dumped the contents into her hand. She stared at the exquisitely lovely silver-and-turquoise ring, then picked it up and slipped it on the third finger of her right hand. It was a perfect fit.

Chapter 1

No. Absolutely, positively no. Not now. Not today. Not on this lonely stretch of road. Not when it was ninety degrees in the shade.

Glancing at the red warning signal, Joanna Beaumont groaned. What could be wrong? Her Jeep Ranger was less than four years old and she had it serviced regularly. How dare it cause her a problem when she took such good care of it!

She wondered just how far she could drive with the warning light on before the vehicle quit. She was miles away from the ranch, even farther from Trinidad, and she'd left the reservation behind nearly two hours ago.

Clouds of white steam rose from beneath the Ranger's hood. Damn! That had to mean either the radiator was overheating or one of those stupid hoses had burst.

Admitting defeat, at least temporarily, Joanna pulled the Jeep to the side of the road, cut the engine and sat there fuming for several minutes. Well, no use just sitting. She popped the hood, opened the door, got out and marched around to the front of the Jeep. Water. She heard water dripping. No, she heard water pouring.

Billows of steam gushed from the engine. Joanna kicked the front bumper, then yelped when pain shot through her foot. If it had been a flat tire, she could have fixed it, but this was altogether different.

She gazed up at the midafternoon sun, blinding in its intensity. Elena and Alex were in Santa Fe and wouldn't be home until late, so if she called the ranch, she'd have to ask Cliff Lansdell to help her. It wasn't that she disliked the ranch foreman, it was just that Cliff had a difficult time accepting the fact she wasn't interested in a relationship with him.

When the steam began to subside, Joanna leaned over cautiously and peeped beneath the hood. At first she couldn't see anything wrong, then she noticed a small tear in the radiator hose. Dammit! Well, she didn't have any choice. She'd just have to call Cliff and allow him to play her knight in shining armor.

Perspiration beaded on her forehead. Late springtime in northern New Mexico might be cooler than in the southern part of the state, but daytime temperatures could still rise to smoldering degrees in the month of May. When she'd first come to Trinidad, over four years ago, Joanna would have expected nothing but an arid desert region, had it not been for Annabelle Beaumont's descriptions of the mountains and trees and crystal-clear streams.

Slipping inside the Jeep, Joanna lifted her cellular phone and dialed the Blackwood ranch. The phone didn't ring. What now? Glancing at the phone's digital face, she saw that the battery was low. It was her own fault; she'd forgotten to charge the battery last night. How could she have been so stupid?

Now what was she going to do? Well, there was only one thing to do—start walking. It was a good ten miles to the ranch house, but if she was lucky, someone she knew would come along and give her a lift. Trinidad was a small town and she knew practically the whole population.

Locking the Jeep, Joanna swung her enormous leather purse, containing her 25-mm semiautomatic, over her shoulder and headed straight up the road. She hadn't gone far when she thought she heard the sound of drums—somewhere far away, just a distant rumble. Perhaps it was thunder. Well, rain in New Mexico wasn't impossible. Maybe an electrical storm was brewing. Glancing up, she saw the sky was still clear. And blue, so incredibly blue. Sparse, virgin-white fluffs of cloud floated overhead.

Lowering her eyes to protect them from the glare of the sun, she saw a horse and a lone rider on a nearby flat-topped hill toward the north. Blinking once, twice, she felt certain the image was a mirage. But no. They were still there. A big man astride a magnificent black-and-white Appaloosa.

The sky at their backs, the afternoon sun coating them with a coppery gold glow, man and horse resembled a bronze statue. Joanna's heart pounded. Her palms grew clammy. There was nothing to fear—not in Trinidad, not from the fine people she knew and respected. Surely this man was from the ranch, a hand she would recognize as soon as he rode closer.

But he did not move, simply sat there high above her, staring down at her. She waved at him. He didn't respond.

"Hey, there, are you from the Blackwood ranch?" she called out as she walked off the road and began to climb the hill. "My radiator hose sprung a leak."

The man didn't answer her, but he did direct his horse into movement. She continued toward her potential rescuer; he rode slowly in her direction. Joanna swung her purse across her chest, unzipped the top pouch and felt inside for her gun. She sighed when she felt the cool metal. If this man turned out to be a stranger, he was a possible threat. Joanna never took chances when it came to her safety. Since surviving the brutal rape nearly five years ago, she had purchased a small handgun and taken several self-defense classes.

When the horse stopped a good twenty feet away, Joanna stared at the rider. She didn't recognize the man, had never seen him before in her life, and yet she had the oddest sensation that she somehow knew him. Her whole body trembled, but the quivering riot was contained within, showing only a slight tremor in her hands. She could not stop staring at the man even though the very sight of him created a sense of foreboding.

He was big, wide-shouldered, long-legged and narrow-hipped, and probably well over six feet tall. But it was not the perfection of his body that held Joanna spellbound; it was his gloriously rugged masculine face. Straight, jet black hair that touched his collar at the back of his neck had blown down across his forehead, escaping his tan Stetson. Over his left eye he wore a black patch. He glared at her with his uncovered eye, the look unnerving her. Joanna swallowed, and tried to look away. She couldn't.

In one glance she took in his long, straight nose, his cleft chin, and the hard set of his full lips. Whoever he was, he was Native American, or at least part Native American. If he was Navajo, perhaps he would respond to their standard greeting.

"Yá' át' ééh," she said.

He merely glared at her even harder, and she instinctively knew he had understood her words.

In the four years she had lived in New Mexico, she had accomplished her goals of building a new life and establishing herself as an artist, but her romantic fantasy of finding a man like Annabelle's Benjamin Greymountain had remained an elusive dream. Until now.

Don't be ridiculous, she told herself. Stop acting like an idiot. She forced herself to look directly at the horse. Breathing in deeply, she took several tentative steps in the stranger's direction.

"Can you help me?" she asked. "My Jeep ran hot and I need to get to the Blackwood ranch."

He dismounted slowly, placing one booted foot and then the other on the ground. Joanna swallowed hard. He was a lot taller than six feet. Closer to six-four. And his eye wasn't brown as she'd thought; it was some light shade of amber and almost translucent in its paleness.

He stared at her, unsmiling, his brow wrinkled. He crossed his arms over his chest and inspected Joanna from head to toe. She slipped her hand inside her open purse, clutching her gun. Her instincts warned her that this man was dangerous, but somehow she didn't think he intended to do her any bodily harm.

"Look, I need to get to the Blackwood ranch. The main house is about ten miles from here," Joanna said.

He took a step toward her. Without thinking, she stepped backward. Realizing what she'd done, she stopped, tilted her chin and looked directly at him.

"Can you help me or not?" What was the matter with him? Was he deaf?

"I won't be heading back toward the Blackwood ranch for a while." His deep baritone voice had a gritty quality, a gravelly tone.

"Are you a new ranch hand?"

"No."

She wished he would quit inspecting her. She was beginning to feel like a bug under a microscope. "You realize you're on Blackwood property out here, don't you?"

Just a hint of a smile twitched his lips and then vanished completely, returning his mouth to its former frown. "If you're not in a hurry to get back to the house, you're welcome to come with me. Otherwise—" he glanced at the long, lonely stretch of road "—you'll have to walk."

Was he out of his mind? Did he think she'd go riding off only God knew where, with a total stranger? "Can't you take me to the ranch and then come back and do whatever it is you were going to do?"

"Why should I change my plans?" Uncrossing his arms, he stroked the big Appaloosa stallion's neck.

"I suppose saying it would be the gentlemanly thing to do would have no meaning for you, would it?"

"None whatsoever," he said, turning his back to her. "Well, what's it going to be? Are you riding with me or are you walking?"

She had every intention of telling him she would walk. Removing her hand from her purse, she turned around and faced the road. She glanced over her shoulder and saw him mounting his horse. The sun reflected off the silver ring on the third finger of his right hand. Since living in New Mexico she'd seen countless silver-and-turquoise rings, but none that was identical to the one she wore—Annabelle Beaumont's keepsake of love. The ring the stranger wore was an exact match. Was it possible that it was Benjamin Grey-mountain's ring? But how would this man have come into possession of the ring?

The stranger motioned the Appaloosa forward, coming straight toward Joanna. Slowing the horse to a standstill, he leaned his body to one side.

"Last chance." He held out his hand.

Joanna stared at his big hand, her vision focusing on the silver ring. Her heart hammered in her chest; the beating thundered in her ears. She looked up into his dark face—into that pale amber eye—and swayed toward him. She felt as if he was beckoning her.

"Who are you?" she asked, her heartbeat roaring in her ears like a hurricane wind.

"Who wants to know?" He stared at her, his gaze hard and intense.

"I'm Joanna Beaumont. I live on the Blackwood ranch."

Withdrawing his outstretched hand, he inspected her from head to toe, as if she were a prize piece of horseflesh he was considering buying. Joanna stiffened her back, clenched her teeth and glared at him. Just who did he think he was? He's an arrogant, macho bastard, Joanna answered her own question.

"So, you're the Southern belle from Virginia who converted one of the old bunkhouses into a home."

He focused his attention on her face, then ran his gaze down her throat and to the V of her partially unbuttoned blouse. A wide trickle of sweat cascaded down her throat and between her breasts. She didn't like the way he was looking at her, and yet her body responded to his blatantly sexual appraisal. Her nipples tightened, jutting outward, and she knew he saw their hardened outlines pressing against her damp blouse.

"How do you know who I am?" If he didn't stop staring at her, she was going to scream.

"My sister has sung your praises to me on numerous occasions, Ms. Beaumont."

"Your sister? Elena?"

He nodded. The corners of his lips twitched as if he were going to smile. But he didn't. He just kept staring at her, the heat of his gaze unnerving her.

"Then you're—"

"J.T. Blackwood."

They stared at each other for endless moments, the hot sun beating down on them, an eerie quiet all around.

"If you're not in a big hurry to get back to the ranch, I'll give you a lift." J.T. broke the silence, damning himself for allowing this fiery redhead to arouse him. He had learned long ago that "ladies" fascinated by the "noble savage" were to be avoided at all costs. "When we get back to the ranch, I'll send someone to take care of your Jeep."

Joanna hesitated. She knew all about Elena's older half brother, the owner of the Blackwood ranch. And what Joanna knew about the man, she didn't like. He represented everything she disapproved of in a man. He was a big, rugged, untamed macho guy, a former Secret Service agent who was now a partner in a private security firm based in Atlanta, Georgia. And according to Elena, he had never had a truly serious and meaningful relationship in his life.

"Look, lady, are you riding with me or are you walking back to the ranch?"

He held out his hand to her again. She stared at the silver-and-turquoise ring on his finger. Benjamin Greymountain's ring.

She would be stupid if she walked ten miles when she could ride, wouldn't she? And it wasn't as if J.T. Blackwood was a stranger. She'd be perfectly safe with him. Besides, if he pulled any type of macho stunt, he just might not be safe with her.

She reached out to him; he grasped her arm, lifting her off her feet. He swept her up onto the horse, placing her in front of him and draping his arm around her waist. Joanna closed her eyes, willing her heart to quiet, questioning her own sanity. From what she'd heard, she didn't even like J.T. Blackwood. So why was she aroused by his very nearness?

J.T. guided the horse from a slow trot down the flat-topped hill and into a steady gallop across the road, then up into the wooded area at the very edge of the Blackwood property. Joanna glanced down at his muscular arm that held her close to him. She felt the hardness of his chest, felt the heat from his body and could not mistake the ridge in his jeans that pressed against her hip.

A sudden sense of panic swept through her. Had she lost her mind? Had the past taught her nothing?

"Where—where are you going?" she asked.

"To a small stream a little higher up the mountain here. It's a place I've thought about for years," he said. "I've been gone a long time. I just wanted to see if things were the way I remembered them."

She tried not to lean back against him, but the upward climb made sitting straight impossible. His arm tightened around her. She sucked in a loud breath. "You don't visit the ranch often, do you? I've been living in Trinidad for over four years, and we've never met."

"I come back about once a year," he said.

"It seems your yearly visits the past few years have coincided with my trips to Virginia to visit my mother."

"Yeah, well, I thought it best."

"What do you mean? Are you saying that you deliberately timed your visits for when I was away?"

"Yeah."

"But why? I don't understand."

"My sister's been trying to play matchmaker, wanting to throw the two of us together. Don't tell me you didn't know."

"No, I had no idea." Joanna tensed as he tightened his hold about her waist and the bulge in his jeans pressed harder against her. She tried to scoot away from him, but had no room to maneuver.

"Elena likes you a lot," he said. "I'm not sure why, but since she's determined to see me married off, she's been pitching you as a candidate ever since you two became friends."

"I assure you, Mr. Blackwood, that I had no idea Elena was trying to— Well, I could have let her know I'm not the least bit interested. She's told me all about you, and you're not the type of man I want."

"Is that right?" He whispered the words against her ear, his warm breath fanning the loose tendrils that had escaped her ponytail.

She shivered, the motion completely involuntary. Her body ached with the start of a sweet longing that had lain dormant in her for a long time. For five years. No matter how many men she'd dated—and there had been quite a few—she had never felt any real desire—until now. And she didn't understand why; if and when she gave herself to a man, she would be the one in control. And a man like J.T. Blackwood would never relinquish his power to anyone, most certainly not a woman.

J.T. spread his big hand out across Joanna's waist, resting the tips of several fingers on her stomach. She drew in a sharp breath and squirmed against him. Why the hell didn't she sit still? J.T. thought. He was already so aroused he felt he was going to burst out of his jeans. She had to know how he was feeling. Was she taunting him?

He hated the effect Joanna had on him. He wasn't accustomed to such a strong, instant attraction, not since he'd been a teenager and got hard just smelling a girl's perfume.

And Joanna Beaumont was the last woman on earth he wanted to get all hot and bothered about. She was like the girl old John Thomas Blackwood had picked out for him to marry years ago. The girl who'd laughed in his face and told him bedding an Indian was fun and exciting, but marrying one was something she'd never do. Oh, yeah, he'd known his share of pretty, wealthy socialites over the years—women who couldn't get enough of him in bed, but were ashamed to introduce him to their friends.

As J.T. caressed her waist and stomach, Joanna told herself not to be afraid. If he tried anything, she'd shoot him. She laid her hand over his, halting his caress.

"How do you like living on the ranch?" he asked.

"I love it." His hand beneath hers felt hard and hot and tense.

"I wasn't in favor of your renovating the bunkhouse, but Elena insisted." J.T. threaded his fingers through hers, gripping her hand in his strong grasp.

"Did Elena tell you that we met a few months after I moved to Trinidad and in less than a year we became good friends?" He didn't respond; and he didn't release his hold on her hand. "I persuaded her to rent the unused bunkhouse to me. She said that once you'd seen what I did to it, you'd approve."

"I've seen it," he said. "It's very…Southwestern. You've obviously spent quite a bit of money on the place."

His breath was warm against the top of her head. Joanna hated the way this big, dark man made her feel. It had been such a long time since she'd felt anything close to sexual desire that she had a difficult time understanding her reaction to J.T. Blackwood. But she couldn't deny that she ached and throbbed with a need she thought had died the night Lenny Plott had raped her.

"I make a very good living with my paintings. Oil and watercolor. And my charcoal and ink drawings are in great demand." Joanna jerked on her hand, wanting desperately to free herself from his hold.

He released her hand, but kept his arm around her waist. "Yeah, I suppose you do. You're talented. I'll give you that. I've seen a couple of your paintings. The ones you gave

Elena. You painted them on the Navajo reservation, didn't you?''

Joanna noticed they were moving higher into the mountains, the path becoming smooth near the ridge, the cottonwood trees more abundant. The sun had moved lower in the western sky. Somewhere in the distance she heard the sound of flowing water.

"You didn't grow up on the reservation, did you?" she asked and immediately felt his body tense. Had she said something wrong?

"You knew the minute you saw me, didn't you?" The words growled from his throat.

"Knew what?" she asked.

"Even before I told you I was Elena's half brother, you took one look at me and knew I wasn't a white man, that I wasn't a *bilagáana*. You even called out a Navajo greeting to me."

"Yes, of course, I knew. Considering the part of New Mexico we're in, I assumed you were Navajo, or at least part Navajo." Was that it? Did he resent his Native American heritage as much as Elena said he did? Did he dislike having his ancestry recognized? If so, he was certainly the exception to the rule. The Navajo she had met while living in New Mexico had all been fiercely proud of being one of the *Diné*, as they called themselves. "You should be proud of your Native American heritage."

"So polite," he said. "So politically correct. Not Indian or redskin or savage, but Native American." He clicked his tongue against the roof of his mouth. "Such a Southern lady."

"What gave me away?" She tried to sound teasing, hoping to defuse some of the tension radiating between them. "Couldn't have been my accent."

"What's the real reason a Southern belle like you is living in New Mexico, roughing it?"

She thought the sound he made might have been a begrudging chuckle, but it sounded more like a fractured grunt.

"I'm sure Elena told you that I came out here to paint. I'm fascinated by the land and by the people."

"So you're fascinated by the noble savage, huh? Do you have a particular fascination for half-breed Navajo men?"

"You're being insulting." Joanna resented the way he made her interest in the Navajo seem sordid and ugly. His comment tarnished her foolish dream of finding true love the way Annabelle Beaumont had done.

"For the record, I'm half Navajo and half Scotch-Irish." He eased his arm from her waist down to her belly, his hand pushing her backward, forcing her hips deeper into his arousal.

"Stop it!" She inadvertently squirmed against him as she maneuvered her purse in front of her where she could reach inside. "Take your hands off me. I knew Elena's big brother had a reputation for being a real stud with the ladies, but I didn't think he was the type to force himself on a woman."

"Are you kidding?" J.T.'s laughter was hard and cold. "I've never forced myself on a woman. They usually throw themselves at me."

Joanna jerked out the 25-mm. If this brute thought he could intimidate her, then he had another thought coming. No one controlled Joanna Beaumont except Joanna Beaumont!

J.T. saw the gun in her hand. Hellfire! What did she think she was going to do, shoot him? What was wrong with her, anyway? She'd made it abundantly clear she didn't like him, that his reputation had preceded him and she'd been put off by what Elena had told her about him. But he couldn't control his arousal any more than she seemed able to control her obvious desire for him. But if she thought he was going to force anything on her, she was crazy. He'd assumed she was as hot as he was.

The moment he'd seen her a few yards away from the stalled Jeep, J.T. had known the redhead had to be Elena's friend Joanna Beaumont. His half sister had been trying to pair him up with the Virginia debutante for the past three years. But the last thing J.T. wanted was to be part of some spoiled Southern belle's New Mexico adventure. She wouldn't be the first woman in his life to think a brief affair with a half-breed exciting.

But this trip home to the ranch was going to be a vacation. The first real vacation J.T. had had in the six years since he'd left the Secret Service and joined Sam Dundee's private security agency in Atlanta.

"Put your gun away, lady. I'm no threat to you. I like my women willing, believe me."

"Well, I'm not willing. Not now. Not ever." She clutched the gun tightly. "I want you to take me to the ranch house right this minute!"

"I told you when I offered you a ride that it would be a while before I went back that way." J.T. guided Washington closer to the stream.

"And I just told you to take me back to the ranch house right now. If you're smart, you'll do what I tell you to do. After all, I have a gun and you don't."

"Lady, is this any way to treat a man doing you a favor?"

"I don't consider your coming on to me as doing me a favor. I asked for help, not for you to...to—" she sought for the right word "—for you to proposition me."

He snorted. "I didn't proposition you. I just asked if half-breed men fascinated you."

"And you—you—" He had pulled her against him, making her acutely aware of the fact that he was still very aroused. His nearness created an unnerving sexual awareness in her—the first she had experienced since the rape. And that desire frightened her. When this man, who wore a silver-and-turquoise ring identical to hers, had swept her off her feet and into his arms, her desire for him had unsettled her equilibrium.

J.T. slowed Washington to a standstill, dropped the reins and reached around the woman's body, grabbing her hand. An angry woman with a gun was dangerous. Joanna struggled against his superior strength, but in the end all her fighting did was toss both of them off the Appaloosa and onto the ground. She lost her .25 in the fall, the small handgun clanking loudly as it hit a nearby boulder.

J.T. was thankful the damned thing hadn't fired. A stray bullet could have killed either of them. Now Joanna pelted her small fists against his chest, fighting him like a wildcat, and with absolutely no rhyme or reason to her hysterical battle. No, that wasn't exactly true, J.T. acknowledged. He *was* a stranger. Despite the fact that he was Elena's brother, Joanna really didn't know him. For some absurd reason the woman assumed he was intent on ravaging her, with or without her permission.

"I'm not going to hurt you," he said in as calm and reasonable a voice as he could muster while the two of them rolled around over the uneven terrain. "But you're going to hurt yourself if you don't stop acting like this."

Joanna paid no heed to his warning. All she could think about was the fact that she was lying on the ground, out in the middle of nowhere, with a huge, hard man on top of her.

J.T. grabbed one of her wrists, then managed to grip the other, manacling them both in one of his hands. He pressed his body against hers, cursing himself for being aroused. Squirming beneath him, tossing her head from side to side as she jerked her shoulders in a vain effort to free herself, Joanna glared up at him and let out a bloodcurdling scream.

In one swift move, J.T. stood, dragging the screaming redhead to her feet beside him. He released her immediately. Her breathing deep and ragged, she glowered at him, a pink flush staining her cheeks. Her eyes, such a dark green they appeared almost black in her anger, focused on him with rage as she balled her hands into fists.

J.T. lifted his arms above his head, high in the air, as a gesture of surrender. He hoped she would realize the error of her assumption and calm herself.

"What the hell happened to you?" he asked. "I apologize if anything I said insulted you or made you think I was going to attack you."

"It wasn't—" Joanna gulped for air "—just what you said. It was what you were doing."

"I didn't realize you hated the way I was touching you. I thought—"

"You had no right to touch me, to caress me, to press yourself against me like that!" She couldn't bring herself to look at him, to make eye contact.

"Lady, you didn't protest anything I did until I asked if you had a particular fascination for half-breeds. And then, you go crazy and brandish a gun in my face."

He was right. She had enjoyed his touch, had gloried in the feelings of desire he created within her, even though those strong emotions had also frightened her...frightened her enough to make her threaten him.

Had she overreacted? This wouldn't be the first time. For nearly a year after the rape, she hadn't been able to bear for a man to even shake her hand. But it had been well over three years since she'd allowed a man's nearness to scare her into acting like an idiot. Dear God, she had thought all the irrational fear was over, that she had truly put the past behind her, that she was in control. But J.T. Blackwood had shown her that she was still a rape survivor; a woman who could not trust any man.

"Maybe I did overreact," Joanna said, then immediately qualified her admission. "I'm not saying I did, just that I might have. I don't like your type. I never have and I never will. You think women are fair game, don't you? That all you have to do is show an interest and a woman will automatically succumb to you."

"Can you stand there and tell me that you weren't just as turned on as I was?"

Lifting her downcast eyes, she glared at him, wanting to scream, no, no, no, a thousand times no! But she knew it would be a lie. And he would know she was lying. J.T. Blackwood was a man of the world, a man who'd known a lot of women.

"Look, if it makes you feel any better, I'm not any happier about the situation than you are," he said. "I don't want to be attracted to you. You're not my type, either."

"That's good to know." Joanna couldn't seem to stop herself from glancing down at the zipper in his jeans. Feeling the burning sting of a blush warming her neck, she turned her head.

"A guy can't hide it very well when he's aroused," J.T. told her. "But you've got my word that while I'm at the ranch, I'll steer clear of you. We'll forget about what happened today. If we run into each other, we'll be cordial, but keep our distance. Agreed?"

"Agreed." She watched him walk over, reach down and pick up her gun. Holding her breath, she waited until he came over and handed it to her. "Thank you."

"Put it away, Ms. Beaumont. Guns should be used only by people who know how to use them."

"I know how to use my gun," she said.

"Fine. Just don't ever try to use it on me again."

"Don't ever make me think you're going to attack me."

"That's a promise."

"Fine," she said. "Will you take me back to the ranch, now?"

"Why not?" He grunted. "You've ruined any chance for me to enjoy this place. Whenever I come home, I always ride up here to this stream. It's been a favorite place of mine since I was a kid."

"I'm sorry I ruined your homecoming, Mr. Blackwood, but I didn't plan on our meeting the way we did."

"Call me J.T."

"I'd rather not, since it's obvious we aren't going to be friends."

"Or lovers."

Every nerve in Joanna's body quivered with awareness. "Or lovers," she repeated.

"Come on. Let's head back to the ranch."

She followed him to the big Appaloosa, waited for him to mount, then hesitated when he offered her his hand.

"You can sit behind me," he told her.

"All right." She mounted the horse, sitting behind him, relieved that she wouldn't have to endure the hard pressure of his body against her hips on the ride back to the ranch.

Within a few minutes, Joanna slipped her arms around J.T.'s waist in order to keep her balance as they rode down the side of the mountain. She found herself wanting to lay her head against his broad back and hug herself tightly to his big body.

What she felt was wrong, she thought; her overwhelming need for this man—this stranger. J.T. Blackwood might be wearing Benjamin Greymountain's ring, but he was not Joanna's dream lover. He couldn't be!

Chapter 2

"Not tonight, Elena. Please." Joanna clutched the portable telephone in her hand. "I'm tired from today's ordeal with my Jeep. I just want to take a nice long bath, look over the sketches I did at the reservation, and go to bed early."

"But this is J.T.'s first night home and I've planned a special dinner," Elena pleaded. "You don't have to stay long after we eat. But come over for a while. I was counting on your being here."

"I've already met your brother. Remember, he's the one who gave me a ride back to the ranch."

"I don't know what happened between you two, but whatever it was, I'm sure we can straighten it out tonight."

"I don't want to ruin your plans, but—"

"Then don't ruin my plans. Just come eat dinner and you can leave as soon as we smooth things over between you and J.T."

Joanna breathed a deep sigh. Stepping up on the raised floor of what had once been the back porch of the old bunkhouse and was now her huge bathroom, Joanna began unbuttoning her dirty blouse.

"There's nothing to smooth over between your brother and me. We understand each other perfectly." Joanna leaned over, turned on the faucets and watched the water flow into the big, pedestaled, cast-iron bathtub she'd found at an antique shop in Albuquerque. "Mr. Blackwood and I have agreed that we don't like each other, that we aren't each other's type and that we have no intention of allowing you to play matchmaker."

"Just what did J.T. say to you?"

Joanna opened a bottle of scented bubble bath, sloshed a generous amount into the running water and set the container down on the unfinished, wide-plank floor.

"He told me that you'd been trying to get the two of us together for several years now and he has avoided coming to the ranch except when I was out of town."

"That no-account brother of mine!" Elena said. "He had no right to say something like that to—"

"Why on earth would you ever think your brother and I would be interested in each other? If I were looking for a man, I'd want someone more like your Alex. Gentle and kindhearted. A fellow artist. And someone who loves New Mexico the way I've come to love it."

"Oh, Jo, you need someone special in your life and so does J.T." Elena let out an exaggerated sigh. "All right, so I was wrong to hope you two were a perfect match. Come to dinner and I promise no more matchmaking."

"Not tonight." Joanna finished unbuttoning her blouse and dropped it to the floor, then unzipped her jeans.

"You've become my best friend," Elena said. "And J.T. is my only brother. Even if there can't be anything romantic between the two of you, I'd still like for you two to be friends. J.T.'s taking a real vacation and he's going to be staying a couple of weeks this time."

"If he's going to be here a couple of weeks, then there's no hurry in our getting to know each other, is there?"

"Isn't there anything I can say to get you to change your mind about dinner tonight?"

Tell me your brother isn't going to be there, Joanna thought. "No, I'm afraid not. But...well, I'll come to dinner one night before Mr. Blackwood leaves. Okay?"

"Mr. Blackwood? He must have really made you angry today," Elena said. "Look, his bark is a lot worse than his bite. J.T.'s pretty cynical about life, and he's stubborn as a mule, but underneath, he's a good guy. After Mama died, he came to the reservation and brought me back to the ranch with him. He didn't have to do that."

"Look, Elena, I know how much you love your brother. That's fine and good, but just because you love him doesn't mean everyone else has to."

"Whew! He really pushed all your buttons, didn't he?"

"Drop it, okay? I'm not coming to dinner tonight and that's final." Joanna stepped out of her sandals, slid her jeans to her feet and kicked out of them.

"Okay. But—"

"We'll talk tomorrow. Bye." Joanna punched the Off button on the telephone, tossed it on top of her discarded clothes and removed her underwear.

Standing naked in the middle of the stucco-walled bathroom, she stretched and gazed up at the slanted, split-log ceiling. She wanted to forget all about her disastrous encounter with J.T. Blackwood. She wanted to wash his scent off her hands and arms and face. She wanted to erase the image of him astride his Appaloosa stallion. And more than anything, she wanted to forget the way she'd felt when her body had been nestled intimately against his.

Joanna stepped into the warm, perfumed water, immersing her body beneath the layers of foaming bubbles. Reaching behind her, she lifted a gold washcloth from the black metal rack above the tub. She lathered the cloth with her moisturizing soap and scrubbed her face. After rinsing, she clutched the cloth in her hand and glanced down at the silver-and-turquoise ring on her finger. The ring Annabelle Beaumont's lover had made for her.

Where had J.T. Blackwood gotten the matching ring? The one her great-grandmother had been certain Benjamin

Greymountain wore till the day he died, as she had worn hers. Had some member of Benjamin's family sold the ring years ago? Perhaps they'd given it away. Or—was it possible that J.T. was somehow related to Benjamin?

More than once, Joanna had been tempted to ask Elena if she had ever heard of a Benjamin Greymountain or if she knew how to trace his descendants. But despite her close friendship with Elena, she hadn't been able to bring herself to share the secret affair her great-grandmother had written about—in great detail—in her diary. There were times when Joanna herself felt like an intruder when she read Annabelle's words. Somehow it hadn't seemed right to tell anyone else about Annabelle and Benjamin's scandalous love.

But tomorrow, she would ask Elena about J.T.'s ring and explain her curiosity by saying she'd noted the similarity between his ring and her own. And she would ask Elena to come to her home; that way she wouldn't have to go up to the main house and run the risk of seeing J.T. again.

The sun hung low in the sky, not quite prepared to set and put an end to the day. Approaching twilight washed an orange-gold translucence over the New Mexico landscape Joanna saw outside her windows.

After her long leisurely bath, she'd slipped into a floor-length pink-and-lavender cotton gown. Barefoot, she traipsed into the kitchen, opened the refrigerator and retrieved a large pitcher of iced tea she'd made yesterday. She poured herself a tall glass, added ice cubes and pulled out one of the Windsor armchairs at her dining table. Before she could sit, she heard a forceful knock at her back door. Who could that be? Surely, not Elena.

Walking toward the back door, she peeked out the window over her sink, but couldn't see anyone. "Who's there?" she asked. She never opened her door without taking every precaution, even out here on the ranch where she knew everyone. Even now, there were times when she checked under her bed and inside her closets after returning from a trip.

"It's J.T. Blackwood," his voice thundered, deep, rough and gritty.

"What do you want?"

"A minute of your time."

"Go away." She did not want to see him again. Not now. Not ever. And she certainly didn't want him to see her in her simple cotton nightgown, her face scrubbed clean and her hair pinned atop her head in a disheveled mess.

"Joanna, open the door and talk to me." He waited for her reply and when she said nothing, he chuckled, a dark, tough laugh that rumbled from his chest. "If you don't talk to me, I won't be able to go back to the house and face Elena. She's convinced I was rude and hateful to you and said something that hurt your feelings. She sent me over here to apologize."

"I never told her that you were rude and hateful. I don't need an apology."

"Dammit, woman, open the door, allow me to apologize and then call my sister and tell her you've forgiven me. Otherwise my vacation will be completely ruined before it even starts."

Hesitantly, fearfully, Joanna opened the door. Just a narrow crack at first, but the moment she saw J.T.'s smirky grin, she flung the door wide open. She would not give him the satisfaction of knowing how nervous he made her.

"Come in." She swept her hand through the air in a cordial invitation.

Her heart fluttered and her stomach twisted into knots. He was raw, proud masculine beauty. Every line of his face was hard, chiseled perfection.

He removed his tan Stetson and stepped forward; she stepped backward. He walked past her into her kitchen; she left the back door open.

He had showered and changed into clean faded jeans and a shirt of muted green-and-blue plaid. He smelled slightly of some manly-yet-expensive after-shave.

"Still rustic, but with every modern convenience," he said, glancing around. "Nice. Very nice."

"Thank you." Joanna felt undressed and vulnerable, wearing nothing but her nightgown, and J.T. Blackwood wasn't helping any by looking at her as if he found her greatly desirable. "Now, get the apology over with and then I'll call Elena."

"Aren't you worried about insects?" J.T. nodded toward the open door.

Joanna wanted to slam it shut, but instead, she closed it slowly. "The apology?"

"Right." He walked over to her, reached out and took her right hand in his.

She tried to pull out of his grasp, but he held tightly. "Please release my hand." She glanced down at their clasped hands and saw their twin rings, identical in every way except size.

"What are you so afraid of, lady?" He loosened his hold on her hand, allowing her to pull free.

"I'm not afraid of anything." She enunciated each word clearly and distinctly. "I'm just annoyed that you disturbed me. I like my solitude and I don't appreciate your bothering me."

"This little visit was Elena's idea," J.T. said.

"So you've already told me." Joanna swallowed, then looked her visitor square in the eye. "If you're going to apologize, then do it and leave."

"I'm sorry for whatever I said or did today that might have offended you. How's that? Was the apology good enough for you to tell Elena that you and I are friends now?"

"Friends? You expect me to tell Elena that we're friends?"

"She says that she's given up her plans to unite us romantically, but she still would like to see us become friends. So how about it? Tell Elena a little white lie and get us both off the hook."

J.T. watched the play of emotions on this lovely woman's face, her expression going from one of surprise and agitation to one of amusement. She smiled at him. His stomach tightened; his body hardened. Hell! This wasn't supposed to happen. Women's smiles didn't have this kind of effect on him. Not ever!

"Apology accepted," Joanna said. "I'll call Elena and tell her we're friends now."

"Thanks. It'll make my life a lot easier." J.T. allowed his gaze to follow the lines of her round, firm body, clearly silhouetted by the warm evening sunlight shining in the window and through the thin cotton material of her nightgown. Lord help him, he didn't think he'd ever seen a more beautiful sight. He grew painfully aroused just looking at her.

"Dammit," he muttered under his breath. That was all he needed—for her to notice his arousal. She'd never call Elena and set things straight. And if he couldn't pacify his sister, he'd just have to leave the ranch. In the twelve years since he'd gone to the reservation and brought Elena home with him, J.T. had grown to care for his half sister more than he'd ever thought he could care for anyone. He knew she meant well, trying to fix him up with Joanna. He couldn't make her understand that marriage and family life weren't for everyone.

"How long has Elena been trying to find you a girlfriend?" Joanna asked.

"Oh, she's not looking for a girlfriend," J.T. said. "She's looking for a wife."

"A wife? And she actually thought that I . . . I mean, she considered the possibility that you and I—"

"Despite being twenty-seven, Elena is still rather naive. She doesn't realize that there are a lot of women who cringe at the thought of being married to a half-breed like me."

"Mr. Blackwood, I didn't mean . . ." Joanna gazed into his good eye, that golden brown glittering eye, filled with anger and pain and—passion. "Your Navajo ancestry has nothing to do with why I dislike you." Indeed, his Navajo ancestry beckoned to Joanna, since it was another link, besides the silver-and-turquoise ring, that connected him to Benjamin Greymountain, and to the tender, gentle fantasy man she had dreamed of for over four years.

"I don't care what you meant or why you dislike me." He took several steps toward her.

Unmoving, she held her breath. Reaching out, he stroked her cheek. "You don't like me, but you want me. Oh, yeah, I've known your type before."

Without thinking about what she was doing, Joanna lifted her hand and laid it atop his while he caressed her cheek. "No, you haven't known my type before. You've never known anyone like me." She removed her hand.

He stared at her for a split second, uncertain whether he could believe her or not. Hell, it didn't matter. He wasn't going to allow Joanna Beaumont to get under his skin. While visiting the ranch, he'd find some way to avoid her or he'd cut short his vacation.

He grabbed her chin, tilting her face. "Call Elena and get me out of hot water, then I'll stay out of your way."

Joanna nodded. "I'll stay out of your way, too."

He made no reply, just turned, walked to the back door, opened it and left. Joanna stared at the open door for endless moments, then ran across the kitchen and slammed it shut. What right did a man like that have to wear Benjamin's ring? Benjamin, a man who'd been capable of the deepest, truest, most unselfish love? It was plain to see that J.T. Blackwood didn't know the first thing about love—real love, the kind Benjamin and Annabelle had shared.

After he'd spent several hours tossing and turning, J.T. gave up trying to get any sleep and got out of bed. His grandfather's bed. Old John Thomas Blackwood. The meanest, orneriest son of a bitch who'd ever lived. The man his father had named him for. The man who had forbidden his only son to marry a dirty Indian. The man who hadn't acknowledged J.T.'s existence until J.T.'s father had died and left the old reprobate without an heir. The man who'd come to the reservation when J.T. was five and taken him from his mother.

J.T., naked as the day he was born, threw open the double doors leading from his bedroom to the attached patio.

The cool night air caressed his bronze skin. He ran his hand through his thick hair—hair he hadn't worn long since his first haircut at the age of five.

"Can't have you looking like one of those damned savages," old John Thomas had said. "Bad enough you've got that woman's coloring. But from now on, boy, you're a Blackwood. And that means you're a cowboy, not an Indian."

And that was exactly what J.T. had become—a cowboy. He'd learned to rope and ride and herd cattle. Although there had never been any real love lost between him and his grandfather, he had come to love the ranch.

He supposed that was why—even though he couldn't live in New Mexico, couldn't face being torn between his two heritages—he always returned to the ranch. He loved this land, this wild, untamed wilderness, as much as the old man had loved it; as much as his Blackwood ancestors, who had fought and died to claim the countless acres that now comprised one of the largest ranches in northern New Mexico, had loved it.

And he loved the land as much as his mother's people did. The Navajo. A people he did not know, except through his half sister. A people and a heritage his grandfather had taught him to deny.

From the side patio, J.T. could see the back of the old bunkhouse. Joanna Beaumont's home. How long would it take for a society girl to tire of the West, to tire of painting the natives and return to Virginia where she belonged?

What had ever prompted a woman, whose mother was a Virginia senator and deceased father a renowned trial lawyer, to seek adventure in New Mexico? Had she fled from an unhappy love affair? Had she rebelled against her wealthy family? Elena had told him Joanna had come to Trinidad to paint, that she had chosen the town because her great-grandparents had once lived here for a whole summer while on an archaeological dig.

J.T. caught the glow of a light in his peripheral vision as he gazed out at the night, the land hushed and still. He focused his gaze on the light coming from a long, narrow window in the old bunkhouse. Joanna Beaumont stood in that window, looking up at the main house. What was she doing awake this time of night? Had she been as restless as he? As aroused and needy? Maybe she was thinking of him, and hating herself for wanting him, and yet was powerless to control that desire.

If he went to her now, would she accept him into her home? Into her bed? Into her body? J.T. shuddered with the force of his longing. Closing his eyes, he breathed deeply, drawing the fresh night air into his lungs. Opening his eyes, he took a last look at Joanna's silhouette in the window, then he closed the double doors, turned around and walked across the room.

He fell into the bed. Lying on top of the covers, he stared up at the dark ceiling. Only the faint moonlight illuminated his room.

He had to stop thinking about Joanna. He had to stop wanting her. He'd come home for a good, long vacation, the first in years. He wasn't going to allow some debutante to ruin his stay at the ranch. He would steer clear of her and she'd steer clear of him. And he'd make sure Elena didn't interfere.

Joanna and Elena sat in cane-seated rockers on the front porch of the bunkhouse. Numerous potted geraniums lined the edge of the wooden porch and a trailing ivy vine sat nestled on a rough-hewn table between the two women. Elena downed the last drops of tea, then set the tall crystal glass on the table.

"So, are you going to tell me what happened between you and J.T. yesterday?" Elena asked.

Joanna smiled at her friend. She had met Elena and Alex at an art exhibit in Albuquerque. Alex was a sculptor, whose finest work was exquisite pieces of his beautiful young Navajo wife. The three had become instant friends and they had been thrilled to learn that Joanna had only recently moved to Trinidad.

"Come on, Jo. J.T. isn't talking." Elena crossed her arms over her chest and grunted in disgust. "Sometimes that brother of mine makes me so angry."

"I have a feeling that your brother makes a lot of people angry."

"I thought you two were friends now. That is what you said when you called last night and told me he had come by and apologized."

"We're on friendly terms," Joanna said. "I'm afraid we got off to a bad start when we met. We offended each other."

"How?"

"How?" Joanna stared at Elena, whose big brown eyes had widened with her question.

"Yes, how did you and J.T. offend each other?"

"Well . . . I misunderstood something he said and did. I thought he was . . . But he wasn't."

"He came on to you, huh?" Elena laughed, creating soft lines around her full lips. "J.T.'s pretty irresistible to the ladies, and he knows it. What did you do, slap his face?"

"No, I pulled my gun on him."

Elena's laughter filled the air. She doubled over in the rocker as she covered her mouth with her hand. "I love it. I absolutely love it. You pulled your gun on J.T. Blackwood, who is a private security agent, a former Secret Service agent and an ex-soldier. Good grief, Jo, I'd give a million dollars to have seen the look on his face."

"He was surprised." A hint of a smile played at the corners of Joanna's mouth.

"Okay, so he came on to you and you put him in his place. That's how he offended you. How did you offend him? Did you tell him you didn't find him the least bit interesting and were totally immune to his masculine charms?"

"No. Not exactly." Joanna sipped on her tea, running her fingers up and down the side of the cold, sweating glass. "Despite the fact that I don't like Mr. Blackwood and am not interested in him, I can't say I'm completely immune to him."

"I knew it!" Elena slapped her hands together exuberantly. "You do find him irresistible, don't you?"

"Don't go jumping to conclusions. I just admit that he's very...well, he's very masculine. But I don't like his type, Elena, and I told him so."

"Hey, I can't believe J.T.'s ego is so fragile he couldn't take a rejection. Come on. Give. There has to be more to it than that."

"He said you wanted to find him a wife and I said I wasn't available. He took it the wrong way. He thought I was prejudiced, that I wasn't interested because he was part Navajo." Joanna looked down at her lap, uncertain she could face her friend. "I tried to explain, but he wouldn't listen. He said it didn't make any difference."

"That idiot! He's my brother and I love him dearly, but sometimes..." Elena laid her small hand on Joanna's shoulder. "J.T.'s all mixed up about a lot of things concerning his heritage. He's not really a white man and he's not really a Navajo. I think that's one of the reasons he left Trinidad and the ranch when he was eighteen and joined the army. No matter how hard his grandfather tried to erase everything Navajo from J.T.'s life and from his memories, that part of him still existed."

"Perhaps there's more to it than that." Joanna caught Elena's hand and squeezed. "Maybe some woman he loved broke his heart by refusing to marry him because he was part Native American."

"I can assure you that no one has ever broken J.T.'s heart. He's never been in love." Elena sighed. "I'm not sure J.T. knows how to love. His grandfather gave him everything money could buy, but he never gave him any love and warmth or genuine caring."

"He must have been a very sad, lonely little boy growing up with such a stern old man." Joanna did not want to think of J.T. as a child—an unloved, emotionally neglected little boy.

"Our childhoods were so different," Elena said. "I grew up on the reservation. My father farmed and raised a few sheep. We never had much money, but we were happy and I was loved by my parents. And I was taught a fierce pride in my Navajo heritage."

"And your brother grew up here, on his grandfather's ranch. Wealthy and unhappy."

"The only unhappiness in our lives, before my father died, was Mother's sadness in having lost her son."

"Elena?"

"Yes?"

"I noticed Mr. Bl—your brother wears a silver-and-turquoise ring. Do you know where he got that ring?"

"I wondered how long it would take you to ask about the ring," Elena said.

"You noticed, too, didn't you, that his ring is identical to mine?" Joanna held up her right hand; afternoon sunshine glinted off the ring's surface.

"The first time I met you, I saw your ring. I wondered about it, but didn't ask. I thought perhaps you'd bought it somewhere out here in New Mexico, and several times, after we became friends, I wanted to say something to you about the ring." Elena reached over and traced circles around the three turquoise stones adorning the ring. "I thought it was an odd coincidence. I've never seen another ring identical to the ones you and J.T. wear."

"Where did he get his ring?"

"Where did you get yours?" Elena asked. "Did you buy it after you came to New Mexico?"

"No. The ring has been in my family for years."

"Ah. I see. And J.T.'s ring has been in our family for years."

Joanna's wildly beating heart soared. J.T. was related to Benjamin Greymountain. Somehow she'd already known. But how was it possible that two men, related by blood, could be so very different?

"Whose ring does J.T. wear?" The moment she'd said his name, she wished she could call it back. Calling him J.T.

seemed far too intimate. By referring to him as Mr. Black-wood, she could keep an emotional distance.

"When my mother grew very sick and we knew she was dying, J.T. came to the reservation to see her. I was fifteen and had never met my brother. But the moment I saw him, I knew him." Elena's eyes glazed with tears. "I hadn't seen the ring before that day, but my mother had kept it—saved it—for her son. The ring had belonged to her father and his father before him. Her grandfather was a silversmith."

"What was your mother's name before she married?" Joanna asked.

"Mary Greymountain from the Bitter Water clan."

"Greymountain?"

Elena nodded. "You have heard this name before... before you came to New Mexico?"

"Yes. My great-grandparents knew a Navajo silversmith named Benjamin Greymountain—"

"My great-grandfather!"

"Yes. Your great-grandfather—J.T.'s great-grandfa-ther—made this ring." Joanna lifted her right hand with her left and stared at the silver-and-turquoise band. "This ring belonged to my great-grandmother."

"Ah. That's why you came to New Mexico, to Trinidad, to paint. You came in search of the ring's mate, didn't you? You knew Benjamin Greymountain had made an identical ring for himself. There was love between my great-grandfather and the woman he made the ring for. Isn't that true?"

"Yes. I have her diary. My great-grandmother. Anna-belle Beaumont. She wore this ring until the day she died. I found it in a leather pouch when I found the diary."

"You wear Annabelle Beaumont's ring and J.T. wears Benjamin Greymountain's ring," Elena said. "It is a sign, is it not? I knew, somehow, when I saw your ring, that you were the woman for my brother."

"But I'm not, Elena," Joanna protested. "Your brother is cold and hard and cynical. He's filled with a rage that frightens me. I'm not the woman for him. I want—I need—

a gentle, kind man. A man who wouldn't try to control me, to possess me, to exert power over me."

"J.T. needs a sweet, tender woman to teach him how to love." Elena smiled at Joanna. "You could be that woman, if you're brave enough to try to tame the devil."

"I'm not that brave."

Elena turned her head at the sound of horse hooves. Joanna looked up just as J.T. rode by on his big Appaloosa. He glanced at the two women, nodded and tipped his hat. For one brief moment, his golden brown eye met Joanna's green glare. Heat suffused her body. Tremors racked her stomach.

He rode on, not looking back. Joanna jumped up out of the rocker and walked inside her house. Elena glanced from her brother's retreating back to the open front door through which Joanna had disappeared.

Chapter 3

J.T. Blackwood had been home exactly one week when Elena finally persuaded Joanna to come to dinner. Joanna had known it was a mistake from the moment she'd agreed, but she also knew that Elena wouldn't leave her in peace until she accepted. Although she and J.T. had done everything possible to avoid each other, an occasional encounter had been unavoidable. And Elena, more convinced now than ever that Joanna was *the woman* for her brother, had taken every opportunity to throw the two of them together.

J.T. had shown up on the trail Joanna took for her morning horseback ride. They'd both gotten a good laugh over the fact that Elena had been the one to suggest the trail to J.T., saying he hadn't ridden over that part of the ranch in years. But J.T. had decided to finish his ride by taking another trail, and Joanna had been greatly relieved.

Elena had tried to turn a routine trip into town for groceries into a foursome luncheon date. When Joanna realized J.T. had been included in their plans, she'd apologized for changing her mind at the last minute and stayed at home. She'd driven into Trinidad by herself the following day to pick up her art supplies.

J.T. had only one more week of vacation. Surely she could survive another week. If she could live through tonight's dinner, all she had to do was continue avoiding the man. Maybe now would be a good time to take another trip. She'd been thinking about going back to the reservation to work. One of Elena's cousins, Joseph Ornelas, had promised to introduce her to the old shaman, James Bonito, who, people claimed, was a hundred and ten years old. She'd give anything to paint the man. She could leave tomorrow and stay away until J.T. had returned to Atlanta.

Tonight was the first time she and J.T. had agreed, beforehand, to see each other. Joanna berated herself for taking so long to get ready for a simple dinner with friends. She didn't want to admit that what J.T. Blackwood thought about her actually mattered to her. But it did.

Had Annabelle Beaumont worried so about her appearance when she had sneaked off for her clandestine meetings with Benjamin Greymountain? Had her heart drummed so fiercely? Had her nerves rioted in fear and anticipation?

What had it been like, Joanna wondered, to have Benjamin as a secret lover?

What would it be like to have J.T. as a lover?

Joanna shook her head, loosening her French twist. Damn, what a thought! She didn't want J.T. to be her lover. When she took a lover, he would be kind, understanding and tender. He would be the exact opposite of J.T. Blackwood. She wanted and needed a man who would allow her to set the pace, to be in control, to take charge. J.T. would possess her without loving her. He would take her with fury and passion, but without his heart ever being involved. He would always be the one with the power. Joanna could never allow a man to have power over her, to bend her to his will.

Busily she adjusted her hair, curling the loose tendrils about her face, softening the severity of the French twist. She checked her appearance in the mirror one last time, and approved of the image she saw reflected. She'd chosen to wear a thin chambray skirt with a ruffle around the ankle-length hem, and matched it with a simple short-sleeved white blouse. She picked up the silver-and-turquoise belt she'd bought from a Navajo silversmith and slipped it around her waist.

She took her time walking from the bunkhouse to the main house, humming to herself—something she'd done since childhood to shore up her courage. For the first time since she'd arrived in Trinidad, Joanna Beaumont regretted coming to New Mexico.

She had found a peace here she'd thought she would never know again, and she'd built a successful career doing something she loved. Her life had been content. Why hadn't J.T. Blackwood stayed in Atlanta for the rest of his life, or at least continued to avoid her as he'd done the past few years?

When Joanna neared the main house, a typical Spanish-style stucco with a red tile roof, she glanced up and saw J.T. standing on the wide porch.

Elena had told her that J.T. had gotten his coloring from their mother, but his size was pure Blackwood. Tall and rugged, every muscle well-developed to a whipcord lean-ness. This evening he had discarded his tan Stetson and had dressed in black jeans and a white shirt. A silver-and-turquoise jewel clasped his black bolo tie. His blue-black hair gleamed with a healthy vitality. Joanna visually traced the thin black band that held his eye patch in place.

"Cheer up, Jo, you're coming to dinner, not going to your own hanging," J.T. said.

She bristled at the use of his sister's nickname for her. No one except Elena had ever called her Jo. Somehow, on J.T.'s lips, it sounded far too intimate. But she wouldn't rise to the bait; she knew he'd called her Jo to see how she'd react.

"I feel like this is the condemned person's last meal and I'm that condemned person." She hesitated momentarily, then stepped onto the porch. "I am sorry that a week of your vacation has been ruined. Elena can't seem to let go of the notion you and I belong together. I know it's made your stay here at the ranch very unpleasant."

"You are so damned polite, Miss Beaumont." J.T. stood with one booted foot resting back flat against the wall. "Do you ever stop being a lady and act like a woman?"

Joanna clenched her teeth to keep herself from lashing out at J.T. Maybe he was right; maybe her good-manners-at-any-cost upbringing was so inbred that she could never escape it. But if her succumbing to him for a one-night stand would make her a woman in his eyes, then she didn't want to be a woman. Not his woman. Not ever.

"I don't think I acted much like a lady the first day we met." She tried to keep her voice even and calm, despite her anger. "If you recall, I pulled a gun on you."

"Oh, I'll never forget our first meeting. But even in pulling a gun on me, you were being a true lady. You were defending your honor, weren't you? That's what a lady would do. Or so I'm told."

Rushing out the front door, Elena glanced hurriedly from J.T. to Joanna. "Dinner will be delicious. Alex is barbecuing on the patio. Steaks this thick." She curved her thumb and index finger to indicate a good three inches. "Come on, you two."

Joanna helped Elena prepare the salads while J.T. assisted Alex with the barbecue. Within an hour the foursome settled around a black wrought-iron table in the right-hand corner of the patio located in the center of the stucco ranch house. The evening sun lay low on the western horizon. A soft, bluesy tune drifted from the CD player on the porch that surrounded the house on all four sides and opened onto the patio.

Joanna cut into her medium-rare steak, lifted a piece on her fork and brought the meat to her mouth. She glanced across the table at J.T. He was looking directly at her lips. Swallowing hard, she laid her fork down on her plate and lifted her mug of iced tea, all the while staring at J.T. He moved his gaze from her lips upward, encountering her hard stare. He smiled, an almost smile, just barely curving the corners of his mouth.

He picked up his mug of cold beer, silently saluted Joanna with it and took a deep, hearty swallow. She averted her gaze, turning to look at Elena, who was busy feeding Alex a bite of steak. The act of feeding her husband seemed terribly intimate and sexual. The two smiled at each other as if no one else existed. They were cocooned in their mutual fascination with each other—the skinny, bespectacled, blond sculptor and his lovely, exotic, brown-eyed wife.

Maybe that's what it's like to be in love, Joanna thought. So absorbed in your lover that you are oblivious to anyone else's presence.

Joanna lifted her fork again, but before she could bring it to her mouth, J.T. leaned over and slipped his own fork into her open mouth. Her body jerked. Her heart hammered. She glared at him. The piece of meat in her mouth felt huge and hot and heavy. Her first impulse was to spit it out—to spit it out in his face. Instead she began to chew slowly, keeping her gaze riveted on his.

"I take my steak rare," J.T. said. "I think this is medium-rare, don't you? Looks like we overcooked it a bit."

Joanna forced herself to swallow the chewed meat. "It's medium-rare. No taste of blood at all."

"Well, it's a good steak. I think I can finish it off." He cut another piece, then ate, following his first bite with many more.

By the time the others had finished their meal, Joanna had forced down several bites of her steak and a small portion of her salad. Finally Elena and Alex started a discussion about New Mexico's history, trying desperately to engage J.T. and Joanna in the conversation. The effort failed miserably. Joanna could find no pleasure in discussing Billy the Kid and John Chisum, and J.T. didn't seem to care anything about the fact that Lew Wallace, the author of *Ben Hur,* had once been the territorial governor.

"Come on, Alex, let's dance." Elena held out her hand to her husband, who quickly stood and lifted her into his arms.

J.T. and Joanna sat quietly at the table watching the couple slow dance in a sensual embrace.

"Every time I'm around those two I feel totally unnecessary," J.T. said. "It's been like this ever since they got married five years ago. You'd think they'd be sick of each other by now."

"They're in love," Joanna said.

"They're in heat." Grunting, J.T. shook his head. "I guess you don't know what that's like, do you?"

There was nothing she could do to stop the flush from spreading over her cheeks and down her throat. She'd been cursed with a redhead's pale complexion and a dusting of freckles across the bridge of her nose and over her cheekbones. When she blushed, it showed plainly.

"I've embarrassed you." He spoke the words in a tone of disbelief. "You can't be that naive. You're no teenager. You've got to be at least twenty-five or more. A woman your age is bound to have had several lovers."

"I'm twenty-nine." Joanna deliberately glanced away from him and at the dancing couple. "And how many lovers I have or haven't had is none of your business."

Elena waved at Joanna. "Why don't you two take advantage of this fabulous music and that glorious sunset—" she nodded to the western sky, which was afire with orange-red flames "—and dance?"

J.T. held out his hand. "Come on, Jo, let's dance. It'll make Elena happy, and that's what this night is all about, isn't it? Pacifying my little sister so she'll leave us in peace for a while?"

Joanna hesitated, then stood, walked around the edge of the table and placed her hand in J.T.'s. His grasp was light and nonthreatening. Stepping into his arms, she followed him into the dance. He held her loosely, his grip around her waist barely discernible. She breathed a sigh of relief when she realized that he intended to keep a reasonable distance between them. She'd been so sure he would haul her close to his big body and force her to endure the feel of him, hard and powerful, against her own body.

If she'd been a bit taller or had worn heels, she might have been able to glance over his shoulder. As it was, she had to stare directly at his wide, muscular chest. He was so tall. Too tall. Too big. Too manly.

Even though J.T. did nothing offensive, Joanna felt trapped. She wasn't in control of this situation. He was. If he chose to pull her against him in an intimate fashion, she wouldn't be able to stop him.

Dammit, that wasn't true. All she had to do was tell him to release her and she could walk away. Admit it, she told herself. You aren't afraid of J.T. Blackwood; you're afraid of yourself!

"Are you always so stiff when a man holds you in his arms?" J.T. asked.

"Stop goading me," she told him. "You may find it amusing, but I don't."

"Sorry about that, Jo, but you leave yourself open to my teasing."

Just as she started to respond, the music ended. Joanna pulled away from J.T. He clasped her wrist, halting her escape. She turned abruptly and faced him.

"I'm tired. It's been a long day," she said. "I think I'll head on home."

"Oh, Jo, don't leave yet." Elena, her arm around Alex's waist, strolled over to Joanna and J.T.

"The night's still young," Alex said. "It's not dark yet. Hang around and we'll play a game of Rook."

"Not tonight." Joanna smiled at her friends, then glanced down at her wrist, still trapped in J.T.'s grasp. "Another time."

"Tomorrow night?" Elena suggested, her smile eager. "Come over for dinner again. Tonight was nice, wasn't it?"

"Not tomorrow night." Joanna wished Elena would just let her go home and stop trying so hard to push her into J.T.'s arms.

"The next night, then," Alex said. "I'll whip up some of my world-famous chili."

"I'm afraid dinner and cards will have to wait awhile. I'm leaving tomorrow afternoon to spend a week or so on the Navajo reservation." Joanna kept her phony smile in place—just barely. She felt J.T.'s hard, cold stare boring into her. She wanted to scream, to tell him, yes, a thousand times yes, he *was* the reason she had to escape.

"But why tomorrow?" Whining, Elena stuck out her bottom lip in a childish pout. "The reservation will be there a week from now. Please, wait."

"Leave her alone, Elena," J.T. said, then released his hold on Joanna's wrist. "She's made her plans."

"But she can go to the reservation any time," Elena said. "You're only going to be here another week and—"

"I'll stop by tomorrow afternoon and say goodbye before I leave." Joanna's smile drooped. She sighed, bit her bottom lip, then reached out and hugged Elena. "Please, understand," she whispered.

Joanna hurried off the patio, onto the inner porch and through the house. When she reached the front porch, she stopped suddenly, her vision blurred by a fine mist of tears. She sucked in a deep breath of crisp, clean air.

She felt a big hand gently clutch her shoulder. Gasping, she turned quickly, bumping into J.T. and losing her balance. He grabbed her by both shoulders to steady her.

"Elena's all right," he said. "I promised her that I'd walk you home and try to persuade you to stay on at the ranch."

"Which you won't do, will you?"

He rubbed her shoulders with his big hands. "You're tight as a coiled spring, honey. What's wrong with you? You act like you're afraid of me."

"I told you once before that I'm not afraid of anything, most especially not you."

"Well, that's good to know, because I'm harmless. I'd never hurt you."

Joanna longed to believe him, to take him at his word, but she knew better than to trust a man like J.T. Blackwood.

Any man, for that matter. Joanna hadn't trusted a man in five years. Not since a monster had sadistically raped her in her own apartment. Not since her devoted fiancé had walked off and left her to face the trial and months of therapy without his love and support.

"I'd never give you the chance to hurt me, Mr. Blackwood."

"I thought we were finally on a first-name basis. Remember, I'm J.T.—" he released one of her shoulders and tapped his chest with the tips of his fingers "—and you're Jo." He pointed to her.

"Please, don't call me Jo."

"Elena calls you Jo."

"I know, but that's different," Joanna said. "She's my good friend and you're . . . you're—"

"Not your friend?"

"No, not my friend."

"Then what am I?" He slipped his arm around her waist, urging her closer.

She couldn't seem to breathe. Her head spun. She clutched his arms, feeling firm muscles beneath her fingers.

They both heard a man clear his throat. J.T. glanced over Joanna's shoulder and saw Cliff Lansdell, his ranch foreman, standing in the yard. Turning Joanna around so that she stood at his side, J.T. kept his arm about her waist.

"What's wrong, Cliff?" J.T. asked.

"Sorry to bother you, J.T., but you told me to let you know when Queen Nefertiti was about to foal. I've called Dr. Gray."

"Thanks, Cliff. I'll come on out to the stables in a few minutes. After I walk Miss Beaumont home."

"That's not necessary," Joanna said at the same moment Cliff spoke.

"I'll be glad to walk Joanna home, if you're in a hurry to get out to the stables, J.T."

"I'll walk Jo home." J.T. said her name in a sultry way, tightening his hold around her waist.

Joanna had the oddest notion that J.T. Blackwood had just laid claim to her, that somehow he had warned Cliff that she was out of bounds to any other man.

"I'll see you over at the stables, then." Cliff's shoulders slumped. He glanced at Joanna. "Good night." He tipped his hat, turned and walked away.

"I can get home by myself." She snapped out the words, not caring how she sounded.

"Would you like to come to the stables with me and wait for the blessed event?" J.T. ran his fingers up and down the side of her waist.

Joanna sucked in her breath. "No. No, thank you."

"My Appaloosa, Washington, is the colt's sire and this will be Queen Nefertiti's first. It's a special occasion."

"Then you should go on. Don't waste time walking me home."

J.T. guided her off the porch and across the yard, not saying a word. When they reached her front door, she unlocked and opened it, then turned to him.

"Good night."

"Goodbye." He lifted his hand, touching her face with his fingertips; the caress was soft, hesitant and quickly over. "I'll be back in Atlanta when you return from the reservation, so it could be months, probably Christmas, before I come back to the ranch."

"Goodbye, then. I—I won't see you at Christmas. I plan to go back to Virginia and spend Christmas with my mother."

"If we're very careful, we should be able to avoid ever seeing each other again," he said.

She nodded agreement. They stared at each other for a brief moment before J.T. turned and walked away. Joanna took a deep breath, thankful that he hadn't kissed her, then went inside and locked the door behind her.

J.T. walked by the old bunkhouse on his way back from the stables shortly after daybreak the following morning. He hadn't expected to see Joanna, dressed in jeans and an oversize shirt, sitting on her porch. He had thought—hell, he had hoped— he'd never see her again after last night. He couldn't quite put his finger on what it was, but there was something about Joanna Beaumont that sent up red warning signals inside his head. She meant trouble for him, and J.T. never let a woman cause him trouble.

"Good morning," she called out to him. "Is everything all right with Queen Nefertiti and her colt?"

J.T. walked over and placed his foot on the bottom step leading up to her front porch. "Mother and daughter are doing just fine. When I stopped by and told Washington he was the father of a beautiful filly, he acted as if he knew what I was talking about."

"Maybe he did." Joanna clutched a large, tan mug in her hands. "Sometimes I think animals are a lot smarter than we humans give them credit for being."

"Yeah, you're probably right." J.T. ran his right hand over his face, the overnight's growth of beard scratchy against his palm. "I need a shower and a shave and about ten hours of sleep." He eyed the mug she held. "But first I could use a cup of coffee."

She glanced into the pale brown liquid she'd been sipping on for the past few minutes, then looked down at J.T. "Come on up and have a seat. I'll go inside and get you a cup. How do you like it? Black?"

"Black, but with a little sugar. A teaspoonful will do."

"Okay. I'll be right back."

While she went inside to get his coffee, he walked up the steps and onto the porch, then slumped down in one of the cane-seated rockers. God, he was tired. But it was a good kind of tired. Here on the ranch he could work hard enough to physically exhaust himself, but he didn't have to face the stress and pressure of his job, which was far more exhausting—mentally as well as physically.

"This is high-octane stuff," Joanna said when she returned with his coffee. "If you're planning on going straight to bed, the caffeine could keep you awake."

He accepted the cup she offered, being careful not to touch her hand in the process. "I don't think anything will keep me from sleeping this morning."

Taking a swig of the coffee, he sighed. "Good. And just the right amount of sugar."

She sat down beside him in the other rocker and lifted her mug to her lips. She hadn't expected to see J.T. this morning. She'd had no idea he'd stayed at the stables all night. But there was no reason to panic, no reason to be rude to him. By noon today, she'd be packed and ready to leave, and when she returned next week, J.T. would be gone.

While she was away, she would have to come to terms with her foolish dream of finding real love and happiness in New Mexico. She had met the man who had inherited Benjamin's ring as she had inherited Annabelle's, and knowing J.T. Blackwood had opened her eyes to reality. There would be no fantasy lover come to life for her. There would be no happily-ever-after for a pair of present-day lovers, any more than there had been for the star-crossed lovers over seventy years ago.

"Do you always get up so early?" J.T. asked.

"What?"

"It's barely daylight and you're up, dressed, and have already fixed coffee," he said. "Is this your normal routine?"

"Not always. But sometimes I get up this early and paint. There's nothing more glorious than a New Mexico sunrise, unless it's a New Mexico sunset."

"You're really in love with this country, aren't you? You've fallen under its enchanted spell like so many Easterners have done over the years."

"My great-grandmother fell in love . . . with New Mexico over seventy years ago, when she and her husband spent the summer here on an archaeological dig." Joanna finished her coffee, placed her empty mug on the table between the two rockers, then looked toward the east at the morning sky.

"Yeah, Elena told me the story, or what you told her." J.T. took another swig of coffee, then placed his half-full cup beside Joanna's. "Your great-grandmother was a married woman who had an affair with one of the natives, then left the guy and went back home to her safe, secure life in Virginia as the wife of a well-to-do college professor and renowned archaeologist."

Joanna's spine stiffened; she clutched the arms of the rocker. "There was a great deal more to their affair. They were truly in love. It broke her heart to leave him. She loved him as long as she lived." Joanna thrust her right hand in front of J.T.'s face. "She wore his ring until the day she died."

"If she loved him so damned much, why didn't she leave her husband and stay here in New Mexico with him?" Grabbing Joanna's hand, J.T. twisted the silver-and-turquoise ring around and around on her finger. "I'll tell you why. Because Benjamin Greymountain was good enough to take as a lover, but not good enough to marry. He wasn't good enough for her to give up everything and spend her life with him. That's not love, Jo, that's—"

Jerking her hand out his, she jumped to her feet. "What would you know about love? Listening to you talk about our great-grandparents in that way is a sacrilege. If you had read Annabelle's diary, you wouldn't say such things. You'd know how deeply she loved Benjamin, and how completely she trusted his love for her."

J.T. stood, grabbed Joanna and whipped her around to face him. "You're right. I don't know the first thing about love, but I know all about lust, all about how good it feels to scratch an itch that's driving you crazy." Lowering his head, he nuzzled the side of her face with his nose.

No, no! her mind screamed. She wasn't going to let him do this. She wasn't going to let him reduce the beautiful love Benjamin and Annabelle had shared into some meaningless sexual affair. And she wasn't going to let him prove his point by showing her that the two of them felt those same animalistic urges.

She struggled against his hold, a feeling of panic building inside her. J.T. clutched her waist, pulling her up against him. She gasped when she felt his arousal. "We could have what Benjamin and Annabelle had, if that's what you want. We could spend the next week making love night and day, and then I'll go back to Atlanta and you can write in your diary about how exciting it was, having an Indian lover."

"Let go of me." She glared at him, hating him. Hating him for making light of their great-grandparents' love. Hating him for stirring passion to life within her.

"You don't want the kind of affair your beloved ancestress had?" J.T. taunted her. "Are you saying you didn't come to Trinidad—" he yanked her hand up, entwined their fingers and pulled their hands between their faces so that they could see their matching rings "—with all kinds of romantic notions of a Navajo man fulfilling your sexual fantasies?"

"You don't know anything about me. About my dreams. Or my fantasies."

He lowered his head. She held tightly to his hand, trying to keep their clasped hands in front of her face. He pulled their hands down, leaned closer and brushed a light kiss across her lips. She stiffened.

"I know you want me—as much as I want you," he said.

She didn't fight him, made no protest when he kissed her. She had thought the kiss would be harsh and cruel and savage. But it wasn't. He took her lips with force, but it was a sweet, tender power that swept through her body like a strong but nondestructive wind.

She returned the kiss, opening her mouth, allowing his invasion. Tingling warmth spread from her breasts to the core of her femininity. When he cupped the back of her head with one hand and caressed her hip with the other, pushing her firmly against his hard sex, she slipped her arms up around his neck. She had never known anything like this raging hunger inside her, this overwhelming need to possess and be possessed.

Just when her knees weakened and she trembled with passion, J.T. pushed her away. He stood several inches from her, his breathing ragged, sweat beads dampening his forehead.

Reaching down, she gripped the arm of her rocker for support as she stared at him, not knowing what to say or do. She wanted to lash out at him, accuse him of something horrible, but she couldn't. She had been a willing participant, her need as wild as his.

"Go to the reservation, Jo. Paint your noble savages and your magnificent sunrises and sunsets. But find yourself another Indian to take as a lover. I'm not in the market for a summer fling with a bored debutante."

He glared at her. She stood ramrod straight, unmoving, her face an unemotional mask. When he turned and stomped down the steps, out into the yard and toward the main house, Joanna stayed on the porch, silent and still, until he disappeared from her view. Then she released the tight control she'd been determined to keep over her emotions. Tears filled her eyes. The unbearable pain in her chest burst free when she gulped in a deep breath of air and let out an agonized moan.

Chapter 4

Joanna placed her art supplies in the back of the Jeep, then lifted her small floral suitcase and her matching overnight bag. She'd packed light, taking two pairs of jeans, two blouses, a nightgown and several changes of underwear. She would stay with Elena's cousins, Kate and Ed Whitehorn, who had opened their home to her on several previous occasions. She had telephoned them this morning, apologizing for giving them such short notice, and found Kate delighted to have company.

Joanna glanced down at her watch as she stepped up on the porch. Eleven-twenty. She would double-check everything in the house, making sure no electrical appliances had been left on, then she'd fix herself a sandwich and eat lunch before running up to the main house to say goodbye to Elena. She prayed J.T. would still be asleep so she wouldn't have to see him again.

The telephone rang just as she entered the house. Leaving the front door open, she dashed across the living room. She picked it up on the fifth ring, just in time to keep her answering machine from being activated.

"Hello," Joanna said.

"Joanna?"

"Mother?"

"Yes, dear. How are you?" Helene Beaumont asked.

"I'm fine." It wasn't like her mother to call unexpectedly. Senator Helene Caldwell Beaumont was the most organized person Joanna had ever known. Her mother called twice a month, at nine-thirty on Sunday morning. "Is something wrong? Did Uncle Peter have another heart attack?"

"No, dear. Peter is just fine."

"Then what's wrong? Why are you calling?"

"I—I don't quite know how to tell you this, but—"

"For heaven's sake, Mother, will you just tell me? You're scaring me to death, acting this way." Her mother never stuttered, never hesitated, never postponed till tomorrow what could be accomplished today.

"That policeman, Lieutenant George, came to my office earlier today."

At the mention of Lieutenant George, every nerve in Joanna's body screamed, every muscle tightened. Milton George had been in charge of her rape case and all the other cases involving the serial rapist who had attacked a total of twelve women in the Richmond area before being arrested.

"What did Lieutenant George want?"

"I thought about flying out there to tell you, but—"

"Dammit, Mother, just tell me!"

"Lenny Plott has escaped from prison." Helene let out a long sigh.

"But that's not possible." Joanna couldn't believe the monster who had brutally attacked her was free and running around loose. "He's in a maximum-security prison. It would have been impossible for him to escape."

"I know what a shock this must be for you, dear, but I'm afraid it's true. Lenny Plott did escape. And—and I'm afraid there's more."

"More?"

"He escaped less than forty-eight hours ago and he's already found Melody Horton."

"What do mean he's 'already found' Melody?" Melody was the twenty-year-old college student who, along with Joanna and two other victims, had testified against their rapist and sent him away to prison for the rest of his natural life.

"She was kidnapped. A neighbor recognized the man she drove off with. She identified him from police photographs. It was Lenny Plott."

"Have the police found her?"

"Yes." Helene's voice was so low, Joanna could barely hear her.

"Is she . . . ?"

"She was strangled to death," Helene said, her words spoken unquaveringly. "Lieutenant George wanted you and Claire and Libby to know that Plott is on the loose and has already killed. . . . Please, come home, dear. Your life is in danger. Come home and I'll hire a bodyguard for you."

"Lenny Plott has no idea where I am now," Joanna said. "He doesn't know I moved to New Mexico and he doesn't know where Claire and Libby are. I don't even know where Libby is."

"Lieutenant George is afraid Lenny will somehow find out where the three of you have moved. He thinks Lenny will hunt y'all down."

"How could this have happened? When Lenny Plott went to prison, our nightmare was supposed to have ended. I won't—I can't live in fear. Not again. Not ever again!"

Joanna would never forget those first few weeks after her rape when she lived in fear the man would return and rape her again. Even after Lenny Plott had been arrested, she hadn't felt safe. To this day, she knew there was always a possibility that it could happen again, but she had learned to face the fear and put it in its proper place. She was careful, always cautious of strangers and new acquaintances. She'd bought a gun and learned how to use it properly. She'd taken self-defense classes and had undergone months of therapy. No, by God, she would not allow Lenny Plott's escape to destroy the life she'd built here in Trinidad. She would not run scared.

"Joanna, are you still there, dear? Please, say something."

"I'm all right. I'm staying where I am. I'm safe here. I'll tell Elena about Lenny Plott. I should have told her a long time ago, but I wanted to pretend it had never happened. Out here, no one knows about the rape."

"But what if Lenny finds you?"

"He won't." Joanna tried to reassure her mother, but in the back of her mind, doubts swarmed like angry killer bees. "I'll tell Elena and she can explain to Alex. There are dozens of ranch hands around this place, macho guys who know how to use guns. And Trinidad is a small town. Everybody knows everybody. If a stranger were to show up, I'd hear about it."

"Lieutenant George is going to call you later today," Helene said. "He's promised to keep us updated. They...the police have a statewide manhunt under way. They're going to catch that monster and put him back in prison where he belongs."

"Yes, of course, they will. He probably won't get out of Richmond."

"I wish you'd come home."

"I'm safer here, and Trinidad is my home now."

"Call me every day, just to let me know—" Helene's voice cracked.

"Every day. I promise."

"I love you, Joanna. You know that, don't you?"

"Yes, Mother," Joanna said. "And I love you."

"Take care, dear. And let me know if there's anything I can do."

"I will, Mother. Goodbye."

"Goodbye."

Joanna hung up the phone slowly, then slumped down on the apricot-gold leather sofa. For just a minute she felt completely numb, as if her body and mind had frozen instantly. Then, just as quickly, the feeling returned. She shivered, suddenly cold. Her hands trembled. The quivering sensation spread up her arms, down her legs. A tight fist clutched her chest. She couldn't breathe.

Dear God, no, please, no. A sour taste, salty and hot, rose in her throat. Memories—horrendous memories—flashed through her mind. Memories she had buried so deep she thought they could never resurface. She had spent five long, difficult years recovering from that night, putting every thought of Lenny Plott and what he'd done to her out of her mind. Forgetting had been the most difficult thing she'd ever done, but she had forced herself to forget, had forced herself to go on with her life. She was too strong to allow what had happened to her defeat her.

Joanna broke out in a cold sweat. Her heart thundered at a frantic pace. Doubling over, she clutched her knees, drew them up against her body and rocked back and forth. Heavy, painful tears lodged in her throat.

"If you scream, I'll kill you." He had whispered the words in her ear as he held the sharp knife blade to her throat.

"No! Don't do this to yourself," Joanna cried.

Squeezing her eyes shut, she tried to capture her tears, to stop them from falling.

Piercing blue eyes glared down at her. Hard, bruising hands clutched her breasts. A bony knee thrust between her legs. The strong odor of stale whiskey breath covered her mouth. She tried to shove him away, tried to scream. The knife blade nicked her throat. Blood trickled down onto her chest.

Joanna's eyes flew open. She shook from head to toe as she kept rocking back and forth. "Stop this! Don't remember! Please, don't remember.... Don't—"

The loud pounding on the front door sounded muffled to Joanna's ears, overpowered by the sound of her own heartbeat. Her mind was so filled with pain, the pain of trying not to remember, that it took her a few minutes to realize that someone was knocking at her door.

"Jo? Hey, Jo. Are you about ready to leave?" Elena called out as she walked into the living room.

Elena. Her friend. Someone who cared about her. She mustn't let Elena find her like this. Move, dammit, move! Sit up straight. Stop crying.

"My God, Jo, what's wrong?" Elena rushed over to the sofa. Dropping to her knees, she grabbed Joanna by the shoulders. "What's happened? Are you sick?"

Joanna managed to shake her head, but when she tried to respond, she couldn't. "Are you hurt?" Elena asked.

Shaking her head again, Joanna opened her mouth and tried to speak. The sound was a squeaky gasp.

"Try to tell me what happened." Elena shook Joanna soundly. "Come on, talk to me, Jo. You're frightening me." Elena reached out and wiped the tears off Joanna's cheeks, then slipped her arms around her and hugged her.

Joanna gulped several times, then groaned. Her body relaxed. She eased her hands off her knees and slid her feet onto the floor. Elena held on tight, continuing to hug her.

"Five—five years ago, I was raped," Joanna whispered.

"Oh, Jo... Jo. I'm so sorry."

"I left Virginia and came out here to New Mexico to start a new life." Joanna hugged Elena, then pulled away from her. "I didn't want anyone out here to know. I should have told you, after we became such good friends, but by then I'd put what happened behind me. I worked so hard at trying to forget."

Elena rubbed Joanna's arms. "What happened today? Did you have some sort of flashback?"

"My mother called. It seems the man who raped me... Oh, God!" Joanna jumped up off the sofa and paced back and forth. "This can't be happening!"

"What can't be happening?" Elena asked, standing and following Joanna around the room in her frantic stroll.

"The man who raped me—Lenny Plott—was what the police refer to as a serial rapist. I was his eleventh victim. After he raped his twelfth victim, the police caught him."

"Then he's in prison, isn't he?" Elena swirled about in front of Joanna, forcing her to halt. "Isn't he?"

"I testified against him. Claire Andrews, Libby Felton, Melody Horton and I. We made sure he would never rape another woman."

"I know it took a lot of guts to do what you four did. But you did the right thing."

"Yes, we did the right thing," Joanna said. "And when our rapist was sentenced to life in prison, we all went on with our lives. Melody stayed on in Virginia and finished college. Claire moved back home to Missouri. Libby just left town. We never heard from her again."

"And you came to Trinidad."

"Elena, Lenny Plott escaped from prison."

"What?"

"He escaped about forty-eight hours ago." Joanna covered her mouth with her hands.

Elena grabbed Joanna's hands and pulled them away from her face. "What are you not telling me?"

"He kidnapped Melody Horton and murdered her. The day the judge sentenced him, he swore that somehow he'd get free and hunt us all down. He swore he'd kill us."

Elena put her arms around Joanna, hugging her fiercely. "You're safe here, on the ranch, with us. He doesn't know where you are. He can't find you here."

"But what if he does?" Joanna, her eyes dry and dazed, looked at her best friend. "I'm scared, Elena. I'm so scared."

Elena rubbed Joanna's back. "I know. I know. But everything's going to be all right. J.T. will know exactly how to handle this situation. He'll take care of—"

"J.T.? No, please, I don't want your brother to know about this."

"Don't be silly," Elena said. "J.T. knows more about protecting someone than anybody in the whole wide world. He was a Secret Service agent until he got shot in the head and blinded in one eye. For the past six years, he's been a partner in a private security agency."

"Mother wants me to come home. Back to Virginia. She's offered to hire a bodyguard for me. I'm sure, if I asked her, she'd hire someone and send him out here."

"But don't you see, there's no need to hire another bodyguard when we've got J.T. It's what he does for a living."

"No, Elena, I—"

"We're not going to argue about this. You're going to stay here on the ranch and live every day as normally as you possibly can. J.T. is an expert on private security. He'll know what to do to keep you safe."

"I can't tell J.T. that I was—"

"Don't sell my big brother short. He'll understand. You can count on him. Trust me, Jo. Please. And trust J.T."

Trust J.T.? How could she trust him? How could she trust any man?

"This agency in Atlanta," Joanna said, "are there other agents? Someone J.T. could send back here when he returns? Mother will pay for—"

"What do you mean when he returns! Once I tell him about your situation, he'll stay here and guard you himself."

"I wouldn't ask him to do that." She wasn't sure what she feared most, Lenny Plott finding out where she was or J.T. Blackwood agreeing to act as her bodyguard. If he found her, Plott could kill her. But if she allowed herself to become involved with J.T., he could completely destroy her emotionally.

J.T. dismounted, dropped the reins and spoke softly to Washington, who followed behind him while he walked along the bank of the stream—his favorite spot on the ranch, high in the hills, secluded and quiet, close to nature.

The rage inside him simmered. A hot fury that he barely controlled consumed him. Part of the anger he felt was directed at himself for being such a macho jerk, such a total idiot. He should have known there was more to Joanna Beaumont's skittish nature and wariness than just an instant dislike of him. His damn ego had gotten in the way of his usual keen perception. His ego and his male libido.

He wasn't sure he had ever wanted a woman the way he wanted Joanna.

J.T. pulled his rifle from its leather holster attached to the saddle and removed the cloth bag he'd hung over the saddle horn. He ordered Washington to stay, then began a slow, steady climb up the mountainside. When he reached the summit, he braced his rifle against the side of a huge rock, then opened the cloth bag and removed a varied assortment of bottles and cans. He lined them up across the top of the rock formation, then lifted his rifle and walked backward, close to the edge of the summit. He aimed his rifle and fired repeatedly, destroying the row of inanimate objects he pretended were Lenny Plott. When he finished, he stood there and stared up at the blue sky, the afternoon sun blinding in its intensity.

"Joanna was raped five years ago." J.T. heard his sister's voice. *"She testified against her rapist. He has escaped from prison and already killed one of the women who testified against him. He swore he'd hunt all four women down and kill them."*

J.T. let out a bloodcurdling cry as savage and brutal as the primitive emotions he felt.

"I told her that she'd be safe here on the ranch. I assured her that you'd know what to do to protect her."

Protect Joanna. Yeah, he knew all about protecting people. He'd spent most of his life acting as someone's bodyguard. He had laid his life on the line every day he'd been a member of the country's Secret Service.

After the army and college, he'd spent more than a year undergoing exams, interviews and a complete investigation into his background before being hired in Washington. He had served time in field offices from Omaha to New Orleans, which had taken him from tediously boring assignments to stakeouts of underworld counterfeiting operations. He had guarded presidential candidates more than once, and had even pulled White House detail for several years.

His last assignment had nearly cost him his life—*had* cost him the vision in his left eye. But it had gotten him the Medal of Valor and an early retirement.

For the past six years, he'd worked with Sam Dundee, a man who had become his best friend. Dundee's Private Security was one of the most respected and successful private security businesses in the country.

Oh, yeah, J.T. Blackwood was a security expert. Acting as a bodyguard was what he did best. There was only a couple of small problems associated with guarding Joanna Beaumont. The woman hated him, although he didn't much blame her. And he wanted her, but didn't have the vaguest idea what a woman who'd been brutally raped would need from a lover.

He'd be a fool to take this assignment. He was far too personally involved. Despite Elena's insistence that he take the job himself, J.T. wondered if it wouldn't be wise to bring in another man from the agency. Simon Roarke was available and Gabriel Hawk would be finishing up an assignment within a week.

But then, J.T. doubted an around-the-clock bodyguard was needed at this point. At least not a professional. There were enough hands on the Blackwood ranch to see that Joanna was kept under watch. If and when Lenny Plott discovered her whereabouts would be the time for a trained bodyguard to step in.

He had put off talking to Joanna long enough. He'd present her with several alternatives, assuring her he would guarantee she was safe on the ranch, then he'd let her decide what she wanted done.

J.T. climbed down the mountainside, returned his rifle to its sheath and mounted Washington. It had been a long time since he had dreaded anything as much as he dreaded facing Joanna, now that he knew what had happened to her five years ago. What if he said or did the wrong thing? What if— Hell! What was the matter with him? When had he suddenly become the sensitive, emotional kind? He hadn't! Not now. Not ever. It was just that there was something about Joanna, something so gentle and tender and compelling, that he couldn't get her out of his head.

When he returned to the ranch, he turned Washington over to one of the stable hands instead of caring for the Appaloosa himself as he usually did. No point waiting any longer to confront Joanna.

He found her and Elena sitting on the front porch of the converted bunkhouse, both of them swaying back and forth in the rockers. Hesitating at the foot of the steps, he looked up at Elena.

"Where have you been?" his sister asked. "You rode off in a big hurry."

He glanced at Joanna; she stared down at her hands resting in her lap. Where was her fiery spirit? he wondered. Her face was too pale. She was too quiet. And she hadn't looked at him.

"I needed some time alone. To think."

"Lieutenant George called," Elena said. "The policeman from Virginia—"

"You've already told me who he is," J.T. said. "Did he have any updated information on Plott?"

Elena shook her head. "No. He pretty much just repeated what Mrs. Beaumont had told Joanna earlier when she called."

J.T. walked up the steps, stopping beside his sister. He placed his hand on her shoulder. "I need to talk to Joanna. Alone."

"Why alone?" Elena asked. "She needs me here. I don't want to leave her—"

"It's all right," Joanna said. "You go on home. I'll be fine. Really."

Elena stood, then pointed her finger in her brother's face. "Don't you dare be anything but gentle and understanding. Do you hear me?"

"I'll do my very best." But would his best be good enough? He might be able to manage understanding, at least up to a point. But he didn't know much about being gentle. There had been very little gentleness in his life and few occasions when he'd been called upon to show any tenderness. J.T. wasn't sure there was a gentle side to his nature.

Turning around, Elena bent over and hugged Joanna. "I'll do anything you need for me to do to help you through this." She squeezed J.T.'s arm as she passed him and walked down the steps and into the yard.

"Why don't we go inside," J.T. said. "It'll be more private."

"Why do we need privacy?" Still, Joanna stared down at her hands, avoiding making eye contact with him. "If I stay on the ranch, we won't be able to keep this a secret. Everyone will have to know."

"Fine." J.T. shrugged, then sat down in the rocker his sister had just vacated. "Do you or do you not want me to take charge of this situation?"

Joanna sighed. "Elena says that you're the very best at what you do—at being a bodyguard."

"I've spent years protecting people."

"I'll arrange with my mother to transfer whatever funds are necessary to cover your expenses." Joanna lifted her hands out of her lap and gripped the rocker's arms.

"I'll be here at the ranch another week anyway, so there'll be no charge." J.T. removed his Stetson, crossed his legs and perched his hat on his knee. "If you want me to stay on after my vacation, we can discuss my fee then."

"You'll stay on and take this assignment yourself?"

"If that's what you want." She looked so fragile, so vulnerable and helpless sitting there in the rocker, her small, delicate hands clutching the rocker's arms, her body wound as tight as a bowstring. "Or if you'd prefer, I can have one of the Dundee agency's best men fly out and take over the assignment."

"Elena wants you to be my bodyguard."

"What do you want, Jo?"

She raised her head, tilted her chin and stared him directly in the eye. "I want none of this to have happened. I want to go back five years and erase the past."

"Yeah, well...that's not possible, is it? All I can do is try to keep you safe now, in the present." J.T. wished he'd been around in the past to protect her. Scum like this Lenny Plott would never have touched Joanna, because if he had, J.T. would have personally annihilated him.

"Look, I'll be honest with you." Joanna released her death grip on the chair arms and stood, striding to the edge of the porch. She kept her back to J.T. "Before the—" she swallowed "—rape, I was fairly trusting and thought the world really was a wonderful place. My life had been almost perfect. I grew up as the only child of wealthy, successful parents, both of whom loved me. After I graduated from college, with a degree in art, I got a job at a small art museum in Richmond. I met and fell in love with an up-and-coming young lawyer in my father's law office and we became engaged. The only unhappy time in my life was when my father died of a heart attack about a year before... before the rape."

"What happened to your fiancé?" J.T. lifted his Stetson off his knee, stood and placed the hat on his head.

"I'm getting to that."

He walked up behind her, close, a hairbreadth away, but not touching. "Go on."

She tensed when she realized he was so close—so close she could feel the heat emanating from his big, powerful body. "The rape and what happened afterward changed me forever. Despite counseling, despite moving away and starting a new life out here in Trinidad, despite everything I've done to get over what happened to me, I've never been able to trust anyone easily again."

"I can understand how you might feel that way, at least for a while."

"Not just for a while." She wished he wasn't standing so close, wished she didn't have the almost-overwhelming urge to turn around and ask him to hold her in his arms. "After I was raped, my fiancé had a difficult time dealing with what had happened to me. When I needed him most—needed his love and support—he walked out on me."

"The bastard!" J.T. clasped her shoulders gently. Dear God, she was sprung so tight she was close to the breaking point. He was afraid that if she broke, she would fly into a million pieces. "You're better off without him, honey."

"Yes, I know." She wished J.T. hadn't touched her. Wished that his touch wasn't so firm and yet so gentle. Wished that his touch didn't make her want to lean back against his chest and have him surround her with his strong arms. "But Todd's desertion only made things worse for me. If I couldn't trust the man who had professed to love me, who had asked me to be his wife, who could I ever trust?"

"You can trust me, Jo." J.T. ran his big hands from her shoulders to her elbows and back up again, soothing her, his touch strong, gentle and nonthreatening. "Trust me with your life."

She shivered in his arms, the involuntary movement relieving some of the tension coiled so tightly inside her. More than anything, she wanted to trust J.T., but she wasn't sure she could.

"I don't want you to have another bodyguard sent from Atlanta." She leaned backward, allowing her body to just barely touch his. "I want you to stay in Trinidad and . . . I want you to protect me, J.T." She took a deep breath, then let it out slowly. "I promise that I'll try to trust you."

J.T. lowered his head, bringing his lips close to her ear. "And I promise I'll do everything possible to earn your trust."

Closing her eyes, Joanna pressed her shoulders into his chest, tilting her head back to rest against him. "I'm scared. I'm very scared."

"I'll keep you safe," he vowed. "We'll stay here on the ranch and I'll make certain someone is with you at all times, until Plott is captured and sent back to prison."

"But what if—"

"If by some chance he finds out where you are and comes after you before he's caught, then I'll stay at your side night and day. And if he comes near you, I'll kill him."

"Oh, J.T., you can't imagine what it was like for me that night." Opening her eyes, she glanced over at his big hand caressing her arm. "And afterward . . . at the trial, when . . . when I had to tell all about what he'd done to me."

"Hush, honey. Don't talk about it. Don't remember." Dear God in heaven, he didn't think he could bear to hear any of the details. Knowing only the basic facts was enough to make him crazy. Learning that some sick pervert had forced himself on Joanna made J.T. want to hunt the bastard down and castrate him.

"It wasn't my fault. It wasn't! Maybe I should have fought harder. Maybe I should have just let him slit my throat with his knife." Tremors racked Joanna's body. "Todd blamed me. He—he thought I could have prevented it, somehow. He couldn't even bear to look at me—afterward. That made me feel as dirty as I had right after the rape."

"Any man who truly loved a woman would never blame her," J.T. said. "What happened to you was Lenny Plott's fault. His and no one else's. I promise you that if it's necessary, I'll move heaven and earth to make sure he never hurts you again."

Breathing in the sweet, clean scent of Joanna, J.T. buried his face in her hair that hung loosely about her neck. He kissed her on the temple, then wrapped his arms around her and held her close against his chest. She didn't resist. They stood there on her porch for a long time, J.T.'s arms draped around her, cocooning her from the world. Protectively. Caringly. Possessively.

Chapter 5

Joanna wasn't sure what had been the most difficult adjustment in the five days since her mother's phone call. Having to deal with painful memories and haunting fears she had thought were long since buried was a challenge she felt she was strong enough to handle. Losing a great deal of her privacy and freedom annoyed her greatly. She wasn't used to the ranch hands paying much attention to her, at least not since she'd first moved into the bunkhouse three years ago. Now, J.T. had a revolving shift of men keeping an eye on her. She certainly wasn't accustomed to someone knowing her whereabouts twenty-four hours a day. She'd been told she couldn't leave the ranch without an escort. She couldn't even go horseback riding on the ranch without one of the hands going with her. Elena and Alex had been wonderful—sympathetic, caring and understanding. The caring and understanding she appreciated; the sympathy she could do without. She felt sorry enough for herself without being weighed down by other people's pity.

She wasn't sure how she felt about J.T. knowing everything concerning her past. Relieved mostly, she guessed, but a little apprehensive, too. When he'd held her in his arms on the front porch and promised to keep her safe, he had said and done all the right things. Oddly enough, he'd been gentle and kind and supportive. She'd been so sure he would react the way her ex-fiancé had; that he would assume the worst about her. Todd certainly had. But J.T. wasn't Todd McAllister. The two men had absolutely nothing in common. Todd was a seventh-generation Southern gentleman; cultured, refined and, she realized now, an elitist snob. He would have been revolted by Annabelle and Benjamin's love affair. He never would have understood. Todd hadn't approved of "fornicating" outside one's own social circle.

Joanna laughed aloud. How could she have been in love with Todd? Pretty-boy Todd, with all his money and good breeding, had been shallow, conceited and selfish. She supposed she'd been drawn to him because they had seemed to have so much in common, her background being very similar to his. He was a fourth-generation lawyer, and her father had been one of the most respected lawyers in Virginia. Todd's uncle was a state senator and so was her mother. She and Todd had had numerous friends in common. In fact, that was how they'd met. A fraternity brother of Todd's had been dating Joanna's cousin, Diane.

Dammit! She hadn't thought much about Todd since she'd moved to New Mexico. After months of mourning his desertion five years ago, she had finally realized she was better off without him. Now, here she was, tormented not only by memories of her rapist, but by memories of her ex-fiancé's callous rejection.

Joanna jerked the piece of ninety-pound Saunders paper from the tray of water. Holding the piece by the edges, she shook off the surplus water and laid it on a drawing board, then dried her hands on her smock and stuck the edges of the paper down with strips of brown paper tape. Reaching into her pocket, she retrieved the thumbtacks and promptly stuck one in each taped end.

She needed to stretch several pieces and have them ready for the three watercolors she had been commissioned to paint for a dealer in Santa Fe. Last week she had stretched the canvases for her two commissioned oil paintings, one of which already had a buyer.

She hadn't painted at all in the past few days. Instead, she'd busied herself with preparations for work, done some in-depth housecleaning, rewatched a dozen videocassettes—her favorite musicals from the thirties and forties—and read Annabelle Beaumont's diary through, from beginning to end.

When she had planned to visit the reservation to escape J.T., she had thought she could do enough sketches to foster some new ideas for the commissioned works. She wanted to try something different from her usual landscapes and portraits of the Navajo in typical settings. She had wanted to capture something of the Navajo spirit that had eluded her in her earlier work. No matter how diligently she tried, she couldn't seem to see past the surface, into the soul of New Mexico and the proud Navajo, the way her great-grandmother had done. But then, Annabelle had not focused her attention on a whole nation of people, but only on one man. A man she had loved as no other. It had been Benjamin Greymountain's spirit she had captured in her heart and then transformed the essence of her feelings into the words written in her diary.

But Joanna's trip to the reservation had been canceled. J.T. had said it was best to postpone any and all excursions for the time being. She knew he meant until Lenny Plott had been apprehended.

Slumping down in the overstuffed tan, green and apricot plaid chair, Joanna picked up her sketch pad from the hand-carved pine table to her right. In the early-dawn hours these past five mornings, when she'd been unable to sleep, she had told herself she should be painting, should be accomplishing something. Instead, she'd retreated to her sketch pad, using her charcoal pencils to fill page after page with hastily rendered images of J.T. Blackwood. In some sketches he wore his Stetson, in others his head was bare. Many were half-finished profiles, most from his right side, but several from the left, depicting his sinister-looking eye patch.

Flipping through the pad, she stopped and glared at the sketch she'd done this morning. This charcoal rendering was different from all the others. This was John Thomas Blackwood, rugged, hard, unsmiling. Neither white man nor Native American. Only primitive male.

She slapped the pad closed, then threw it on the floor at her feet. What ever had possessed her to fill half the sketch pad with drawings of J.T.? What would he think if he saw them? He might get the wrong idea and assume she—

No! She did not feel anything for J.T., except maybe gratitude. She was exceedingly thankful that he was in charge of keeping her safe; that if necessary, he would become her personal bodyguard. She prayed the necessity would never arise, that the authorities would arrest Lenny Plott and return him to prison before he was able to find her. Or Claire. Or Libby.

The second week of J.T.'s vacation would end soon, but he had promised to stay on at the ranch. Even though she had seen him only at a distance the past few days, she felt reassured by his presence. She knew that he was keeping close tabs on her and taking every precaution for her safety.

But there seemed to be no immediate danger. No one knew where Lenny Plott was. He could still be in Virginia. Or he could already be in New Mexico. Or he could have gone to Missouri to hunt down Claire Andrews. Or he could somehow have discovered Libby Felton's whereabouts. Only God knew what slimy rock that monster had crawled under.

No, there was no immediate danger from Lenny Plott, a man the authorities couldn't find. Joanna's only immediate danger came from her ridiculous thoughts of J.T. Blackwood. She was confused and overly emotional, her nerves strung to the breaking point. That's why I'm thinking the way I am, she decided. All right, so he'd been tender and understanding about the rape. And he had made a promise her heart wanted to believe he would keep—that he would protect her from all harm. Still, that was no reason for her to start thinking of him as some knight in shining armor, as a man equal to his great-grandfather, a man capable of fulfilling her romantic dreams.

The loud knock on the front door startled her. She jumped, then her body stiffened. Don't react this way, she told herself. She had to stop thinking every bump, every creak, every unexpected sound might be Lenny Plott. The man would hardly come to her door and knock, would he?

The knocking continued, then ceased abruptly. "Joanna? Are you all right?" J.T. called to her.

She opened her mouth to answer, but only a quivering squeak came out. Her mind issued orders, but her body didn't respond.

"Joanna!"

By the time she had convinced herself she could move, that her legs could actually hold her weight and walk across the living room, J.T. had used the spare key she'd given him to unlock her door. He stormed into her house, scanning the huge expanse of combined living and dining areas. She met him in the middle of the room. He glared at her, then reached out and grabbed her by the shoulders. She knew he wanted to shake her, and realized how much control he was exerting to keep from doing just that.

"Why the hell didn't you answer me?" He squeezed her shoulders, then released her.

"I'm sorry. I—"

"Are you all right?"

"I'm okay. What do you want? Why did you stop by?"

"I came by to see if you'd like to take a ride with me," he said. "You haven't been off the ranch in five days. I thought maybe you'd enjoy an outing."

"Oh, I see. Was this Elena's idea? Did she tell you that I've been complaining about feeling hemmed in?"

J.T. grinned—a half smile, really, not showing any teeth. "She mentioned you were used to coming and going as you pleased, to taking off for hours at a time to sketch or paint."

Joanna nodded.

"Elena fixed a picnic basket," J.T. said. "Sandwiches. A thermos of iced tea. That sort of stuff." He glanced at Joanna, taking note of her appearance. "Have you been in your gown all day?"

"I'll go change." She whirled around, then saw her sketch pad on the floor. "Where are we going?" She walked by the plaid chair, stuck out her foot and kicked the pad under the chair.

"I thought you might want to go out past Trinidad to the old archaeological dig where your great-grandparents worked the summer they lived here."

Halting in the doorway to her bedroom, Joanna swung around and faced J.T. "What? I tried to get permission from the man who owns the land, to go out to the old site, but I could never get anywhere with him. He said he had enough trespassers traipsing around on his property, stealing artifacts and—"

"That old man was my grandfather's worst enemy. It seems Hezekiah Mahoney married the woman my grandfather had picked out for himself and John Thomas never forgave either of them. I think it pleased Hezekiah to see my grandfather taken down a peg or two when he had to claim a half-breed as his heir."

"Are you saying—"

"I'm saying Hezekiah and I have always understood each other." J.T. walked over and sat down in the plaid chair. "I've done him a few favors over the years, and he owes me one or two. He isn't unreasonable. He allows archaeologists and archaeology students to work out at the old dig."

"And he gave us permission to visit the site?"

"Yep. So hurry up and change clothes."

"Can we stay out there for the rest of the day?" she asked. "Do you have the time? I'd love to take a sketch pad and do some work while we're there. I need some fresh ideas for the paintings I've been commissioned to do."

"We can stay until the sun goes down, if that's what you want," J.T. said. "You can look the place over. We can eat Elena's lunch. And you can draw to your heart's content."

"Thanks, J.T."

He liked her smile. Real. Honest. Warm. "Jo, while we're out there, we need to talk. Okay?"

Her smile disappeared, and J.T. wished he'd waited to mention anything about their needing to talk. But he wanted to prepare her, get her ready for what he had to tell her. No matter what happened in the days and weeks ahead, he was not going to lie to her. Not about anything.

"Okay," she said, then hurried into her bedroom.

J.T. laid his Stetson on the hand-carved table to his right. Leaning over, resting his elbows on his thighs, he let his hands dangle between his spread legs.

Today's excursion out to the old archaeological dig on Mahoney's ranch *had* been Elena's idea. She'd been after him for two days to call old Hezekiah and arrange to take Joanna on this special outing. After his talk with Lieutenant Milton George and his telephone calls—one to Sam Dundee, and another to an FBI friend, Dane Carmichael— J.T. had decided it might be easier for him to discuss hard, cold facts with Joanna while she was relaxed and enjoying herself.

In the five days since he'd accepted responsibility for her safekeeping, J.T. had taken precautions to keep Joanna Beaumont as safe as possible without actually placing a twenty-four-hour-a-day guard at her door. He had suggested she should move into the main house. After all, they had more than enough room. But she hadn't wanted to leave her own home. He supposed he understood how she felt. But if Plott did make a move, J.T. would have no choice but to insist she stay with him. Or—and he really didn't want to think about his other choice—he would have to move into the renovated bunkhouse with her.

He had lived in close confines with a beautiful woman more than once and been able to remain completely professional and emotionally uninvolved. But Joanna Beaumont was more than just a client. She was someone he desired. That could pose a major problem for him—wanting a woman he had sworn to protect. A woman who, by her own admission, didn't completely trust him.

Staring down at his booted feet, J.T. noticed the edge of some sort of book sticking out from underneath the chair. He reached down, pulled out the large notebook, and picked it up. Leaning back in the chair, he laid the sketch pad on his lap and opened it to the first page. The bottom dropped out of his stomach. He turned the page, then sucked in a deep breath and let it out. Hurriedly, he flipped through the pages, and on each, he saw himself. They were rough, obviously hastily sketched likenesses, but there was no mistaking Joanna's chosen subject. When he looked at the last sketch, about halfway through the pad, he closed his eyes, blotting out what he saw. In that one drawing, she had come too close to capturing the real J.T. Blackwood. A man at odds with himself. Hard. Cold. Cynical. A man torn between two cultures—the one his grandfather had forced him to accept, and the one the old man had taught him to be ashamed of and to completely reject.

J.T. closed the pad and slipped it back under the chair. He wished he'd never seen the damned thing. If Joanna was sketching him, over and over again, seeing past the facade he presented to the world and getting too close to the angry, disillusioned man inside him, that meant she had allowed all the romantic nonsense concerning their great-grandparents to make her think— Hell! He had to put a stop to this before it started. He wasn't averse to the idea of having an affair with Joanna, now that he realized she wasn't just another spoiled rich girl out for kicks. But no way did he want her to think of him as some dream lover who could fulfill all her fantasies.

It would be better for both of them if he set her straight today. He didn't know a damn thing about romance or happily-ever-after or making love to a woman who needed the utmost tenderness.

He wondered if there had been a man in her life, someone she had trusted enough to take into her bed, since the night Lenny Plott had raped her. What did it do to a woman to be brutalized that way, to lose all sense of power and control? What would I have done if I'd been her fiancé? J.T. asked himself. He knew he would have wanted to hunt Plott down and kill him with his bare hands. And he knew he never would have deserted Joanna. If she'd been his woman, he would have— But she hadn't been his woman, wasn't his woman now. And for both their sakes, he had to keep it that way.

"I don't know how to thank you, J.T." Joanna spread her arms open wide as if somehow she could embrace the land and the sky, and perhaps even grasp the moment and hold on to it forever. "It still looks so much like Annabelle described it and yet so very different, too. They lived in tents right here on the site, and went into Trinidad for supplies."

"Your great-grandfather was the archaeologist. Why did he bring his wife along with him? This is some pretty rugged country, even now. It could hardly have been a suitable place for a Virginia society matron." J.T. lifted the thermos from the picnic basket he had placed beside him when he'd sat down atop the huge, oddly shaped rock formation.

Joanna looked down into the valley below. Such a wide-open space. Such an incredible view. Steep-walled canyons. Never-ending blue sky. And colors so sharp and vivid, they took her breath away.

"Annabelle was a lot more than a society matron. She was a site artist and photographer. She kept a detailed record of the artifacts her husband found, photographing or sketching every discovery. And, for your information, Ernest Beaumont wasn't just an archaeologist." She turned and smiled at J.T. "He was a world-renowned archaeologist, and he counted among his friends both Earl H. Morris and Alfred V. Kidder. He took part in Kidder's Pecos conference in 1927." Suddenly realizing she was babbling, Joanna hushed, shook her head and laughed. "I admit that, after reading Annabelle's diary, I found out everything I could about my great-grandparents."

"Did you discover the reason your great-grandmother committed adultery?" J.T. asked.

Her laughter died as quickly as it had been born. She sat down on the rock beside J.T. and watched while he poured iced tea into plastic cups. He handed her a cup. She accepted it, being careful to neither touch him nor look at him.

"Ernest Beaumont had been a contemporary of Annabelle's father, who had arranged the marriage for Annabelle, his only child, shortly before his death." Joanna sipped her tea. "She was eighteen when she married. Ernest was forty-two. She was a dutiful wife, who gave him two sons, and often accompanied him on his archaeological digs, working with him. They had a contented marriage, but not a passionate one."

"So Annabelle met Benjamin and saw her chance to put a little passion into her life." J.T. unwrapped a ham-and-cheese sandwich. "She had a summer affair with a wild savage, then returned to her safe, secure life in Virginia and wrote beautiful prose about her 'great love.'" J.T. grunted, his cynicism obvious in both his words and the cold expression on his face.

"She *did* love him. She never forgot him. Never loved anyone else."

"Yeah, sure. Look, Jo, if she'd really loved Benjamin, she'd have given up everything and stayed out here in New Mexico with him."

"How could she have done that? It wasn't as if all she had to do was pack her bags and leave her husband. She had two children. And it was Benjamin who told her she couldn't sacrifice her children for him. That if she did, someday she'd grow to hate him."

"Annabelle's diary sure has you hooked, doesn't it?" J.T. handed her a sandwich. "Elena packed chips and pickles. Want some?"

"No, thank you." She unwrapped the sliced sandwich, lifted one of the halves to her mouth and took a bite.

"Hey, there's no need for you to get upset with me or pout," J.T. said. "You and I disagree about our great-grandparents' affair. You think it was some grand passion, some eternal love, and that they're up in heaven now, reunited and happy. I, on the other hand, think they had the hots for each other, sneaked off together every chance they could, but when the summer ended, they went their separate ways without a bunch of mushy sentimental exchanges or broken hearts." Joanna chewed slowly, swallowed, and took another bite. She turned her back on J.T., not wanting to listen to him make light of their great-grandparents' tragic love affair. Obviously, the man didn't have a romantic, loving bone in his body.

J.T. grasped her shoulder. She jumped, then jerked around and faced him. "You don't know the first thing about love. Real love. The kind Annabelle and Benjamin shared."

"Let's drop the subject." He squeezed her shoulder. She glared at his hand. Immediately, he slipped his hand down her arm. His touch was light, but sensual. Joanna shivered. J.T. lifted his hand, clutched her chin and tilted her face. "Besides, we've got more important things to discuss than our ancestors."

Joanna held up her right hand in J.T.'s face. "You might not believe in mushy, sentimental exchanges or passionate, everlasting love, but Benjamin Greymountain did. He put his whole heart into crafting this ring." She grabbed J.T.'s right hand, lifting it in hers. "And this one. These rings symbolized everything he felt. Everything he and Annabelle had shared."

J.T. glared at her. Her heart pounded, the beat drowning out every other sound. He grasped her by the back of the neck, sliding one hand under her long ponytail while gripping her waist with the other, and drawing her toward him.

"What do you want me to say, Jo?" He lowered his head, his lips so close to hers that he felt her breath on his mouth. "Okay. Maybe Annabelle and Benjamin were in love. How do I know? What the hell difference does it make? Just because you and I inherited their rings, doesn't mean there's some special bond between us."

Who was he trying so damned hard to convince—her or himself? He wanted to deny it, wanted to pretend it didn't exist. But it did. There *was* some sort of bond between him and Joanna. There had been since the moment they met. But it wasn't what she thought it was, wasn't what she wanted. It was plain, old-fashioned lust. And J.T. would bet his last dollar that lust had been the overriding emotion between Benjamin and Annabelle.

J.T. wanted to take Joanna. Here. Now. On this hard, hot rock in the middle of nowhere, with only the birds and the insects and the big blue sky as witnesses. And perhaps the ghosts of two long-dead lovers. Had his great-grandfather felt this way about Annabelle? Had his blood run hot every time he'd touched her?

J.T. took Joanna in his arms, kissing her as he had longed to kiss her since the day they met. A wild, hungry passion ruled his actions. He was neither gentle nor patient. When she did not respond, but sat in his arms, stiff and unyielding, he thrust his tongue into her mouth and cupped her hip with one hand while he held her head in place with the other.

He ended the kiss abruptly, resting his forehead against hers. His breathing was ragged and harsh. Taking her shoulders in his hands, he held her at arm's length. "I'm sorry, Jo. I didn't mean to be so rough. I'm not used to taking things easy or being gentle."

She looked directly at him. "You think I need to be handled with kid gloves, don't you? Because of the rape. You think I'm not normal anymore, that I can't react the way a normal woman would."

"I don't think any such thing." He rubbed her shoulders. "I just think my kiss might have been a little too brutal. You froze solid in my arms, honey."

"For your information, you aren't the first man who's kissed me since.... I have dated. There have been other men. Is your ego so enormous you think all you had to do was kiss me and I'd fall at your feet, that you would be the only one who could sexually arouse me?"

"Did you respond to any of these men you dated?" His touch on her shoulders softened. "Did you have sex with any of them?"

"I—I don't think that's any of your business."

He ran one hand across her shoulder, then draped his big fingers around the side of her neck, caressing her with tenderness. "I made you a promise to protect you, to keep you safe. Now, I'm going to make you another promise. I promise that I'll never take your power and control away from you. That even if I possess you completely, it will be only because you've given me the right."

Joanna shivered. He was telling her that he wanted her, that he expected them to become lovers. Did she want him? Was she prepared to be his lover? "There hasn't been anyone since... My former fiancé and I—"

Releasing her, not touching her at all, J.T. lowered his head and kissed her again. This time his mouth moved over hers with soft, tender passion. When she made no protest, he deepened the kiss by slow degrees. Joanna slipped her arms around his neck, encouraging him, responding, hesitantly at first, but soon taking charge of the kiss. When she was breathless and trembling, she eased away from him and stood.

The bright afternoon sun coated her with warmth. She breathed deeply, then smiled at J.T. "You're a man of your word, aren't you, J.T. Blackwood?"

"I try to be," he said. "If I give a promise, I keep it."

She nodded, then turned away from him and looked back down over the wide expanse of northwestern New Mexico's rugged yet fiercely beautiful landscape. Did believing J.T. was a man of his word mean that she trusted him? She wanted to trust him—indeed, needed to trust him—and perhaps, on some level, she did. But not completely, and never with her heart.

"Before we left the ranch this morning, you said we needed to talk, and I know it wasn't about Annabelle and Benjamin," Joanna said.

He stood, walked over to her and drew her back up against his chest. She relaxed against him.

"I talked to Lieutenant George." Joanna tensed in his arms. "He has contacted Claire Andrews and Libby Felton."

"How did he find Libby?" Joanna asked.

"It wasn't difficult. She has a driver's license, a couple of credit cards. She files income taxes."

"Oh, I never thought about how easy it would be to find her. Where is she living now?"

"Texas," J.T. said.

"What else did Lieutenant George tell you?"

"Plott seems to have disappeared, and left no trace." J.T. hugged her to him. "And even if Plott has more trouble than the authorities had getting the information he needs on you and the other two women, it won't be impossible for him to get it."

"What are you saying? That if Plott wants to find us, he can?"

"I'm afraid so. I contacted an old friend of mine, Dane Carmichael. He's an FBI agent. You realize the Feds are already involved. They were called in when Melody Horton was kidnapped."

"And?"

"Hell, Jo. Why didn't you tell me Plott had millions of dollars at his disposal? The guy is some sort of Virginia blueblood whose name is really Leonard Mayfield Plott III, and he comes from the same kind of wealthy, aristocratic background you do."

"I know." She crossed her arms over J.T.'s where they wrapped around her. "But I don't see what his background has to do with—"

"A guy with that kind of money can pay to get any information he needs. God knows how much he paid out to engineer his escape from prison."

"He's going to find me, isn't he? And when he knows where I am, he'll come after me."

"Yeah, there's a good chance that sooner or later he'll come to Trinidad. But we'll be ready for him. I'll keep you safe."

They stood there, looking down at the canyon below them. Joanna thought she heard the sound of drums somewhere off in the distance, but when she saw a streak of lightning on the far horizon, followed by a low rumble of thunder, she realized she had imagined the drums—just as she had imagined them the first time she'd seen J.T.

At sunset, J.T. drove up to the ranch house and parked, then rounded the vehicle, lifted Joanna's sketch pad from her lap and assisted her.

"J.T.!" Elena ran out into the yard. "I was just going to call you on your cellular phone when Alex heard you drive up."

"What's wrong?" Joanna asked.

Alex stepped off the porch. Elena turned to him, her eyes pleading. Alex looked directly at J.T. "That Lieutenant George just phoned from Richmond. It seems Claire Andrews received a phone call from Lenny Plott this afternoon. He warned her that he was heading west, that he had business in Missouri and he'd be seeing her soon."

Joanna gasped, then covered her mouth with her clutched fist. J.T. put his arm around her and pulled her up against him.

"He's found out where Claire lives," Joanna said. "How long will it be before he finds me, too?"

Chapter 6

*H*is hand closed over her mouth, silencing her scream. He gazed down into her eyes and laughed when he saw the terror she could not hide.

"I promised I'd get out of prison and hunt you down, didn't I?" Lenny Plott's grin widened as he laid the knife across her throat. "I warned you that you'd be sorry if you testified against me. You and the other three."

She struggled to free herself, pushing up against him, but he pressed her down, trapping her with his body.

"You can't get away from me. There's no one here to save you." He removed his hand from her mouth, then kissed her hard, thrusting his tongue inside.

Joanna moaned. He slipped his hand under her gown, inching his way up her leg.

No, please, dear God. Not again. Not ever again! She prayed he would go ahead and kill her. She felt his fingers, painful and probing, and felt the knife at her throat.

Joanna's scream rent the night air. She jerked straight up in bed. Sweat coated her body, drenching her nightgown. Trembling from head to toe, she grasped the bottom sheet with both hands as she tried to slow her harsh, accelerated breathing. Reaching out a trembling hand, she switched on the bedside lamp.

A dream. Only a dream. But it had seemed so real. Too real. Had it been a premonition? Was it inevitable that she faced Lenny Plott again?

With his 9-mm Glock pistol held firmly and ready to fire, J.T. flung open the bedroom door and quickly scanned the area for an intruder. When he saw none, he turned to Joanna.

"What happened?" Replacing his gun in the shoulder holster he was wearing, he walked toward the bed. "You scared the hell out of me."

"Where did you come from?" Sliding to the side of the bed, she slipped her legs off the edge.

"I decided to have the ranch hands take turns standing guard outside. Starting last night. I woke up early and came over to relieve Chuck Webb." J.T. sat down beside Joanna. "I hadn't been here more than ten minutes when I heard you screaming."

Joanna scooted away from J.T., not thinking rationally, only feeling vulnerable and insecure. "It was just a dream. A nightmare, really."

"Must have been some nightmare," J.T. said. "Want to tell me about it?" Joanna was acting skittish, like a spooked mare, he thought. If only she would let him, he'd take her in his arms and hold her, but he could see plainly that she didn't want to be touched. Not right now.

Joanna shook her head. "I'd like to forget it."

"Think you can go back to sleep?" he asked.

"No." She wondered if she'd ever sleep again without fearing the return of the nightmares. For months after the rape, in fact for nearly a year, she had seldom slept the whole night through. "What time is it?"

"It's about five o'clock. If you don't think you can go back to sleep, I'll fix us some coffee."

J.T. stood, but stopped abruptly before taking a step when he felt the tentative touch of Joanna's fingertips against his hand. He looked down at her hand reaching out for him. His chest tightened; his stomach knotted. Turning his hand upside down, he offered her his open palm. Damn, but he wanted to grab her, drag her into his arms and hold her close and safe. Instead he waited, holding his breath.

She laid her hand in his, threading her fingers through his fingers, clasping their hands together.

Nothing in his life had prepared him for the feelings that coursed through him at that precise moment. Desire softened by overwhelming tenderness. A fierce protectiveness that made him want to fight the world for her. And a primitive possessiveness that shouted, *This woman is mine!*

He could not bring himself to look at her, uncertain what he would see in her eyes, and afraid of what he might do.

Holding tightly to his hand, she eased off the bed and stood. "Thank you, for being here."

He lifted his downcast gaze, drinking in the sight of Joanna, all feminine beauty in her teal silk nightshirt. Her rich, dark red hair tumbled around her shoulders in a thick, fiery mass. She stared at him with earthy, moss green eyes.

He grew hard and heavy, the very sight of her arousing him painfully. "Joanna—"

"Let me put on my robe and I'll go fix our coffee." She released his hand, turned and picked up her matching teal silk robe from the corner chair. "I have some banana-nut muffins I made fresh yesterday."

The moment she pulled away from him, he felt bereft, as if he'd been robbed of the tentative closeness blossoming between them.

"Muffins and coffee sound good to me," he said, and followed her out of the bedroom.

She flipped on a lamp in the living room as they passed through, then turned on the fluorescent light in the kitchen. J.T. sat down in a Windsor chair at the table.

"Are you sure I can't help you?" he asked.

"Thanks, but I know where everything is and can do it quicker without any help."

He sat and watched her as she prepared the coffee and warmed the muffins. He couldn't keep his eyes off her. Damn! What was wrong with him? He hadn't been this horny in years. If he needed a woman, he could solve that problem easily enough. But that was it. He didn't want just any woman. He wanted Joanna Beaumont. And despite her denials and her brave show of strength, she was vulnerable and fragile and filled with distrust. There was a raging bull inside him, a rutting animal. But the object of his desire needed a patient, gentle and understanding lover. Hell, what a mess!

He traced the lines and shapes on the table cover, then noticed it was a woven cloth of Navajo design. He'd seen enough Navajo rugs and blankets and other items to recognize them. When he'd given Elena permission to redecorate the ranch house after she'd married Alex, she had used various Navajo items in almost every room.

Joanna placed two mugs of piping-hot coffee down on the table, then removed the huge muffins from the microwave and laid each on a separate plate. Placing a plate in front of J.T., she sat down opposite him. She tore her muffin in half, broke off a piece and popped it into her mouth. Chewing slowly, she swallowed, then washed the morsel down with a sip of coffee.

J.T. lifted his mug. The coffee smelled good. He always started his mornings with a pot of coffee. But this morning, he'd been too anxious to bother with it. His gut instincts had told him he should be near Joanna. Somehow he had known she was going to need him.

Holding the mug in both hands, he sipped the coffee. "Was your dream about Plott?"

She gazed down into the dark liquid in her mug. "Yes. He had found me and was—" Joanna looked at J.T. and drew in a deep breath when she saw him staring at her, an odd expression on his face. "He was raping me...before he killed me."

"No wonder you woke up screaming." J.T. laid his hand, palm up, on the table. "It's not going to happen, Jo. You're safe with me. Plott may find out where you are, but he'll have to go through me to get to you. And tougher bastards than Plott have found out it's not so easy to get through me.''

Joanna glanced down at his outstretched hand. He was offering her comfort and support, the way he'd done in the bedroom. He wasn't grabbing, wasn't taking, wasn't forcing anything. He was just waiting for her to make the first move. She laid her hand in his. With gentle strength, he encompassed her hand with his.

She looked up at him and smiled. He returned the smile and squeezed her hand.

"I'm all right," she said. "I'll admit that I'm scared, but I'm dealing with it. I've had to deal with it before. For a long time after the rape, I had nightmares. I kept reliving what had happened over and over, and each time it got worse. That first year, even after I came out here to New Mexico, I seldom slept the whole night through.''

"Yeah, I can understand," he said. "I had a few nightmares after this." He pointed to his black eye patch. "The bullet severed the optical nerve and screwed things up pretty bad inside my head. I was lucky I didn't die or wind up some sort of vegetable.''

"The eye patch suits you. Makes you look roguish and a little dangerous.''

"I am dangerous, Jo. You might do well to remember that.''

"Are you trying to warn me about something?'' she asked.

He squeezed her hand, released it and stood. Lifting his coffee mug, he took a swig of the warm, sweet liquid, then set the mug back down on the table. "You're a sentimental, romantic woman. You need something I can't give you. I don't want to wind up hurting you, but I could, if you let me.''

He walked into the living room, propped his booted foot on the hearth and stared up at the portrait hanging above the fireplace. A beautiful woman with coppery red hair, cut in a fashionable twenties bob, stared down at J.T. with compelling blue-green eyes.

"That's Annabelle Beaumont." Joanna walked into the living room. "I painted her portrait, using some old photographs to go by and from studying the portrait of her that was painted when she was sixteen. Her father had it done and it hangs in one of the guest bedrooms at Mother's house."

"I can see why Benjamin Greymountain wanted her," J.T. said. "She was a beautiful woman." Turning his head, he ran his gaze over Joanna's face. "As a matter of fact, you look a bit like her."

"Yes, I know. I resemble my father a great deal, and he was told he took after his grandmother."

J.T. wondered what she'd say if he told her that he looked a bit like Benjamin Greymountain, that although he'd never seen any photographs of his ancestor, and didn't even know if any existed, he had seen Benjamin's likeness. When his mother had given him the silver-and-turquoise ring, she had also given him a yellowed sketch, the edges of the paper frayed and the charcoal drawing somewhat faded. She had told him that the sketch went with the ring, that both had belonged to her grandfather, Benjamin Greymountain, a Navajo silversmith and a revered leader to his people.

J.T. paced around the living room, knowing he should leave before he said or did something he would regret, but he didn't want to desert Joanna. If he left, she'd know he was running from her. And where could he run? Outside to stand guard? He had the oddest notion that there was nowhere on earth he could run to get away from Joanna, to escape the way he felt about her.

He stopped at the easel set up before the row of windows looking out onto the front porch. Glancing down at the sketch, he caught his breath. Damn! Yesterday when he'd taken her to the site of the old archaeological dig, she'd spent a couple of hours sketching and several times he had caught her watching him. But he'd had no idea she was using him as subject matter.

Hell, he shouldn't be surprised. She'd already filled half a notebook with rough sketches of him. But this was not a rough sketch. This was a completed work. And there was something about the way he looked in the picture that greatly disturbed him. He couldn't quite put his finger on it, but there was something—something alien to him.

"I didn't mean for you to see that." She walked up beside him. "I suppose I should have asked your permission before drawing you."

He grabbed her wrist. She gasped. "Why would you have bothered to ask my permission to do another sketch, when you'd already filled a notebook with sketches of me?"

She jerked away, glaring at him, her mouth rounded in surprise. "How did you know? When did you see my sketches?"

"I found the pad yesterday while I was waiting for you to change clothes. It was sticking halfway under the chair I sat down in."

"Why didn't you say something then?"

"I didn't want to embarrass you."

"You didn't want—" Joanna laughed. "You're so damn egotistical, J.T. Blackwood. Those sketches aren't what you think. And neither is that one." She pointed at the completed sketch on her easel. "If you think I'm some lovesick fool—"

"I never said you were a lovesick fool. Just a sentimental, romantic fool. You've got it in your head that because your great-grandmother had an affair with a native, you're destined to do the same."

"I wish I'd never told anyone, least of all you, about Annabelle's diary!" Spinning around, she marched over to the easel, ripped off the sketch and threw it to the floor, then lifted her foot and stomped on the torn paper.

"There's no need for you to get violent. I didn't mean to upset you, only warn you not to build any romantic fantasies around me."

J.T. grinned, a stupid, smirky, macho grin, and Joanna wanted to slap that silly smile off his face. "For your information, I have five commissioned works to do, all with a Native American theme. I've built my career on creating unique oil and watercolor paintings as well as finely detailed sketches. But somehow I've never been able to truly capture the spirit of this land or the Navajo people. Using you as a subject has helped me focus on your ancestry. In a couple of sketches I've come so close to putting my emotions on paper, in delving deep enough inside myself to find the truth.''

''What the hell are you talking about?''

''You might have been raised as a cowboy, J.T., but when I try to sketch you as a cowboy, I know something is missing. In this sketch—'' she stomped her foot on the object under discussion ''—I somehow captured the real you. A man who is both cowboy and Indian, and yet is truly neither.''

He grabbed her, not heeding the warning voice inside his head, listening only to the primitive needs inside him and to the whispers of his heart. Pulling her up against him, he glared at her. ''You see too much, Jo. You understand too much.''

''I'm not afraid of you,'' she said, tilting her chin defiantly as she stared directly at him.

''You should be,'' he told her. ''But heaven help me, I don't want you to be.'' Lowering his head, he took her mouth in a hot, bold kiss that quickly had her clinging to him.

The moment she responded, giving herself over to his ravenous attack, he gentled the kiss, then cupped her buttocks and drew her up against his arousal. He ached with the need to take her, to be inside her.

Lifting her in his arms, he gazed into her questioning eyes, then carried her over to the apricot leather sofa. He laid her down, untied her robe and spread it apart, revealing her silk nightshirt. Pulling the robe down her arms, he paused to kiss one and then the other shoulder. Joanna trembled.

''Easy, honey.'' He removed her robe and tossed it on the floor. Then he brought his body down on the wide sofa, placing his legs on either side of her. He braced himself by laying his hands flat on the cushion, one on each side of her head.

She raised her arm, reached out and caressed his face. "I'm not sure I can do this. There hasn't been... I don't—"

"Only as far as you want to go." J.T. kissed her forehead. "Trust me just a little, Jo. When you tell me to stop, I'll stop. It may kill me, but I'll stop. I promise. Just don't deny us some pleasure. I need this, and I think you do, too."

Nodding agreement, she tried to smile, but couldn't. Although she longed for J.T. to touch her intimately, to lead her along a passionate path to fulfillment, she wasn't sure that at some point she wouldn't freeze in his arms. And if she did, what would he do? Could she trust him to keep his promise?

He unbuttoned her nightshirt—slowly, kissing each inch of newly exposed flesh, painting a moist trail down her throat, between her breasts, over her stomach, then stopping just below her navel. He raised his head and looked at her. With the utmost gentleness, he spread apart her nightshirt, exposing her naked body completely.

"Joanna." He had never seen anything as beautiful as the woman who lay beneath him, all slender curves and creamy flesh.

He ached with wanting, his need urgent and painful. Patience, he told himself. Patience!

He slid over onto his side, lifting her as he turned. She gasped, grabbing him, holding on to his shoulders as he placed her on top of him. Raising her body up, she stared down at him. He slipped his hand beneath her nightshirt to caress her buttocks. Joanna sighed and closed her eyes, savoring the sensations his touch aroused in her.

Capturing her nipple with his teeth, J.T. tugged playfully. Joanna moaned, then shivered. He licked and suckled one breast, then moved hurriedly to give the other equal attention. And just when she thought she could bear no more of the torturous pleasure, he stopped and kissed her throat. Lifting his arms, he slipped the fingers of his right hand through those of his left and placed his hands behind his head.

"J.T.?" With labored breathing, she spoke his name in a harsh whisper.

"I've been doing all the work," he said. "It's your turn."

"My turn?" What did he mean? What did he expect her to do?

"Undo my shirt."

"Oh." She obeyed his command instantly, her nervous fingers working quickly to unsnap his shirt. Sliding her hands beneath the chambray material, she spread his shirt back, revealing his chest the way he had revealed hers. She sucked in a deep breath. Dear God, *he* was the beautiful one. All sleek, hard muscle and hot bronze flesh. Lowering her head she licked one tiny, pebble-hard nipple, then kissed it. He groaned. She repeated the process on the other nipple.

He reached around and grabbed the back of her head in one hand, threading his fingers through her hair. She dotted kisses all over his chest, moving steadily downward until her mouth reached his belt buckle.

Grasping her shoulders, he pulled her upward until her breasts scraped over his chest. He took her mouth, thrusting his tongue inside. Her breathing quickened and she responded with a fervor that astonished her.

He drew away from her, and whispered against her lips, "Would you like to unbuckle my belt, honey?"

Nodding her head, she smiled, then sat up on top of him, resting her hips on his legs. She clutched her hands into fists, trying to stop the trembling. Taking her hands into his, he lowered them slowly to his belt. He helped her undo the heavy silver-and-turquoise belt buckle, then released her hands and waited for her to make the next move. She touched the zipper tab, then jerked her hand away.

"I—I can't," she said.

"Then don't," he told her. "It's your call, Jo."

Clasping the zipper tab between her thumb and index finger, she eased the zipper down and laid her hand over his throbbing sex. Only his thin cotton briefs separated her hand from his naked flesh. J.T. groaned deep in his throat. Heaven help him, he was about to lose it. She had no idea what she was doing to him, what torment she was putting him through.

Cupping her hips, he pressed her downward, positioning the apex of her thighs directly on his arousal. He pushed upward gently, allowing her to become accustomed to the feel of him. Her whole body trembled, then instinctively undulated against him.

He couldn't take much more. Her innocent explorations were driving him crazy. "I want you, Jo. I want to make love to you." He kissed her hard, hot and hungrily.

She quivered beneath his touch, responding fervently, but when he eased his fingers inside her warm, damp body, she tensed. Bracing her hands on his shoulders, she pulled away from him.

"I can't. Please. I can't." Tears filled her eyes. She knew she had disappointed him, that he was on the verge of losing control.

He shoved her up, lifting himself into a sitting position at the same time. Settling her in his lap, he put his arms around her and hugged her close to him. "It's all right, honey." He nuzzled her neck with his nose and kissed the side of her face. He pulled her nightshirt together, then buttoned the three middle buttons, just enough to hold the material in place.

"I'm sorry." She choked back the tears.

"You have nothing to be sorry about," he said, holding her with a gentle protectiveness. "What we gave each other was enough for now. We both needed some loving. When you're ready for more, you'll let me know."

"Oh, J.T." Covering her mouth with her fist, she took several deep breaths and gulped down her sobs.

He sat on the sofa and held her in his arms while she cried. He ached unbearably. He had never wanted a woman the way he wanted Joanna. But he didn't want to hurt her, in fact, he would do anything to make sure she was never hurt again, especially not by him.

Was this the way Benjamin Greymountain had felt about Annabelle? Had he wanted her with a desperate, all-consuming passion? If so, J.T. understood why his great-grandfather had taken another man's wife. What he didn't understand was how Benjamin could ever have let her go.

Elena Gregory squirmed on the stool where she sat perched, her waist-length black hair swaying softly with her movements. "I need a break, Jo. I'm sore from sitting in one position for so long."

Sighing, Joanna laid her brush aside. Elena had a difficult time sitting still for longer than fifteen minutes at a time. Joanna was beginning to wonder if she'd be able to complete Elena's portrait in time for Alex's birthday.

"Okay, we'll take a break. I could use some iced tea." Joanna wiped her hands on her jeans and walked around the easel. Glancing down at her watch, she realized it was after one o'clock. "Hey, we might as well take a lunch break. I didn't know it was so late."

"There's no need for me to go back up to the house for lunch," Elena said. "Alex started on a new sculpture yesterday, and you know how he is when he starts a new project. I'll be lucky if he comes out of his studio for dinner."

"Then stay and have lunch with me. We can fix sandwiches."

"I'll help you." Elena glanced down at her clothes. "Maybe you'd better get me an apron. I didn't bring a change and I don't want to get anything on my outfit."

Elena had chosen an ankle-length gathered skirt and a long-sleeved blouse made of the same red cotton material—simple in design, but a striking contrast to her dark coloring. She wore an abundance of silver-and-turquoise jewelry; several rings and bracelets as well as dangling earrings. She had chosen a squash-blossom necklace with *naja* pendant because it had been crafted by Benjamin Greymountain and given to Elena by her mother.

Elena followed Joanna into the kitchen. She took the bread and baked chicken breasts out of the refrigerator while Joanna set the table.

"How are things going between you and J.T.?" Elena asked.

"Things are fine." Joanna tossed Elena a large tan apron trimmed in ecru crocheted lace. "I feel much safer knowing he's handling the security around me. I guess you saw Tim Rawlins outside when you came in, didn't you?"

"Yes. J.T. told Alex and me last night that he planned to put a man on guard duty around the clock." Elena sliced the cold chicken into strips and prepared their sandwiches. "J.T. took over guard duty bright and early this morning, didn't he?"

Joanna dropped the bag of potato chips on the table. "Yes. Fairly early." She cast her gaze downward, not wanting to face Elena, who was sure to suspect something if she could see Joanna's eyes.

"He was in an odd mood when he came back up to the house for breakfast." Elena returned to the refrigerator for ice, then filled their glasses. "He was just about as talkative as you are now when I asked him about it."

"About what?" Joanna asked.

Elena poured the tea into their glasses and brought them to the table. "Something must have happened between you and J.T. to make you both so secretive."

Joanna forced a quick laugh. "Just because you've had this plan to get your brother and me together for several years, doesn't mean J.T. and I have any intention of going along with your plans."

"Something did happen! I knew it. Confess. Did he kiss you?"

Someone knocked on the front door. Joanna jumped and Elena gasped. Both women turned around and faced the living room.

"Boy, we're as nervous as a couple of cats in a room full of rocking chairs," Elena said. "I'll go see who it is."

"No, you finish getting lunch ready and I'll go to the door."

Joanna crossed the room, opened the front door and sighed with relief when she saw Cliff Lansdell standing on her front porch.

"Afternoon." Cliff removed his hat. "I just wanted to stop by and see how you're doing. I hope I'm not intruding."

"Not at all, Cliff." Joanna stepped back to allow him entrance. "Come on in. Elena and I were just about to have lunch. Would you care to join us?"

"Done had mine, but thanks."

Joanna had liked Cliff since they'd first met, but despite his rugged good looks and gentlemanly manners, she had called a halt to their budding relationship after half-a-dozen dates. Cliff's feelings for her had been much deeper and far more sexual than hers had been for him.

"How about a glass of tea?" Elena called out from the kitchen.

"Don't go to any trouble, Elena. I can't stay long. I just dropped by to say... well, to let you know, Joanna, that I—" he transferred his hat from one hand to the other and then back again "—I'll do anything I can to help J.T. keep you safe and not let that Plott fellow get anywhere near you."

Joanna reached out, laid her hand over Cliff's and gave it an affectionate squeeze. "Thank you. I appreciate your concern and—"

The telephone rang. Joanna tensed. Dammit, she had to stop this! Every time someone knocked at the door or the telephone rang or she heard an unusual sound, she overreacted.

"Want me to get it?" Elena asked.

Joanna nodded. Cliff placed his hand on her shoulder. She glanced at him and felt somewhat comforted by his friendly, caring smile.

"Hello," Elena answered the telephone. "Oh, hi there, Mrs. Beaumont. Yes, Joanna's right here." Elena held out the phone.

Hesitantly, Joanna walked over and took the phone out of Elena's hand. "Hello, Mother. How are you?"

"How am I?" Helene asked. "I'm worried sick about you, that's how I am."

"I'm perfectly all right," Joanna said. "There's no need for you to worry."

"My dearest girl, how can you say that? I know Lenny Plott has already discovered where Claire Andrews lives and has called and threatened her. It's only a matter of time until he finds out where Libby Felton is and where you are."

"I realize that's a possibility, Mother, but we can't be certain."

"Of course, we can be certain." Helene sighed. "Lenny didn't become a pauper when he went to jail. His family has millions, and that idiot mother of his will make sure he can put his hands on however much money he needs. Money can always buy information, Joanna. You know that as well as I do."

"I'm well guarded here at the ranch. J.T. has posted ranch hands outside my house day and night."

"A wise decision on Mr. Blackwood's part, I'm sure, but I'd feel much better if you came home to Virginia. Mr. Blackwood could escort you home, if you'd like, or I could send a bodyguard to get you. We'll hire around-the-clock guards here. Please, Joanna, come home."

"Mother, I am home." Joanna bit her bottom lip, then rolled her eyes heavenward. "I plan to spend the rest of my life here in New Mexico. I'm not ever going to move back to Virginia."

"But surely, someday—"

"Not now. Not ever."

"You'll change your mind," Helene said. "When you decide to marry and have children, you'll come back to Virginia to find a suitable husband."

"What makes you think I couldn't find a suitable husband out here in New Mexico?"

"Joanna, there isn't anything going on between you and this Blackwood man, is there?"

Joanna gripped the telephone with white-knuckled strength. "Why would you ask such a question?"

Joanna noticed Elena staring at her, questioning her silently with her eyes. She glanced over at Cliff, who seemed equally puzzled.

"I know how totally enamored you were with that diary of your great-grandmother's. I told myself when you decided to move all the way to New Mexico that it was a temporary move. You needed to get away from...after the...after what happened to you. I understood. And I even went along with your romantic notions about Annabelle Beaumont and that illicit love affair she had with some Indian. But I never thought you'd stay out there or that you'd actually become involved with...well, with one of those people."

"One of those people? Native Americans? Is that what you mean, Mother?"

"I've had that Blackwood fellow thoroughly checked out," Helene said.

"You did what? How dare you!"

"When it comes to your safety, I'd dare almost anything. Besides, the man seems to be the very best at what he does and the firm in which he's a partner is considered one of the top private security firms in the nation."

"Then you have no reason to worry about me or want me to come back to Virginia, do you?"

"You didn't answer my question about you and Mr. Blackwood. Have you become personally involved with him? I know that he is Benjamin Greymountain's great-grandson."

"My God, Mother, when you said you had J.T. thoroughly checked out, you weren't kidding. You must have spent quite a bundle on private investigators." Joanna glanced back and forth between Elena and Cliff, and wished she wasn't having this conversation in front of an audience. Especially not Elena.

"If you won't come home to Virginia, I'm coming out there," Helene said.

"No, Mother, don't do that!"

"I'll fly out tomorrow and see if I can't talk sense to you, face-to-face. At a time like this, you should be at home."

"What are you so worried about, Mother?" Turning her back toward Elena and Cliff, Joanna lowered her voice. "What has you the most upset, the fact that Lenny Plott might find me and try to kill me, or that I might fall in love with J.T. Blackwood and ask him to marry me?"

"You're being irrational. There's no point in our discussing this anymore. You can expect me tomorrow."

"No, Mother, don't come out—" The dial tone hummed in Joanna's ear.

Cliff Lansdell walked across the room and placed his hand on Joanna's back. When she turned toward him, he slipped his arm around her shoulders. She rested against him, glad to have someone to lean on.

"I take it that we can expect a visit from Senator Helene Beaumont," Elena said.

Joanna nodded her head. "She'll be here sometime tomorrow."

"Are you all right, Joanna?" Cliff asked.

Slipping her arm around his waist, she hugged him. "I'll be fine as soon as I cool off and calm down. I love my mother dearly, but she has always tried to run my life."

Elena untied the apron she wore, folded it and laid it on the back of the sofa. "You never told me your mother was a bigot."

Joanna laughed. "She certainly doesn't consider herself one, but she is. She's horrified at the idea I might—"

"Who's horrified at what?" J.T. Blackwood stood in the arched opening leading into the kitchen.

They hadn't heard him enter the house. All three of them turned and stared at the intruder.

"You left your back door unlocked," J.T. said. "From now on, make sure it's locked." He walked into the living room. His eyes focused on Cliff Lansdell's arm draped across Joanna's shoulder. "What's going on here? Who were you talking about being horrified at something you might do?"

"My mother just called," Joanna told him.

"Mrs. Beaumont is worried about Joanna's safety," Cliff said.

"She's horrified at the thought Joanna might be hurt." Elena didn't look at her brother when she spoke.

"Are you worried about your safety?" J.T. walked up behind Joanna and glared at Cliff.

Cliff removed his arm from Joanna's shoulder and took a step away from her. Joanna watched the silent exchange between J.T. and Cliff, and couldn't help feeling a bit sorry for Cliff. At that moment, she realized few men would have the courage to stand up to J.T. and confront him. There was something powerfully intimidating about J.T. Blackwood; something other men obviously sensed instinctively. Cliff was a big guy, rugged and strong. She had seen him riding and roping and issuing orders in his duties as ranch foreman, but he hadn't dared make a stand against J.T.

"Guess I'd better be going," Cliff said. "If you need me for anything—"

"She won't need you," J.T. interrupted.

Cliff nodded, then made a hasty retreat out the front door.

"That show of machismo wasn't necessary." Joanna whirled around to face J.T. She placed her hands on her hips and glared at him.

"She's got you there, big brother," Elena said. "All Cliff was doing was giving her a little comfort."

"If you two will excuse me, I'm going into the bedroom for some privacy." Joanna patted Elena on the arm when she walked past her. "I'll call Mother back and see if I can persuade her not to fly out here tomorrow."

The moment they were alone, Elena turned to J.T. "You didn't hide your feelings very well."

"What the hell are you talking about?"

"I'm talking about your proprietary attitude toward Joanna. If you could have seen the look on your face. I thought for a few minutes you were going to rip Cliff's arm off."

"You're talking nonsense."

"Am I?" Elena smiled. "I don't think so. Cliff got the message. Everyone in this room got the message, including Joanna."

"What message?" J.T. asked.

"You've staked a claim on Jo and were sending out No Trespassing signals, loud and clear."

"You're reading too much into what happened."

"Look, Joanna doesn't need you acting like some macho jerk right now. She just had a rather unpleasant conversation with her mother. Senator Beaumont wants Jo to come home to Virginia, and she wants to hire another bodyguard. She's afraid her daughter might be getting a little too personally involved with the wrong sort of man."

"The wrong sort . . . you mean me?"

Elena shook her head. "Joanna really let her mother have it. She disagrees with the way her mother thinks. Joanna isn't like that."

"Senator Beaumont doesn't want her daughter to become seriously involved with a half-breed. That's it, isn't it? Well, the woman has nothing to worry about. Whatever happens between Joanna and me won't be serious. Her mother doesn't have to worry about her marrying—"

"I couldn't get through to Mother." Joanna stood across the living room, staring at J.T., her face pale, her eyes glazed with a fine mist of tears.

Damn, he hadn't meant for her to overhear his conversation with Elena. Joanna looked as if he'd slapped her. He had hurt her with his careless words. Why hadn't he been more cautious? The last thing in the world he wanted to do was cause Joanna any more pain.

"Jo, we need to talk," J.T. said.

"No, we don't need to talk." Joanna glanced at Elena. "I'd like to be alone for a while. Please."

"I'm not going to leave like this, not until we've talked." J.T. took a tentative step toward Joanna.

Elena grabbed him by the arm. "Call me later, okay?" she asked Joanna, then tugged on her brother's arm. "We're leaving now," she told him.

J.T. hesitated, but when he saw the anger and pain etched on Joanna's face, he turned around and walked out of the house with Elena.

Joanna went back into her bedroom, sat down on the edge of the bed and covered her face with her hands. The tears were trapped inside her, choking her, restricting her breathing.

Whatever happens between Joanna and me won't be serious. Won't be serious. Won't be serious.

She'd been a fool to think that just because J.T. wanted to make love to her, he might actually care about her. Maybe her mother had been right all along. Hoping to find the kind of love Annabelle Beaumont had found with Benjamin Greymountain was a fool's fantasy.

Joanna twisted her great-grandmother's ring around and around on her finger. Sometimes she wished she'd never found the old diary and the leather pouch containing the ring. Maybe it would have been better if she'd never come to New Mexico, searching for a new life and dreaming of finding true love.

One thing was certain—J.T. Blackwood most definitely wasn't the man Benjamin Greymountain had been. But then, maybe she wasn't half the woman Annabelle had been.

Chapter 7

J.T. nodded at Tim Rawlins when he stepped up on Joanna's front porch. Standing at the door, he hesitated before knocking. He'd given Joanna a couple of hours to be by herself and calm down, but he'd waited as long as he could. His patience had run out.

He hadn't meant for her to overhear his conversation with Elena. He could have kicked himself when he'd seen the look of hurt and disillusionment in her eyes. But who knows, he told himself, maybe it's better this way. At least now, she knew exactly where they stood. He wanted Joanna, wanted her in the worst way a man could want a woman. But if she was expecting love and "forever after," she had the wrong guy. *Love* wasn't a word that existed in his vocabulary. And there was no such thing as "forever after." He lived his life a day at a time.

Joanna opened the door, took one look at J.T. and started to close the door in his face. He stuck his foot over the threshold and grabbed the edge of the door.

"May I come in?" he asked.

She glared at his hand, then down at his foot. "Doesn't look like I can stop you." She stared directly at him.

"I'd like to come in and talk to you, but I won't crash my way in if you say no."

"Come in." Turning her back on him, her spine stiff as a board, she marched into the living room.

J.T. followed her over to the easel supporting Elena's portrait. "You're capturing my sister's earthy beauty."

"We didn't get a chance to do much work today," Joanna said. "I need only a couple more sittings to be able to finish it. Elena wants it for Alex's birthday present."

"Well, it'll certainly be something he'll treasure."

"I hope so."

J.T. stared at the unfinished portrait. "Elena looks a lot like my mother. The way I remember her from my early childhood. When I saw her again after so many years, she was dying and had aged terribly."

"You and Elena resemble each other some, enough to recognize the fact you're brother and sister." Joanna covered the portrait.

"Elena was fifteen before I ever met her, before I even knew I had a half sister. One of my mother's relatives called and told me my mother was dying." J.T. strolled around the living room, surveying the changes Joanna had made in the old bunkhouse. She'd turned a ramshackle old building into a warm, comfortable home.

J.T. glanced at the portrait of Annabelle Beaumont hanging over the mantel, and wondered if he should show Joanna the picture he had of Benjamin. His gut instincts told him that Annabelle had been the artist who had drawn his great-grandfather's likeness in a stark, totally male black-and-white sketch. Suddenly J.T. noticed a small fire burning in the fireplace.

"It's too hot a day for a fire," he said.

"I needed to burn some trash." She sat down on the leather sofa. "Is there a reason you came over here to see me?"

J.T. took a closer look at the "trash" she had decided to burn. A tight knot formed in his throat when he recognized the notebook she had half-filled with sketches of him. Dammit! She must hate him. And he didn't want her to hate him. All he wanted was for her to accept this thing between them for what it was. Lust. Good old plain lust. Nothing less, but nothing more.

"Maybe you should go back to Virginia the way your mother wants you to," he said.

Snapping her head around, she frowned at him. "Why?"

"Why? Well, you'd be better off without my being involved in the case. I think it's pretty obvious that things aren't going to work out between us. Our expectations are different."

"Oh, I see. So, you're saying that if I return to Virginia and get a different bodyguard, I won't wind up making a total fool of myself over you."

"Dammit, Jo, that's not what I said." J.T. slumped down in the overstuffed plaid chair across from the sofa. "If you go back to Virginia, neither one of us will wind up making fools of ourselves. I want something from you that you're not willing to give, and you want something from me that isn't in me to give. It's as simple as that."

"Nothing's ever that simple."

"If you want to go home to Virginia, I'll call Simon Roarke and have him fly out here tomorrow and go back to Virginia with you whenever you're ready to go."

"Who's Simon Roarke?"

"He's been an agent with Dundee's Private Security for several years. He's top-notch. You'd be safe with him." J.T. grinned, but there was no mirth in his smile. "Besides, your mother might approve of him. He's pure Scotch-Irish all the way back to Adam. Not a drop of impure blood in him that I know of. But his folks were poor Southern farmers. Think that will disqualify him?"

"It might disqualify him as husband material," Joanna said, "but I think Mother would approve of him being my bodyguard."

"Then I'll call him and have him catch the first flight—"

"There's no need to call Mr. Roarke. I'm not going anywhere. I'm staying right here in Trinidad, New Mexico, on the Blackwood ranch, and I'm holding you to your promise to stick around as long as I need protection." She smiled, just barely turning up the corners of her mouth. Her green eyes glistened with triumph.

"Your mother isn't going to be happy."

"I really don't care. I'm just sorry that you and Elena and Alex will have to endure her visit. She's a charming Southern lady on the surface, but beneath that Virginia-belle facade, beats the heart of a born politician. She's not above saying or doing whatever she thinks is necessary to get her own way."

"And that includes taking potshots at me."

"I'm not worried about you." Joanna stood. "Your hide is pretty tough. I'm worried about Elena. She's very protective of you, and she'll jump to your defense if Mother casts aspersions on your ethnic heritage." Joanna walked toward the front door. "I think we've discussed everything we needed to, don't you?"

J.T. stood. "Here's your hat. What's your hurry?" he said jokingly. "One question before you kick me out."

Shrugging, she nodded agreement. "All right. One question. Then you'll leave."

He glanced at the notebook, now almost totally consumed by the blaze in the fireplace. "Why did you burn the sketch pad?"

Every muscle in Joanna's body tensed; her nerves jangled like a zillion tiny bells. She couldn't bear the way J.T. was looking at her, as if accusing her of something sinful. How could she possibly answer him without lying? His thoughtless remark that nothing serious would ever happen between them had cut her to the quick. She didn't want to admit to him how much he had hurt her. But he already knew. The burning sketch pad was all the evidence he needed to know the depth of her anger.

"I understand exactly where we stand," she said. "We are not our great-grandparents. There is no grand love affair in our future. You don't want a serious relationship with me, and I don't want any type of relationship with you, other than in a strictly business capacity."

"You're a hard woman, Joanna Beaumont. You want all or nothing, don't you?"

"I'm afraid so."

"I'll keep a guard posted outside around the clock, and I'll check in with you from time to time." He walked over to her, hesitated momentarily; then, when she didn't respond to his gesture, he opened the front door and stepped out on the porch.

Just as she started to close the door, the telephone rang. She rushed across the room, grabbed the receiver and said hello. J.T. stood in the doorway and waited.

"Hello," she said again.

"Hello, Joanna."

"Who is this?"

"Don't you recognize my voice, baby doll?"

"No—no, I don't." But she did. She would never forget that cultured Southern drawl, that soft, effeminate voice or the "baby doll" endearment.

"I've already talked to Claire and Libby. I told each of them that I'd be paying them a little visit any time now. I didn't want you to find out about all the attention I'm giving them and get jealous."

J.T. stepped back inside and closed the door behind him slowly. He watched Joanna. Her face paled. She clutched the telephone fiercely.

Joanna glanced over at J.T. He mouthed the words, "Who is it? Plott?"

She nodded her head. J.T. cursed softly under his breath.

"What's the matter, baby doll?" Lenny Plott asked. "Surely you're not surprised to hear from me. After all, you knew it would be only a matter of time before I'd look up all my old friends. I suppose Lieutenant George told you what happened to poor little Melody."

"You strangled her."

"Is that all he told you?" Lenny Plott laughed—that shrill, diabolical laugh Joanna would never forget. "You know what else I did to her before I strangled her, don't you, Joanna?"

There was no way Joanna could keep Plott on the phone long enough to run a trace. From everything he'd found out about Leonard Plott III, J.T. knew the man might be deranged, but he wasn't a fool.

"I'll be seeing you," Lenny said. "But you don't know when. You don't have any idea who I'm coming after next. Will I go to Missouri or Texas or New Mexico? Who knows, maybe I'll throw darts at a map."

"If you come after me, you'll be sorry," Joanna said. "I'll kill you before I'll ever let you touch me again."

"So brave, aren't you, darling girl? Well, just remember this, you won't recognize me when you see me. I've changed my appearance. I doubt my own mother would recognize me."

The line went dead. Joanna replaced the telephone receiver. J.T. grabbed her by the shoulders.

"What did he say?"

"He said he had changed his appearance enough that I wouldn't recognize him, and that he knows where all three of us—Claire, Libby and I—are. We don't know which one of us he'll come after next."

"Look, Jo, he just told you that to try to frighten you even more than you already are. Our boy Lenny sounds like the type who likes to play head games."

"Phone Lieutenant George and let him know about this call," Joanna said.

"I'll phone from the main house." He rubbed his hands up and down her arms, soothing her. "Will you be all right here by yourself until I get back?"

"Tim Rawlins is still outside. And I have my gun." She pulled away from J.T. "There's no need for you to come back over here."

"You're wrong about that, honey. Plott knows exactly where you are now. I'm moving in here with you. It's time for me to start acting as your private, around-the-clock bodyguard."

"No!" She backed away from J.T. "That's not necessary."

"This isn't up for discussion. We're not taking a vote. From now until Lenny Plott is arrested, I'm not leaving your side. Do you understand?"

Reluctantly, she nodded her head. Dear God, how had her life come to this? Lenny Plott had escaped from prison and was threatening her life. And J.T. Blackwood, a man she both desired and despised, was moving in with her.

Joanna stared at the shaving kit sitting on the left side of the vanity in her bathroom. She had never shared a bathroom with a man. Even when she'd been engaged to Todd, they hadn't lived together. Having J.T. sleeping in the room next to hers, the two of them together twenty-four hours a day, seemed far too intimate. She might not like the idea, but she wasn't going to ask J.T. to leave. In the sea of fear and uncertainty her life had become, J.T. was her lifeline— the one person standing between her and a deadly enemy.

Dragging her gaze away from the leather kit, Joanna picked up the jar of cleansing cream, unscrewed the lid and delved her fingers into the solution. Smearing the cream on her face, she glanced in the mirror. Her green eyes stared back at her, mocking her, telling her she was a fool. Although her body longed for J.T. and her romantic heart cried out for his love, she knew they were all wrong for each other. She was a permanent type of woman; he was a temporary kind of guy. She believed in love; he didn't. And to complicate matters further, she could not bring herself to fully trust J.T. She didn't doubt his sincerity when he promised to protect her from Lenny Plott, but she didn't dare trust him with her love. Of course, it didn't really matter. He didn't want her love. All he wanted was her body.

She wiped off the face cream, washed her hands and lifted her silk robe from the wooden wall peg. She had thought about going to bed early, but had decided she would not stay in her room to avoid J.T. She had work to do, a life to live, an orderly routine to her days. She'd go crazy if she couldn't maintain some semblance of normalcy in her life. She'd just have to get used to J.T.'s presence.

Before leaving the sanctuary of her bathroom, she glanced back at the shaving kit.

She found J.T. standing in front of the fireplace in the living room, gazing up at Annabelle Beaumont's portrait. Joanna sucked in her breath. The sight of him, partially disrobed, left her breathless. He had removed his boots and socks, leaving his big feet bare. His unbuttoned shirt hung loosely about his hips. In that one brief moment before he turned and looked at her, Joanna saw a glimpse of what she thought might be the real J.T. Blackwood. Pensive, brooding and yet somehow vulnerable. And in desperate need of love.

"I have something to show you," he said. "Something you can have, if you want it." He reached down in the plaid chair, picked up a large yellowed, frayed piece of paper and held it out to her.

"What is it?" she asked, noticing that it seemed to be a sketch of some sort.

"Here. Take a look."

He handed it to her. Holding the sketch by the edges, she gasped when she saw the strikingly bold features of a handsome Navajo man. Obviously the drawing had been done years ago. Over seventy years ago?

"This is Benjamin Greymountain, isn't it?" Joanna had always wondered what he'd looked like, if he'd truly been as handsome as Annabelle had thought. He had been.

"Yep. That's him."

"Where did you get—"

"My mother. When I went to see her, shortly before she died…" Pausing for a split second, he swallowed hard. His jaw tightened, then relaxed. "She gave me her grandfather's ring and this sketch of him. She told me the ring and picture went together."

"You know Annabelle sketched this," Joanna said. "She couldn't keep it, couldn't take it back to Virginia with her and look at it day after day."

"What makes you think that? More than likely, she knew she'd have no use for it once she left New Mexico. She probably wanted to put her summer affair behind her."

"That's where you're wrong." Joanna stared down at Benjamin's image. There was the hint of a resemblance between J.T. and his ancestor; a similarity in the eyes, in the cheekbones, in the full lips. "I knew that Annabelle had done several sketches of Benjamin. She wrote about them in her diary. She gave him one—" Joanna glanced down at the treasured portrait in her hands "—this one, as a keepsake, and she destroyed the others before she returned to Virginia. She said it was best if the only picture she had of him was the one forever etched on her heart."

J.T. swore under his breath. Snapping her head around, Joanna glared at him. She carried the sketch over to her work desk in front of the row of windows overlooking the porch. Reverently, she laid the image of Benjamin Greymountain down on top of the desk.

"From what you just told me, I'd say your great-grandmother was quite a romantic." J.T. hooked his thumbs under the waistband of his jeans and laid his palms flat on his hips. "She must have had a really miserable marriage to have spent so much time idealizing some summer affair she'd once had."

"I found the diary in an old trunk in my parents' attic," Joanna said. "I looked for things to occupy my mind after... Well, needless to say, I was intrigued by my great-grandmother's tragic love affair. Believe me, J.T., what she shared with Benjamin was far more than just some summer affair."

"I don't see what was so damned tragic about it." J.T. padded softly across the wooden floor, easing up behind Joanna.

She knew he was hovering over her, only inches away. And he was waiting for her to turn on him, to denounce his insensitivity. Keeping her back to him, she glided her fingertips around the edge of the sketch.

"If you're right, and they weren't deeply in love, then there was no tragedy. But if I'm right, just imagine how they felt—how you'd feel if you'd gotten to spend only a couple of precious months with the one true love of your life."

J.T. couldn't imagine. He'd never been in love, didn't believe in the nonsense and wished Joanna didn't. If she were less of a romantic, their relationship would have a better chance. If only she could admit that wanting each other was enough, without clouding the issue with sentimentality.

"Let's agree to disagree," J.T. said, wanting more than anything to ease her into his arms, untie her robe and slip it off her shoulders. She had such pretty shoulders. Soft, pale skin, with a light dusting of freckles just like the freckles that dotted her cheeks and the bridge of her nose.

"If you read the diary, you might change your mind." Joanna felt his warm breath on her head. If she turned, would he take her in his arms? She pivoted slowly, facing him. "Would you like to read Annabelle's diary?"

"No, I wouldn't. And you'd be better off if you locked the thing in a drawer and forgot about it." He touched her then. Hesitantly. Tenderly. Reaching down, he lifted her hands into his. "I want you. You want me. There's nothing wrong with that. As a matter of fact, I think it would be wrong if we denied ourselves the pleasure we can give each other."

J.T. held their clasped hands between their bodies. When Joanna glanced down, all she saw was their matching rings, the old silver gleaming faintly in the lamplight. She was tempted. Dear God, how she was tempted. But when their affair ended, what would she have left? Memories, some inner voice told her. But her memories would be tarnished, not golden the way Annabelle's had been. Love made all the difference. It had to Annabelle. It did to Joanna.

"Would you consider making a bargain with me?" Joanna asked, wondering if she'd lost her mind even considering the proposition she was about to make.

"What sort of bargain?" Lifting her hands to his lips, he kissed each fingertip.

Joanna shivered. "You're interested in an affair. Nothing serious. Nothing permanent. You'd just like for us to become sexual partners while you're acting as my bodyguard, then when your services are no longer required, we both go our separate ways. No regrets or recriminations on either side."

"What are you getting at?"

"I'm willing to consider what you want, to give us both a chance to see exactly what there is or isn't between us." Joanna already knew. She'd gone and done the unforgivable. She was falling in love with J.T. How stupid could she get? She wanted tenderness, understanding, patience, and a man interested in a lifetime commitment. J.T. offered nothing she wanted—nothing except himself. And *he* was what she wanted most of all. Even if he could be a part of her life for only a few weeks.

Cocking his head to one side, J.T. grinned. "What's the catch, honey?"

"I want you to read Annabelle's diary," Joanna said.

"You want me to do what?" He released her hands, dropping them quickly, as if her touch had burned him.

"You read Annabelle's diary, one entry at a time, and I'll give you the chance to persuade me to become your lover."

"You're serious." He laughed, the sound deep and hearty. "By God, you are serious."

"Is my asking price too high?"

"Go get that damned diary!" He pulled her into his arms, lowered his head and whispered against her lips, "I'd read a hundred diaries for the chance you're offering me."

She shoved him away gently, then took a step backward, her hip bumping into the easel holding Elena's portrait. She grabbed the easel, steadying it.

"Not tonight. Too much has happened today. Discovering that Lenny Plott knows where I am. Having you move in with me. And knowing Mother will arrive tomorrow and start issuing orders." Joanna groaned. "Tell me, J.T., am I making a deal with the devil? I really don't trust my own feelings. And I don't trust you at all. At least not when it comes to—" she'd been about to say *love* "—our having a physical relationship."

"You handle things with your mother and I'll take care of Lenny Plott. You trust me to keep you safe, don't you?"

"I want to trust you completely," she said. "I know you seem to be a man of your word, a man who keeps his promises, but I... Well, I don't know if I'll ever be able to completely trust a man again. Not after the rape. Not after Todd's desertion."

"I'd like to be the man who teaches you to trust again," J.T. told her. "And I'm not the devil, honey. I'm just a man. A man who's going to keep you safe. And that is a promise."

And I'd like to be the woman who teaches you how to love, Joanna thought, but said, "Promise me something else, J.T."

"What?"

"Promise me that, no matter what happens, you'll try to open up your heart and your mind to your mother's people. Elena told me that you know practically nothing about the Navajo."

"What is it with you? You want me to read Annabelle's diary. You want me to get in touch with my Native American roots. You want to change me, Jo. I swear, a person would think you don't like the man I am now."

"I'm not sure I do like you," Joanna admitted. "At least, not the J.T. Blackwood you present to the world. I want to get to know the man inside you, the real J.T. Blackwood."

"Don't kid yourself. The real J.T. Blackwood is who you see right here in front of you."

"What I see when I look at you is only the physical, and I like that just fine. What I want to get to know is the spirit, and that's the part of you that you keep hidden from everyone. Even from yourself, I think.''

"I'll read Annabelle's damned diary.'' J.T. marched across the living room, his bare feet slamming against the wooden floor. When he reached the hallway, he stopped and turned around. "And if it'll make you happy, I'll let Elena give me 'Navajo lessons.'" J.T. grunted. "But I'm warning you that reading some old diary filled with a lot of mush and learning more about my mother's people won't change me.''

"Maybe. Maybe not," Joanna said. But in her heart she hoped that while J.T. was putting his life on the line to protect her, she could help him discover the man he really was beneath all the bitter cynicism—a man capable of giving and receiving love.

Chapter 8

*W*e have been in Trinidad a week now. Ernest is quite pleased to be here, although the heat seems to bother him terribly. Yesterday's find, though not of prehistoric origin, was enough to pacify him. He and his assistant, Horace Grisham, discovered several items of Spanish origin—iron, copper, glass and porcelain. Ernest says that finding these items at this site is a result of the Pueblo Indians having taken refuge here with the Navajo after the revolt against the Spanish in the late seventeenth century.

The boys are doing well, running and laughing and playing as boys their age will do. They're quite a handful at eight and twelve. But they are the joy of my life, my beautiful sons.

We met a most interesting man today. He is a Navajo silversmith, and without a doubt the most handsome man I've ever seen. He came riding into our camp on his big Appaloosa stallion. I must say that horse and rider were a spectacular sight.

His name is Benjamin Greymountain, and his father is a member of their tribal council. Although he wore white *man's clothing, his black hair, which he had tied back off his face with a bandana, hung to well below his shoulders. He is young—I suspect, a good ten years younger than I.*

I feel extremely foolish admitting this, even to myself, but the first moment I saw Benjamin Greymountain, I thought I heard drums beating somewhere off in the distance, and when he looked at me, the most extraordinary feelings spread through me. I am a bit afraid of those feelings. I must, of course, control them.

Benjamin's father sent him to our camp to offer his services as a guide, if any of our party should wish to take excursions about the countryside. It seems there are some Indians here who hate the archaeologists who are poking and digging about in their heritage, and the senior Mr. Greymountain hopes that he can prevent any unpleasantness between his people and ours.

I cannot help wondering how I will handle seeing this young man every day for the next two and a half months. I am a married woman of thirty-four, with children. I must remember who I am. But the memory of those black eyes staring at me, devouring me, almost, makes me think that Benjamin experienced the same jolting emotions that I did.

"Joanna's mother is here," Elena called from the hallway. "Aren't you coming out to meet her?"

J.T. closed Annabelle Beaumont's diary. An odd, queasy feeling hit him in the pit of his stomach. No wonder Joanna had become so engrossed in her great-grandmother's diary. The woman certainly had a captivating way of expressing herself. And it was apparent that she had been sexually attracted to Benjamin Greymountain from the first moment she saw him and had been determined to fight those feelings.

Placing her hands on each side of the doorframe, Elena leaned into J.T.'s study and gave him a hard look. "Well, are you coming or not? I'd think you'd want to make a good impression on Joanna's mother."

"I'll be there in a minute. Go on without me. By the time Alex escorts the senator into the house, I'll be there."

"Joanna could use a little moral support," Elena said. "She's waiting in the living room, pacing the floor. She really didn't want Mrs. Beaumont to come out here. When Joanna lived in Virginia, her mother tried to run her life. From what Joanna's told me, the woman is a first-class manipulator."

"Has Mrs. Beaumont ever visited Joanna before?" J.T. asked.

"No, not once since she moved to New Mexico. Joanna goes back to Virginia two or three times every year." Dropping her hands from the doorframe, Elena stepped into J.T.'s private domain—the study that had once belonged to old John Thomas. J.T. had changed it very little, adding only the modern conveniences of a computer and a fax machine. "But Joanna's life has never been threatened before. I believe Mrs. Beaumont loves Joanna and is genuinely concerned."

"I'm sure she is." J.T. sat down on the edge of the huge oak desk. "But she must know Joanna wouldn't be any safer back in Richmond than she is here in Trinidad. At least, not any safer from Lenny Plott."

"What are you not saying, big brother?"

"I don't know what Mrs. Beaumont suspects is going on between Joanna and me, but whatever it is, she doesn't like it. My guess is the senator's visit to New Mexico has more to do with my presence in her daughter's life than with Lenny Plott's escape from prison."

"Just what *is* going on between you and Joanna? You're my only brother and she's my best friend. You already know I'd like nothing better than to see you two get together, but... You seem to mix like oil and water."

"If you're so interested in Joanna's relationship with me, why haven't you asked her?"

"I have asked her," Elena admitted. "She said you were her bodyguard, and when I asked if there wasn't more to it, she said to ask you."

Hearty laughter rumbled from J.T. Elena's eyes widened; her mouth fell open.

"Joanna and I aren't lovers. Not yet, if that's what you're asking, nosy little sister." J.T. stood straight and tall, the remnants of a smile still on his face.

"Don't you dare hurt her." Elena slipped her arm through her brother's. "She's very special, you know."

"Yeah, I'm beginning to see just how special."

J.T. led Elena out of his study and down the hall, pausing when they heard voices coming from the foyer.

"I'm almost as nervous as Joanna," Elena said. "I want Mrs. Beaumont to like us. I've planned a wonderful dinner, in the dining room, for this evening."

"Come on, then, let's go meet the queen bee." J.T. hoped, for Elena's sake, that Mrs. Beaumont proved his suspicions wrong and didn't show herself to be the "just-slightly prejudiced" person she was.

When they entered the living room, they found Alex preparing Mrs. Beaumont a drink, while mother and daughter seated themselves on the sofa. Joanna glanced up, a tentative, strained smile on her face.

"Please, come and meet Mother."

Joanna stood and held out her hand to Elena, who rushed across the room. Helene Beaumont looked directly at J.T., who waited in the arched doorway. She sat up just a bit straighter, squaring her shoulders. When she turned her head to greet Elena, her chin-length, salt-and-pepper hair flared outward. Impeccably dressed in a neat little red designer suit, she looked every inch the wealthy, successful woman she was.

"Mother, this is Elena." Joanna clasped her best friend's hand.

Helene lifted her hand, offering it to Elena, who accepted the older woman's firm handshake. "I'm simply delighted to meet you, my dear. Joanna just raves about you and your Alex. You can't know how pleased I was when she finally made some friends out here in this wilderness. In all honesty, I didn't think she'd end up staying out here permanently. Joanna's always been a city girl, you know."

"Well, we've pretty much turned her into a country girl," Elena said, her smile warm and genuine. "We're glad she decided to make Trinidad her home. Like Alex, she's found this land an inspiration for her work."

"My, yes," Helene said. "I'm so proud of my little girl's success. Of course, with talent like hers, she would have been a success anywhere."

J.T. glanced down the hallway when he heard the back door open and then slam shut. Before he could go check on things, Alex called out to him.

"That's just Willie bringing in Mrs. Beaumont's luggage," Alex said.

"Did you tell Willie where to put her things?" Elena asked.

"I'm staying here?" Helene turned to Joanna. "I thought you'd told me you had two bedrooms in your house."

"You'll be very comfortable here with us, Mrs. Beaumont," Elena told their guest. "We have tons of room and if you'd like breakfast in bed, all you need to do is ask."

"Why aren't I staying with you?" Helene tilted her sharp little chin upward, glaring at her daughter.

"Well, Mother, you see, it wouldn't be convenient. There just isn't enough room right now."

"I'm afraid I don't understand. I took time away from my work to come out here to be with you, Joanna." Helene glanced up, smiling at Elena and then at Alex. "As much as I appreciate the Gregorys' offer to stay here, I'd much prefer staying with you."

"Mother, that's impossible. If you stay with me, you'd have to sleep on the sofa."

"Why would I have to sleep on the sofa?"

J.T. strolled into the room. "You wouldn't, if you have no objections to my sharing Joanna's bed."

Joanna sucked in a deep breath. Elena gasped. Alex covered his mouth to hide a chuckle.

"J.T. is staying in the second bedroom at my house," Joanna said. "He moved in last night, after I received a telephone call from Lenny Plott. J.T. is going to be with me twenty-four hours a day until Plott is back behind bars.''

"I see." Helene glowered at J.T., then quickly centered all her attention on her daughter. "If Plott knows where you are, if he's found you here in New Mexico where you thought you might be safe, there's no reason for you to refuse to come home with me.''

"Let's discuss this later. Please." Joanna knew she would have to stand her ground with her mother or she'd be run down like a steamroller. Helene Beaumont liked things her own way, and she was happiest when she controlled the lives of everyone around her.

"Very well," Helene said. "Perhaps, you'll stay long enough to show me to my room.''

"Here you are." Alex handed Helene the vodka collins she had requested.

"Thank you, Alex." She sipped her drink, then smiled with approval. "Perfect, simply perfect.''

"Mother, I'll be staying here until after dinner," Joanna said. "Elena is preparing something special, just for you.''

"How delightful." Helene's campaign smile returned in full force, brightening her dull gray eyes and softening her sharp features. She took another sip of her drink, then stood. "I'm dreadfully tired after my plane ride. Why don't you show me to my room, dear, and then stay and we'll have a little talk while I rest?''

Joanna grimaced, dreading the upcoming confrontation with her mother. The only time she had ever won a battle with the formidable Senator Beaumont was when she had decided to move to New Mexico four years ago.

"Dinner will be at six," Elena said. "So there's plenty of time for a nap, if you'd like.''

Helene blessed everyone in the room with her gracious smile, even J.T. Slipping her arm through Joanna's, she held the vodka collins in her other hand. "I'm looking forward to dinner. We'll see you around six, then.''

Joanna gave Elena a pleading look, asking for her friend's understanding. Helene tugged on Joanna's arm, the action so subtle, no one else noticed.

"I'll be with Mother for a while," Joanna told J.T. as they walked past him. "I won't leave the house."

"I'll be close by." J.T. looked directly at Joanna, avoiding eye contact with her mother.

The minute the Beaumont ladies were out of earshot, Alex blew out a huffing breath. "Well, well, isn't she something! I can see why Joanna doesn't want to go back to Virginia."

"You're being unkind," Elena said.

"Unkind, my rear end." J.T. crossed his arms over his chest. "Instead of giving Joanna her complete support and understanding, Mrs. Beaumont is here to create problems. It's obvious she doesn't give a damn what Joanna wants, and she certainly doesn't like me."

The corners of Elena's mouth twitched. "You deliberately baited her with that comment about sharing Joanna's bed."

"I'm wealthy. I'm successful. I'm highly trained to protect her daughter. What could the woman possibly have against me?"

The partially-formed smile on Elena's face vanished. "You're half Navajo. You think that's the reason she doesn't like you, that she's prejudiced because of your Navajo blood."

"If the shoe fits," Alex said, as he slipped his arm around his wife's shoulders. "Kind of makes you wish you hadn't planned such a special dinner for her tonight, doesn't it?"

"Well, no matter what, she's Joanna's mother and I'm going to be nice to her for Joanna's sake." Elena cuddled against Alex.

"Let me know when that special dinner is ready," J.T. said. "I'll be in my study."

* * *

Helene tied the belt around her silk dressing gown, then sat on the edge of the bed and held open her arms to her daughter. "Come give me a hug."

Joanna obeyed. She adored her mother—her beautiful, brilliant mother—but sometimes she didn't like her very much. Helene had been the "perfect" wife and mother, always doing what she thought best. But there had been times when Joanna had wondered how much of that "perfection" had been an expression of love and how much had been just for show. What the world thought of Helene meant a great deal to her and she had spent her life presenting herself and her family in the very best light.

Helene hugged Joanna, released her and patted the bed beside her. "Sit with me for a while and let's talk the way we used to when you lived at home."

Sighing, Joanna acquiesced to her mother's request and sat down on her right. "I can save us a lot of arguing back and forth. There's no need for us to have a talk. I'm not returning with you to Virginia. I'm staying here in New Mexico. This is my home now."

"But Plott knows where you are."

"Lenny Plott will find me wherever I am and we both know it. With his kind of money, he can buy whatever information he needs to track us down. I doubt there's a place on earth we can hide that he couldn't eventually find us."

"What are you saying?" Reaching down, Helene covered Joanna's hand with hers.

"Sooner or later, I may have to come face-to-face with Lenny Plott, and if that happens, J.T. will be there with me. I won't feel safe anywhere without J.T."

"The man's just a bodyguard, dear. I can hire half-a-dozen bodyguards for you, if having them around will make you feel safe."

"I don't want just any bodyguard. I want J.T."

"What's going on between you and that man?" Helene released Joanna's hand. "Somehow he has convinced you that he's the only person who can protect you."

Joanna stood, walked across the bedroom and looked out the window at the far distant horizon. "That's what this is all about, isn't it, Mother? This little trip isn't about keeping me safe, about protecting me from Lenny Plott. It's about getting me away from J.T. Blackwood. That's it, isn't it?"

"I'm not blind," Helene said. "I can see plainly why any woman would be attracted to him, but don't you realize how wrong he is for you?"

"Just what are you so afraid of?"

"I'd think you'd be the one to be afraid." Helene laid her open palms flat on each side of her hips, pressing down against the bed. "To my knowledge, you haven't been with a man since the night that monster brutalized you. Do you honestly think J.T. Blackwood is the kind of man you need as your first lover? I've had his background checked out. Putting aside the fact that he was illegitimate and his mother was a Navajo, the man has spent his life in one brutal business or another. First the marines, then years as a Secret Service agent and for the past six years, he's been a private security agent. The man is practically a hired killer. Just how gentle and kind and patient do you think a man like that will be in the bedroom?"

"My love life is none of your business." Joanna kept her back turned on her mother. "I know you love me and you want what you think is best for me. Maybe you really do believe I need a more gentle lover, but let's be honest, shall we? You're far more concerned that I might marry J.T. Then how on earth would you ever explain it to your friends? Oh, it might be all right to speak out for and even vote for racial equality, to have friends and associates who aren't pure WASPs, but you don't want your daughter marrying outside the inner circle, do you?"

Knotting her hands into fists, Helene jumped up from the bed. "It's that ridiculous diary of your great-grandmother's, isn't it? Someone should have burned that thing long ago. To think that woman actually filled a book with details of her illicit love affair with some wild savage."

"We aren't going to agree on this." Joanna turned slowly, took a deep breath and faced her mother. "You are not in charge of my life now. I am. I choose where I live. Not you. And I decide who I love, and who I marry."

"Has he asked you to marry him?"

"No, Mother, he hasn't, but that doesn't mean I won't ask him, one of these days."

"I don't know what's happened to you since you left Richmond. You were always such a sweet, easygoing child. You made all the right choices. You had a wonderful fiancé, a good job, a bright future."

"I did everything you wanted me to do," Joanna said. "You made all my decisions for me. You planned my life. But you didn't plan on Lenny Plott beating me half to death and raping me, did you?"

"I would give anything if I could change what happened." Tears misted Helene's eyes.

Joanna walked over, wrapped her arms around her mother and hugged her. "I know you would. But what happened can't be changed. I'm a different person now. I'm stronger. I can never go back to being your sweet little girl."

"I want only what's best for you." Pulling back from Joanna, Helene cupped her daughter's face in her hands. "I truly believe J.T. Blackwood is the wrong man for you."

"Let me make that decision," Joanna said. "If I get hurt, I'll have no one to blame but myself."

Joanna had thought dinner would never end. She had forgotten what it felt like to watch her mother preside over a gathering, commanding all the attention, issuing orders and playing the Southern belle to the hilt. She only hoped that while she and Elena cleared the table and straightened the kitchen, her mother wouldn't say or do something unforgivable.

Joanna stacked plates in the dishwasher while Elena hand-washed the pots and pans.

"I think your mother enjoyed dinner." Elena placed a copper pot in the drainage rack. "She said she loved the spicy chicken and she raved about the homemade ice cream.''

"No one could find fault with your cooking," Joanna said. "If anyone ruined your dinner party, I did. Or perhaps J.T. He didn't say ten words the whole time."

"He thinks your mother doesn't like him."

"She doesn't know him, she just thinks she does." Joanna placed the dirty glasses in the top rack of the dishwasher. "But I'm beginning to think that I really don't know J.T., either. He acts like he's two different men. Every time we get a little closer to understanding each other, he withdraws and we wind up in an argument."

"J.T. *is* two different men," Elena said. "Maybe even three different men. One part of him is the man John Thomas Blackwood made him, while another part of him is Navajo, and then I think another third of him is the man he longs to be, a man at peace with the other two-thirds of himself."

"I suppose there's more than one person inside all of us, isn't there?" Joanna filled the detergent dispenser, closed the door and turned on the dishwasher. "There's still a part of me that's the proper young lady my mother raised me to be and part of me is the independent, confident woman I've become since moving to Trinidad. But there's also a dark, frightened part of me. That's the part Lenny Plott and Todd created nearly five years ago. No matter how hard I try, I can't completely let go of that fear and anger and distrust."

"I can only imagine what it must have been like for you, but you must know that even when Lenny Plott is arrested and put back in prison, you'll never be free from him until you can destroy that dark part of you he created."

Joanna dried her hands, then tossed the towel to Elena. "I thought I had destroyed most of it, until he escaped and forced me to face the past, to face the truth about myself. I have so much love to give the right man, but I can't trust enough to completely give my heart and my body to anyone."

Elena laid the towel on the countertop, put her arm around Joanna's waist and gave her a hug. "Let's join the others and see if your mother and J.T. have drawn swords yet."

Joanna laughed, but the sound was hollow. When they reached the end of the hallway, Joanna heard her mother's voice. Jerking Elena back against the wall, she held a finger over her lips, silently asking Elena not to speak.

"Joanna has always been a very sensitive girl," Helene said. "She hated confrontations of any kind. She always cried whenever she overheard her father and me arguing. Not that we argued very often."

"I'm sure Joanna's sensitivity is a great asset to her in her work," Alex said. "Most of us artists have sensitive souls. We seem to feel things more deeply. I suppose we have to be able to do that in order to put a part of our souls into our work."

"No doubt." Helene cleared her throat. "But I'm afraid that, in some people, sensitivity makes them rather weak and vulnerable, and thus easily hurt."

Joanna clenched her teeth tightly. What was her mother doing? There was always a method to her madness, a scheme behind the most innocent-sounding conversations. Elena squeezed Joanna's hand.

"Surely you're not talking about Jo." J.T.'s voice sounded deeper, darker and rougher than usual.

"I'm afraid I am," Helene said. "She was always fragile and sensitive and a bit naive. Then, after Lenny Plott attacked her, she went completely to pieces. It took months of therapy before she'd go out of the house in broad daylight without someone with her."

"Isn't a reaction like that fairly normal?" Alex asked. "I'm sure different women react differently after living through such an experience."

"Jo isn't weak," J.T. said. "She's one of the strongest people I've ever met. It's obvious to me that you don't know the woman your daughter has become."

"You're quite wrong about that, Mr. Blackwood. I know my daughter far better than you. She's still just as fragile and sensitive and vulnerable as she was before she left Virginia four years ago, and I worry that she's going to be hurt and terribly disappointed if she continues living in this dreamworld she's created for herself."

"I'm afraid I don't understand," Alex said. "Joanna is a very sensible woman. She—"

"You're referring to her interest in Annabelle Beaumont's diary." J.T. grunted. "And my connection to Benjamin Greymountain."

"Joanna needs the right kind of man. Someone as sensitive and gentle as she is. Another artist, perhaps. Someone who can offer her a safe, contented life." Helene's sweet Southern drawl sharpened into a louder, rather sour tone. "I thought that sooner or later she'd experiment with having a brief affair with some Indian and then she'd see the foolishness of having built some ludicrous fantasy around her great-grandmother's illicit love affair."

Joanna ripped away from Elena and flew into the living room. "Go home, Mother! Go back to running the state of Virginia and leave me alone."

Helene's face lost all color. She held out a hand to her daughter. "Joanna, my dear, I didn't mean for you to hear. I'm so sorry. I simply thought it best for Mr. Blackwood to understand."

"To understand what, Mother? That I'm some weak, helpless, fragile little girl who lives in a fantasy world? That's what you just told him, wasn't it?"

"Don't upset yourself this way." Helene took a tentative step toward Joanna. "I'm only trying to protect you from being hurt."

Joanna backed away from her mother. "In your own subtle way, you were trying to warn J.T. to stay away from me because I'm so fragile that if he dares to touch me, I'll break."

"Joanna, dear, let's not turn this into an ugly scene," Helene pleaded.

Hysterical laughter rose from Joanna's throat, tearing holes in the tension-filled atmosphere. "No, we wouldn't want to do that, would we? Whatever would people think? Wasn't that your greatest concern after Lenny Plott raped me? Oh, you were heartbroken for me and hovered over me, smothering me with attention, but I knew. Damn you, I knew! You were so ashamed. Ashamed that your daughter had let herself become front-page news in a serial rapist's trial. Ashamed to have to face your friends. Ashamed that I wasn't strong enough to cope without therapy!"

Joanna turned and ran from the room, into the hallway and out the front door. Elena called after her.

J.T. looked directly at Helene Beaumont with his one good eye. "Call tonight and make reservations for the first flight to Richmond tomorrow. Alex will have one of the hands drive you to Santa Fe."

Without a backward glance, J.T. exited the living room, walked down the hall and entered his study. He flipped on the overhead switch, bathing the room in light. Quickly he picked up Annabelle's diary, shoved it into his pocket and rushed down the hall and out the front door. He saw Joanna several feet away, standing in the middle of the yard, her arms wrapped around her middle.

"Joanna," he called out to her.

"Go away!" Spinning around on trembling legs, Joanna faced him. "Leave me alone."

"I can't leave you alone, Jo. I'm your bodyguard. Remember?"

"Oh, that's right. I hired you to protect me from Lenny Plott because I'm so weak and frightened and fragile and sensitive and—"

"Stop talking nonsense." J.T. walked down the steps and into the yard. "Your mother doesn't know who the hell you are. She's the one living in a fantasy world, a world where she can control you."

"She did control me. All my life. And I let her."

"She doesn't control you now. You make your own decisions. Right?"

"You know what the funny thing is, J.T.?" She watched, unmoving, while he walked toward her. "As different as you and Helene Beaumont are, you do agree on one thing."

"What's that?" he asked, halting a couple of feet away from her.

"You both think Annabelle Beaumont was a foolish adulteress and the great love she and Benjamin shared was nothing more than a lonely, unhappy matron's fantasy."

"I've just started reading the diary," J.T. said. "I'm not sure what I believe. Not anymore."

"Don't you dare try to pacify me with lies, John Thomas Blackwood. Don't pretend something you don't believe."

"Nobody calls me John Thomas. I'm J.T. John Thomas was my grandfather."

"Sensitive, are we?" she taunted.

J.T. grabbed her and held her by the arms, keeping a good foot of space between their bodies. "Yeah, honey, I'm sensitive about some things. Everybody is. And it's all right for you to be sensitive." Still holding her arm with one hand, he grasped the back of her neck with the other. His touch was strong, yet gentle. "Your sensitivity is one of the things I like about you."

"Don't you dare be nice to me out of pity!"

"Pity has nothing to do with the way I feel about you."

His kiss, like his touch, was strong yet gentle. Her momentary resistance disappeared as quickly as smoke in the wind. By the time his tongue entered her mouth she eagerly accepted him, responding with a desperate hunger.

He ended the powerful kiss, but pulled her into his arms and pressed her face against his chest. "I want to make love to you, but I don't want you to agree as an act of revenge against your mother."

"If and when I agree to make love with you, it will be for only one reason," she said. "Because I want you."

"Why don't we go to the bunkhouse? I'll fix us both a drink and you can tell me more about Annabelle and Benjamin."

"You're willing to do anything to cheer me up, aren't you?" she said teasingly.

J.T. let out a deep breath, pleased to see her smile. "Just about anything."

"All right, why don't we go home to the bunkhouse? You can fix us both a drink, then you can tell me about what it was like in the Secret Service, and I'll tell you something you want to know about me."

"What's wrong, Jo, are you afraid if we talk about our great-grandparents, we might find ourselves following in their footsteps and—"

She laid her index finger over his lips. "Shh."

J.T. kissed her forehead. "I read Annabelle's first entry in the diary. The day she met Benjamin."

Pulling out of J.T.'s arms, Joanna backed away from him. "The day we met, when I first saw you sitting astride Washington, I thought I heard drums." Joanna turned and ran across the yard and toward the bunkhouse.

J.T. raced after her, catching her on the front porch. Grabbing her, he slowly turned her around. "You're hell on a man's nerves. Why did you have to go and tell me something like that?"

"What difference does it make?" she asked. "You don't believe I heard drums any more than you believe Annabelle heard them."

"I told you that I don't know what I believe. Not now."

"Come on, let's go inside and talk. You tell me about the Secret Service and I'll tell you about—"

"You tell me about your art. About when you first realized you wanted to be an artist and how you could draw better than anyone else in kindergarten."

She slipped her hand into his. "Thanks, J.T."

"For what?"

"For not paying any attention to my mother. For not letting her run you off."

"Nothing and no one is running me off. I made you a promise, and it's a promise I intend to keep. You can't get rid of me, honey. I'm sticking to you like glue."

Hand in hand, they entered the bunkhouse—a woman who, more than anything, wanted to be able to trust this man; and a man who, for the first time in his life, wondered what it would be like to truly love a woman—this woman.

Chapter 9

Joanna awoke with a start. At first, she had no idea what had awakened her and then she vaguely remembered hearing the front door open. Was J.T. awake? Had he gone outside? She got out of bed, slipped into her thin silk robe and walked into the living room. The floor lamp behind the plaid chair was on, and an open book lay, spine up, across the overstuffed armrest. Undoubtedly, J.T. had been unable to sleep and had been reading. She glanced over at the front door, which stood open, with only the screen door closed. The shadowy outline of J.T.'s broad shoulders caught Joanna's eye. He stood on the edge of the porch, staring out into the dark night sky.

When Joanna neared the plaid chair, she realized the book perched on the armrest was Annabelle's diary. Had J.T. been reading another entry? Joanna picked up the diary, turned it over and glanced down at the open page.

I know I should feel great shame for having committed such an unpardonable sin. But I feel no shame, only an overwhelming joy. How could loving someone the way I love Benjamin be wrong? I knew we would consummate our

*love today. He took me to a cave in the mountains, high
above the world, quiet and secluded. I was far more nervous with Benjamin than I had been on my wedding night
nearly sixteen years ago. He sensed my unease, my doubts,
my fears, and he soothed me with sweet words that I did not
understand because he spoke them in his own language. But
my heart knew their meaning.*

*When we came together, it was as if we had both been
waiting a lifetime for the moment. Benjamin seemed to
know me better than I knew myself. Sheer instinct seemed
to guide him, telling him what I wanted, what I needed. The
love we shared, I have never shared with another, and know
in my heart I can share only with him. Benjamin. My Benjamin. My tender, passionate lover, who taught me the
meaning of ecstasy.*

Tears gathered in Joanna's eyes. She closed the diary and
hugged it to her breast. Had J.T. read a third of the diary
tonight, or had he skipped through parts of it, coming to
this account of the first time Annabelle and Benjamin made
love?

Joanna padded across the room, her bare feet quiet on the
wooden floor. She opened the screen door, stepped outside
and let the door slam shut behind her. J.T. didn't flinch. He
had known she was there; he had probably heard her stirring about inside.

"Did I wake you?" he asked, keeping his back to her.

"I'm not sure," she said. "I think I might have heard the
front door open, but I wasn't sleeping soundly anyway."

The moonlight combined with the glow from the lone
lamp in the living room, creating a muted illumination that
cast everything into soft shadows. J.T. wore nothing except
a pair of faded jeans. His broad, muscular back looked like
polished leather. Joanna barely controlled the urge to reach
out and touch him. She wanted this man, wanted him in a
way she had never wanted anyone or anything. He stirred
needs in her that were new and powerful and frightening in
their intensity. Yet, as much as she wanted J.T., she was

afraid of the very virility and masculine power that attracted her to him.

"If I weren't working, I'd go somewhere and get riproaring drunk." J.T. gripped the banister that bordered the front porch. "I never had any idea it was possible to want a woman as much as I want you."

Joanna went hot all over; a flush of excitement and pure feminine exhilaration spread through her body. She reached out and touched his shoulder. He flinched. She withdrew her hand.

"You read some more of Annabelle's diary, didn't you?" Joanna's voice sounded strange to her own ears, its quality low and earthy and undeniably sensual.

"Yeah, I read a couple of entries after the first one, then I just flipped through the pages."

"You read about the first time they made love." Joanna laid her hand on his bare back. Dear God, how she longed to wrap her arms around him, to cuddle up against him and hug him close to her.

He whipped around, knocking her hand off his back in the process. "I wish I'd never made that bargain with you. I wish I'd never read a word in that damn diary."

Joanna's heart roared in her ears. She swayed slightly. J.T. grabbed her by the elbows, steadying her. She looked up at him, and suddenly the whole world condensed into this time, this space, this one man.

"It's painful, isn't it?" Joanna realized that Annabelle's words had touched J.T.'s heart. "Reading about how she felt, how much she loved him and how hopeless their love was, always makes me cry. And of course, they'd both realized, from the very beginning, that they had no future together."

J.T. knew what Joanna wanted him to say. She wanted him to admit he'd been wrong and she'd been right about their great-grandparents' summer love affair.

After reading her diary, it had become obvious to J.T. that Annabelle Beaumont had been deeply in love with

Benjamin Greymountain, and that it had broken her heart
knowing they couldn't spend the rest of their lives together.

How had Benjamin felt? What pain had he suffered? J.T.
wondered. Unlike Annabelle, whose emotions lived on in
her words, Benjamin's thoughts and feelings had died with
him. Had he suffered the way she had? Had he lived out his
life yearning for a love that could never truly be his, except
in his memories? And how had he felt having an affair with
a woman, knowing he had nothing to offer her? He'd been
a poor Navajo silversmith and she a wealthy Virginia so-
cialite. How many nights had Benjamin stared up at the
stars and raged against heaven?

"Would you do what Annabelle did?" he asked, drawing Joanna into his arms. "Would you risk everything for a
brief affair with a man who could offer you nothing more
than heaven in his arms?"

"Yes." She slipped her arms around his waist and laid her
head on his chest. Silently she added, "If I loved him, I
would risk everything."

"I promise that I won't hurt you. Not now or ever," J.T.
vowed. "I want you, Jo. I want to lift you into my arms and
carry you to bed and make slow, sweet love to you all night
long."

"I want that, too, but—"

"You take charge, honey. You tell me what to do. Every
step of the way. I won't do anything without your orders."

He was promising her what she wanted to hear, assuring
her that she would be in control of the situation. But could
she trust him? J.T. looked like a man on the edge, a man
ready to explode. He might promise her anything right now
to gain her acceptance, but what would he do in the throes
of passion?

"I'm not sure. I want you, too, J.T. I want you till I ache
with the wanting. But I'm afraid."

"Trust me to be true to my word."

Lifting her head, she stared up at him. "You're so big and
strong and . . . if I asked you to stop and you didn't, I'd be
powerless."

"If you ask me to stop, I'll stop. I promise."

Closing her eyes against the sight of him, against the temptation of his pure masculine beauty, she took a deep breath and choked back her tears. Reaching into the depths of her soul she sought and found courage—Annabelle Beaumont's kind of courage; the courage to risk loving a man who could promise her nothing more than the moment.

"Hell, Jo, take your gun to bed with us if that'll make you feel safer!"

Tears escaped from her eyes, trickled down her cheeks and into her mouth. She smiled at J.T. "You want me so much you'd risk getting shot?"

If she refused him, he'd die. But if she accepted him, making love to her slowly and tenderly would kill him by degrees. He wanted her wild and furious this first time, wanted her passion to equal his. But if he acted on his instincts, he'd scare the hell out of her. "Yeah, I want you that much."

"Then take me to bed," she told him.

He thanked God that she hadn't denied him, and at the same time prayed for the strength to be the lover Joanna needed, to be man enough to relinquish the power to her and allow her to make love to him. It was the only way, and he knew it. Yet every primitive, masculine instinct in him cried out for him to take her, possess her, dominate her and make her yield to him.

He swept her up in his arms, swung open the screen door and carried her into the living room, then closed and locked the front door. Joanna kept her arm draped around his neck as he carried her down the hall and into her bedroom. After laying her down, he stood by her bed and waited.

"I'm not sure what to tell you to do next," she admitted. "I haven't done this sort of thing before and I... J.T., what do I do?"

"What do you want to do?"

"I want to touch you."

His already aroused body stiffened painfully. He sat down on the edge of the bed. "How's this?"

She scooted over toward him, wrapped her arms around his waist and laid her cheek on his back. "You're hot." She ran her fingers up and down, over his stomach and chest.

J.T. sucked in his breath. Her hands stilled on his chest. He laid his hands over hers gently. "It's all right. You didn't do anything wrong. I love having your hands all over me."

"Would you . . . would you lie down and let me look at you?"

Slipping out of her arms, he rolled over and lay down flat on his back, then raised his arms and crossed them behind his head. "How's this?"

Joanna edged backward, easing her knees up in front of her and hugging her arms around her legs. "You're a beautiful man, J.T. The most beautiful man I've ever seen."

He grinned. She smiled. And the bottom dropped out of his stomach. "And I'm all yours," he told her. "Putty in your hands. Yours to command."

"I guess I'm just a bit overwhelmed with all this power."

She surveyed him from the top of his head to the tips of his bare feet, taking inventory of every inch of his big, hard body. He lay there watching her watch him. His arms bulged with muscles. She reached out and ran her fingertips over one arm from elbow to armpit, then slid her nails down his side and over across his broad, sleek chest. When she touched one tight little nipple, he made a sound, and Joanna knew he was trying to stifle a groan.

She wondered if his body ached the way hers did; if he throbbed with desire, wanting her the way she wanted him.

She couldn't mistake the evidence inside his jeans—the truth about the way he felt. His body revealed his need for her. "Would you take off your jeans?" she asked.

"Why don't you help me take them off?" He took her hand, brought it over to the snap on his jeans and placed it directly over his zipper.

Her hand trembled. She'd never touched a man this way. Shaking like a leaf, she unsnapped his jeans and undid the zipper, then jerked her hand away.

He lifted himself up off the bed, tugged his jeans down his legs and tossed them on the floor. Joanna watched his every move, becoming more and more fascinated by the sheer masculine glory of J.T.'s body.

"I suppose I should take something off, shouldn't I?"

"Only if you want to, honey." J.T. wasn't sure he had the strength to resist his need to take this woman. But, God in heaven, he had to resist. He had to be strong for Joanna. He had to give her all the power; otherwise, she'd be lost to him forever.

Joanna removed her thin silk robe. She sucked in several deep breaths, then dropped the robe on the floor and edged her way closer to J.T. Sliding close to his side, she eased one leg up over his and rested her elbow on the bed as she leaned over and kissed his chest. She explored his body, touching, kissing, licking him from forehead to feet.

J.T. could imagine no torture more unbearable. He called upon every divine force in the universe to help him.

Suddenly his prayers were answered when Joanna said, "Touch me, J.T. Please, touch me."

Touch her? Where? How? What he wanted to do to her would be too much too soon. Slow and easy, Blackwood, he told himself. Don't do anything to frighten her, to take away her sense of complete control.

He lifted her up and on top of him, showing her how to straddle him the way she did a horse. He sat her down directly on top of his arousal, allowing her to feel his throbbing hardness through the thin cotton of his briefs.

"Oh," she gasped. Her body clenched and unclenched with pulsating need. She braced herself by placing her hands on his shoulders.

J.T. bucked up against her once. She gasped again. Still clinging to his shoulders, she clenched his hips with her knees.

"Do you like that?" he asked, and circled her waist with both hands, urging her to lean forward.

"I'm tingling all over," she said. "Tingling and aching and—"

Her breath caught in her throat when she felt his hands spreading out from her waist, slowly covering her buttocks. He caressed her through the silk gown, the feel of his big hands gentle yet sensual.

"I'd like to kiss you," he said. "Would that be all right?"

"Yes. Please."

Every muscle in his body strained, every nerve roared like a wounded beast. Take her! Take her now! his body ordered him. Be patient. Wait. Make sure she's ready, his mind told him. While his body and mind fought, his heart won the battle. He brought her downward, inch by inch, until she lay atop the full length of his body. She lowered her head and touched her lips to his.

She played with his lips, licking, nibbling, and then finally enticing him to open his mouth and allow her tongue entrance. Once she had initiated the dance, he fell into step, thrusting and tasting, becoming a full participant in the wild fandango their kiss became.

J.T. eased her gown up her hips, one tiny piece of material at a time. When he slipped his hands beneath the silk and stroked her bare buttocks, Joanna moaned into his mouth and shivered violently.

He ended the kiss. They both gulped in air. She cuddled up against him like a sleek, purring kitten. He wrapped his arms around her.

"I want to kiss your breasts and your belly and taste the sweetness of your body," he said. "Will you let me do that?"

With her head still resting on his chest, she nodded, then whispered her agreement. Gently shoving her upward until she straddled him again, he gripped the hem of her gown, which rested about her hips.

"May I take this off?" he asked.

"My gown? Yes. It's all right. Take it off."

He pulled her gown up over her head, tossed it on the floor on top of his jeans and then rolled her over onto her back. While he anointed her face with dozens of sweet kisses, he ran his hands over her breasts, cupping them, lifting them, caressing their roundness.

Her nipples beaded into hard buds. Her breasts felt heavy and achy. "J.T.?"

"It's all right, honey. I know what you want." While he suckled one breast, he stroked the other between his thumb and forefinger.

Joanna's lower body lifted off the bed, the movement completely instinctive. "Oh, J.T., please, do something. I'm aching so."

He rose over her and looked down at her face, her beautiful face, flushed and damp with passion. His gaze traveled over her breasts, round and full, the nipples tight with desire.

Lowering his head, he kissed her belly. She moaned. He painted a moist trail downward until his lips encountered the fiery red triangle between her legs. "Let me touch you . . . here." He nuzzled her with his nose.

"Yes. Please."

J.T. cupped her softly, petting her, then slipped his fingers inside the hot, wet folds of her body. She quivered uncontrollably for a few seconds, then closed her thighs, capturing his hand.

"Easy, Jo. Easy, sweet darling."

She relaxed her legs and allowed him to part them slowly. After he'd settled himself between her legs, his lips sought and found the secret heart of her. When he kissed her there, she cried out. When his tongue worked tirelessly against her, she clutched his shoulders and wept as her body tightened and released, tightened and released, until she was wound so tight, she was wild with need. With one final stroke, he sent her over the edge, then lifted himself upward to take her cries of completion into his mouth.

She shuddered as spasms of earth-shattering ecstasy claimed her body. Taking her in his arms, J.T. rolled them over, positioning her on top of him. He had to take her—take her now—or he'd die on the spot.

"I want you, Jo. I want you so much."

"Yes. Please. Now," she cried, as the remnants of her release echoed through her body.

J.T. lifted Joanna and brought her down onto him, thrusting inside her. She gasped several times, then whimpered softly.

"Are you all right?" he asked, praying he hadn't hurt her.

"Yes. Oh, yes."

Nothing he'd ever experienced had prepared him for the feel of being inside Joanna, of becoming her lover. She was hot and wet and tight. So very tight. Her body sheathed him like a glove. A perfect fit.

"Take charge, honey," he said. "Do whatever you want to do to me."

"I want to make love to you, J.T., but I'm not sure I know how. I've never... I mean, there wasn't anyone before—"

"You and your fiancé never made love?" Was it possible? he wondered. Had she been a virgin when Lenny Plott raped her?

"No. Todd and I didn't make love. I wanted to wait."

"Then I'm the first," J.T. said.

"You would be, if... if I hadn't been—"

"I'm your first," he told her, moving out and then back in, claiming her as his own. "No other man has ever been your lover."

She wept, tears of joy and of sorrow. Tears that washed away any residue of shame she'd felt. Tears that proclaimed her gratitude. He might not realize the truth himself, but Joanna knew, in her heart of hearts, that J.T. was the other half of her, her life's partner, her soul mate.

"Making love is so easy," he said, "when you want each other the way we do."

"I do want you, J.T. I want you so desperately."

"Then take me, honey. Ride me...hard and fast. Give us both what we want...what we need."

Pure, primitive feminine instinct took over, guiding her into a mating ritual as old as time. She moved, slowly, tentatively, uncertain of herself and of him at first. But as the momentum inside her body gradually built, she gave herself over to the passion, to the basic animal urges she didn't want to control. J.T. stroked and petted her hips and buttocks. He suckled at her breasts, moving from one to the other, paying equal homage. And he whispered sweet, dark, erotic words of praise, and in the moment of fulfillment, he cried out to her, *"Ayóí óosh'ni,"* the words strange to his own ears, the language the Navajo tongue of his childhood.

She whispered his name over and over, telling him that she loved him, as release claimed her only seconds after he fell headlong into completion.

He held her in his arms, atop his sweat-dampened body. She cuddled to him, not wanting to move, wishing they could stay this way forever. Happy, fulfilled, complete, and safe from the outside world.

He spread a line of kisses along her cheek and jaw, then reached down, pulled up the sheet and covered them.

"Shouldn't I move?" she asked. "I can't stay on top of you all night. I'm too heavy."

"I don't want you to move," he said, stroking her hip. "Go to sleep right where you are, honey."

Sighing, she relaxed on top of him, then kissed his chest. "What did you say to me when . . . just as you . . . you know . . . those strange words? Were they Navajo?"

"I don't speak *Saad.*" He kissed the top of her head resting on his chest. "Or at least I haven't since I was a little boy. I don't have any idea what I said. It must have been something I remembered from my childhood."

"Something very wonderful?" she asked.

"If I said it to you, then it had to be something wonderful."

"Thank you, J.T. Thank you for making this so good for me—so special."

"Don't thank me, Jo. I should be thanking you. Do you know how honored I feel knowing I'm your first lover?"

"But that's why... Don't you understand?" She cuddled into him as if she were trying to bore her way inside him, seeking shelter and safety in the harbor of his big, strong body. "Todd wanted to be the first. He wanted a virgin bride."

"I told you, honey, the man was a bastard. And a stupid one, at that." J.T. wrapped her tightly in his arms, cocooning her in his warmth and strength, protecting her in the safe haven of his embrace. "What Lenny Plott did to you had nothing to do with making love. In every way that matters, you were still a virgin until tonight."

"Do you really believe that?" She could not stop the tears, could not keep herself from clinging to J.T., could not keep her heart from bursting with the joy of loving such a special man.

J.T. took her chin in his hand, lifted her face and kissed the tip of her nose. "The way I see it, you gave your virginity to me tonight. I'm your only lover. There's never been another man. Only me."

"Yes. Only you." Only you, J.T. For now and always. My only lover. My only love.

Joanna awoke shortly after dawn in J.T.'s arms and found him watching her. They made love again, lingering over every touch, drawing out every sighed expression. He was as tender, as gentle and as passionate the second time as he'd been the first, and their fulfillment had been even more complete. Joanna had never dreamed loving someone could be so good. Now, she truly understood how Annabelle had felt about Benjamin.

When she roused from sleep the second time, she was alone in bed. She called out to J.T. He answered her from the kitchen, telling her to stay put. She waited patiently for his return. Within minutes he entered the bedroom. Joanna's heart filled with warmth at the sight of him standing there wearing nothing but his briefs and carrying a tray of food. He set the tray at the foot of the bed, then eased himself down beside her.

"Breakfast is served." He dragged the tray up the bed and lifted it on top of their laps. "I whip up a mean batch of scrambled eggs, if I do say so myself."

Joanna inspected the tray, taking note of the white rose lying on her napkin. "You picked one of Elena's prized roses! She'll kill you."

"How's she going to know one's missing?" J.T. shrugged, then picked up a glass of orange juice and handed it to Joanna.

She took a sip. Her eyes widened. "This is fresh-squeezed. I don't believe it. You're a man of many talents."

"Oh, honey, you've just seen a few of my many talents." He slipped his hand under her gown and up the inside of her leg.

"Behave yourself." Joanna swatted at his hand. "We can't play around all day. Mother will be up soon and if I don't confront her up at the main house, she'll be down here trying to move in with me."

J.T. removed his hand from beneath her gown. "I've been trying to forget that your mother is still here." Lifting his mug to his lips, he took a hearty swallow of sweet, black coffee. "Jo?"

"Uh-hmm?" She finished off her orange juice.

"Last night I told your mother to make reservations to fly home to Virginia today."

"I'll bet she loved being ordered to get out of Dodge," Joanna said. "She's probably ready for a showdown this morning."

"I can deal with your mother by myself, if you'd rather not see her again."

"Don't do that." Joanna placed her hand on J.T.'s shoulder. "Don't start trying to fight all my battles, especially not the ones with my mother. I'm not the fragile, helpless creature she made me out to be, even if last night I—"

"You were no fragile, helpless creature last night," he said. "You were a woman filled with powerful emotions who took charge of our lovemaking." Covering her hand with his, he lifted it and brought it to his lips. "You are brave and strong and so very beautiful. You're everything a woman should be. Don't hold it against me because I'm an old-fashioned, macho kind of guy. I can't help wanting to protect you. And not just from Lenny Plott, but from anything or anyone who could hurt you."

She cupped the side of his face with her hand, leaned over and kissed him. "I won't hold it against you, if you're willing to accept the fact that I need to be the one to make my decisions, to be in control of my life, as much as possible."

"I understand." He returned her kiss. The tray on their laps slid off the side of the bed, hitting the floor with a resounding crash.

They looked down at their scrambled eggs and toast scattered across the handwoven rug and wooden floor, then they both laughed. He wrapped his arms around her and pulled her down in the bed, devouring her with kisses. She rubbed her body against his, moaning as ripples of pleasure radiated through her.

The loud pounding on the front door ended their passion before it went any further. They sat up straight in the bed.

"Who the hell?" J.T. grumbled as he got out of bed, picked up his jeans and struggled to get into them as he crossed the room. "If that's your mother, I'll strangle her."

Joanna glanced at the bedside clock. "It can't be Mother. It's only seven o'clock. She's never up and dressed this early unless there's an emergency."

By the time he'd made his way to the front door, J.T. had managed to zip and button his jeans, but his chest and feet were still bare.

"Whoever it is, go away," J.T. said through the closed door. "Everything is fine here."

"J.T.?" a man's voice said, the tone husky, the accent Southern. "Come on. Open up. We need to talk."

J.T. unlocked the door, swung it open and stared into the face of his old FBI friend, Dane Carmichael. "What the hell are you doing here?"

"I've got news on Plott," Dane said. "Bad news."

"Come on in." J.T. held open the door.

Dane walked in, glanced around the living room and then down the hall. "Where's Ms. Beaumont?"

"She isn't up yet," J.T. said. "What's this about Plott? And why didn't you just call me?" J.T.'s gut instincts told him that Dane Carmichael wouldn't be here unless the Bureau had sent him.

"We're going to be sending a man out here to New Mexico and another one to Texas."

"Why?" J.T. asked. "And why just New Mexico and Texas? One of Plott's victims lives in Missouri."

"We've already got people in Missouri," Dane said. "Claire Andrews has disappeared."

"What?" Joanna stood in the hallway, one hand clutching the lapels of her robe where they crossed over her chest, her other hand knotted into a tight fist at her side.

"Jo, honey." J.T. rushed over to her, put his arm around her and guided her into the living room.

"What happened to Claire?" Joanna asked. "Has Lenny Plott kidnapped her?"

J.T. held Joanna close to his side, supporting her trembling body with his strength.

"Ms. Beaumont, I'm Agent Carmichael, with the Federal Bureau of Investigation. And I'm afraid we don't know for sure what happened to Ms. Andrews," Dane said. "Her boyfriend called us when she didn't come home from work yesterday. Claire worked at a local grocery store. Everyone in town knows her, and yet no one has any idea how she simply disappeared when so many people were supposedly looking out for her."

"He found her and kidnapped her and—" Joanna's breathing became fast and frantic "—raped her and killed her. That's what he said he'd do to her...to all of us."

J.T. pulled Joanna into his arms. She buried her face in his chest. He ran one hand up and down her back, soothing her, while he held her hip with the other.

"We're going to put a man in the vicinity. I'm here now doing preliminary planning," Dane said. "I know you don't need help guarding Ms. Beaumont. Our man will be here to do a job—to apprehend Plott—while your job is defending Ms. Beaumont. If we're lucky, we'll catch Plott before he gets anywhere near the ranch."

"Send one of your best men," J.T. said. "I'll consider it a personal favor."

"I'm sending Landers, Hal Landers. You don't know him. He's a fairly new agent, but he's fast become one of our best."

With her arms still wrapped around J.T., Joanna turned her face and looked at Dane Carmichael. "How will your agent recognize Lenny Plott if he's changed his appearance? He could come into town, even come out here to the ranch, and no one would know who he was."

"Landers will be working with the local authorities to keep an eye on any strangers coming into Trinidad," Dane told her. "He'll get settled in town, then he'll stop by the ranch and introduce himself. If you need him before he makes contact, just give me a call."

"Agent Carmichael?" Joanna called out to him.

"Yes, ma'am?"

"Please let me know as soon as you find Claire. No matter what."

"Yes, ma'am, I'll give J.T. a call."

"Thank you," she said. "J.T., why don't you see Agent Carmichael to the door?"

"I'll see myself out," Dane said.

The minute they were alone, J.T. lifted Joanna into his arms, sat down in the plaid chair by the fireplace and held her in his lap. Cuddling in his arms, she rested her head on his shoulder.

"Claire's dead," Joanna said. "I know she's dead."

"Maybe not, honey."

"He's going to come after Libby and me. But which one of us is going to be next?"

"If he comes after you—"

"*When* he comes after me," Joanna corrected J.T.

"When he comes after you, he'll have to face me." J.T. took her chin in his hand and looked directly at her. "I told you before, nobody's going to get to you without going through me first, and so far, nobody's ever gone through me."

She tried to smile, but could manage only a faint curve of her lips. She closed her eyes and sighed. He kissed her closed eyelids, then drew her into his arms, holding her, soothing her, reassuring her.

Why had life played such a cruel joke on her, bringing J.T. into her life at the same time Lenny Plott escaped from prison? She'd spent the past four years in New Mexico, dreaming of and searching for a love of her own to equal the one her great-grandmother had found. Now, when there was a chance of that dream coming true, her life was in danger. And the one person who stood between her and certain death was the man she loved.

Chapter 10

"Please try not to worry about me too much." Joanna kissed her mother on the cheek. "J.T. will do everything possible to keep me safe. And now that there'll be FBI agents in Trinidad keeping a lookout for Lenny Plott, it should be only a matter of time before they arrest him."

Helene hugged Joanna, then released her. Holding Joanna's hands in hers, she smiled. "I can't stay. As much as I would like to be here with you, I have too many obligations back in Richmond. And since you refuse to come home with me, then—"

Joanna squeezed her mother's hands. "There's absolutely nothing you could do if you stayed here. As a matter of fact, we're probably better off with a couple of thousand miles between us. If we were together, we'd only end up arguing. You were too accustomed to running my life when I lived in Richmond, and since moving to Trinidad, I've become used to making all my own decisions."

"I still think you're making a mistake getting involved with J.T. Blackwood," Helene whispered, then glanced over her shoulder at J.T., who stood on the ranch-house porch, watching and waiting for her departure.

"If having an affair with J.T. is a mistake, then it's my mistake, Mother."

"I don't want to see you hurt again. I simply couldn't bear—"

"You'd better get going." Joanna tugged on her mother's arm. "Alex and Elena are waiting in the Jeep."

"They're very nice people," Helene said. "I'm glad you have them as friends. But friends can never take the place of family. Remember that."

"If y'all don't get started right now, Mother, you'll miss your plane," Joanna said.

"I wish you could at least ride into Santa Fe with us."

Joanna opened the Jeep door and assisted her mother inside, then leaned over and kissed her again. "I'll call you often to let you know I'm all right." Joanna closed the door.

Helene waved goodbye as Alex drove away; Joanna watched the departing vehicle until all she saw was a trail of dust.

J.T. put his arm around Joanna's shoulders. "It would be nice if we all had perfect parents."

"I wonder if anyone does?"

"Probably not," J.T. said. "After all, parents are only human beings, with faults and weaknesses. I used to blame my parents for all my problems, for all my unhappiness. But that was when I was a boy. When I grew up, I realized that they were just a couple of kids who fell in love and were too young to overcome all the obstacles in their path. Mainly old John Thomas."

"I'm not sure my parents were ever in love. I think their marriage was more or less a merger of two old Virginia families."

"Marriages have been based on far less."

"Why have you never married, J.T.?" She slipped her arm around his waist.

"I decided a long time ago that I wasn't the marrying kind, honey. I'm a hardheaded, cynical son of a bitch, who doesn't like to compromise. I'd make a lousy husband."

"Have you ever been in love?"

"Nope."

"I thought I was in love with Todd, but I came to realize that what Todd and I had was a lot like what Mother and Daddy had. We were compatible, came from the same social circle and probably would have had a fairly contented life together. At least for a while. Until the day came when I discovered that I needed more in a relationship."

"I suppose that's what happened to Annabelle," J.T. said. "After sixteen years of marriage, she decided she wanted some passion in her life."

"You've changed your mind about Annabelle and Benjamin, haven't you?" Joanna nudged J.T. in the ribs. "Come on. Admit it. You know there was more to their relationship than a summer affair."

"I concede that there might have been more going on." He gave Joanna's arm a gentle yank, guiding her into motion. "Come on. You need to go change into something comfortable for riding."

"We're going riding?" she asked. "Now?"

"It's a beautiful day. Not hellfire hot. Alex and Elena graciously volunteered to take care of your mother for us, so that gives us the day to ourselves."

"What if Agent Landers tries to contact you?" Joanna asked.

"I'll take my cellular phone. I'm sure Dane gave Landers all the numbers where I can be reached. Now quit making excuses and go get changed." J.T. shoved her across the yard. She glared at him, then laughed.

"Where are we going?"

"I thought we'd ride back out to the old archaeological dig, and after that, I have a surprise for you."

What J.T. wanted more than anything was to get her mind off the fact that Claire Andrews had been kidnapped and no one had any idea where she was. Sure, the odds were that

Plott had her, and she was probably dead. But they'd face that reality if and when they found Claire's body. He was sorry for Melody Horton and Claire Andrews. He hoped the feds caught up with Plott before he got to Libby Felton, if Libby was next on his list. But his main concern was Joanna—keeping her safe and sane, until Plott was back behind bars.

"Why don't you go get our horses ready while I change," Joanna said. "I won't be long."

"We've got all day. No need to rush." J.T. followed her up the steps to the bunkhouse porch.

She stopped dead still, turned slowly and looked at him. "You *are* going to stick to me like glue, aren't you?"

"I'm not going to take any chances where your safety is concerned. Consider us temporarily joined at the hip."

She nodded, turned and went inside, with J.T. directly behind her. He waited patiently for her to change into boots, jeans and a cotton shirt. When she came out of the bedroom carrying her hat, J.T. took it from her and set it on her head.

"You look like a real cowgirl now, honey." He kissed her, quick and hard, yet nondemandingly.

She loved the way he smiled when he looked at her, as if he found the sight of her delightful. She and J.T. were lovers now and that should mean they were relaxed around each other. But Joanna found herself trying to second-guess his thoughts and actions. What exactly had their making love meant to him? Was she more important to him than the other women he'd had sex with over the years? Or was she nothing more than his latest affair?

She watched him while he prepared Washington and a spirited mare named Playtime. He checked his rifle before attaching the scabbard to the saddle. He packed his Glock in the saddlebags, along with a couple of flashlights, a flask of water and his cellular phone. Then he tied down a folded blanket.

"Flashlights and a blanket," Joanna said. "I'm getting curious about this surprise of yours."

"Don't start asking questions. Just wait and see."

They rode off Blackwood property and onto Hezekiah Mahoney's. Within an hour they had reached the eastern section of Mahoney's ranch, where the old dig was located near the foothills of the mountain. Although Joanna had painted the vibrant colors of this land time and time again, the breathtaking beauty of the red sandstone canyons, the mushroom-shaped cliffs and the golden cottonwood trees that grew along the arroyos would always make her want to put brush to canvas.

Giving their horses a rest, they walked, hand in hand, over the old archaeological site. The earth had long since given up most of her buried treasures here, leaving only a random find for the occasional student whom eighty-four-year-old Hezekiah allowed on his property.

Joanna tried to imagine what her great-grandfather's campsite would have looked like. Closing her eyes she could almost smell the cook fires burning. Could almost hear the sound of Annabelle's young sons, one her own grandfather, laughing while they played. Could almost see a young Navajo silversmith gazing down from his Appaloosa stallion at the woman who was to become the one true love of his life.

"Hey, wake up." J.T. nudged her. "Where were you? Off in some dream?"

"Just trying to picture what this place must have looked like in 1925, the summer my great-grandparents worked here."

"Fantasizing about Annabelle and Benjamin's first meeting?" J.T. asked.

"Yes, that, of course," she admitted. "But wondering how my great-grandfather could have been so blind. His wife was having an affair right under his nose and he didn't suspect a thing."

"Maybe he did," J.T. said. "Maybe he just chose to keep his mouth shut and pretend nothing was happening."

"But how... why?"

"He must have known she wasn't in love with him, since her father had arranged their marriage." J.T. took Joanna's hand in his while they traipsed around the old site. "He was a lot older than she was, and my guess is they weren't sexually compatible. Ernest Beaumont would have been pretty sure his wife would never give up her sons, and that's exactly what she'd have had to do if she'd left him."

"So, you're saying you think my great-grandfather simply stood by and endured Annabelle's affair, knowing in the end, she'd return to Virginia with him."

"Think about it. It makes sense."

Joanna kicked the dirt under her feet, stirring up some ancient dust. "Can you imagine the intense emotions, the high level of tension? I'm surprised we can't still feel it in the air around us."

"I think you're feeling some of it right now, aren't you, Jo?" He whirled her around and into his arms. "It's all right to get a bit caught up in our ancestors' lives. For the time being, it's good for you to have other things to think about. But keep in mind that these were their lives, not ours. You're not Annabelle and I'm not Benjamin."

"Yes, I know. I'm not a married woman with two children. You're not a poor Navajo youth. The obstacles that kept Annabelle and Benjamin apart don't exist for us. Where their affair was doomed from the start, ours isn't. We're free to do whatever we want with our lives."

J.T. stared at her, his gaze softening. He caressed her cheek. "What I want right now is to show you my surprise."

He didn't want to think too deeply about his feelings for Joanna. She was a woman who deserved far more than he could ever give her. She needed more than his passion, more than the momentary pleasure they found in each other's arms.

"What's the surprise? Where is it?"

J.T. thought she looked like a little girl, bright-eyed, rosy-cheeked and almost giddy at the prospect of being given a secret present. He hoped she wouldn't be disappointed. He didn't think she would be. But often reality dulled beside the brilliance of fantasy.

"It's about a three-mile ride from here. Up the side of the mountain."

J.T. led her to their horses and helped her mount, then guided them up the mountainside. With the jagged peaks high above, the yellow pine and white oak trees kissing the royal blue sky and an almost-holy solitude surrounding them, he dismounted, lifted her off Playtime and held her in his arms. She clung to him, her heartbeat thundering in her ears.

Sliding her slowly down his body, he caressed her. Releasing her, he turned and undid one saddlebag and retrieved two flashlights. He handed one to her. "Come with me."

She removed her hat and hung it on the saddle horn. Then she followed him to the mouth of a cave, partially hidden from view by an outcropping of scrubby bushes.

"Take a look," he said, moving aside to allow her entrance.

Switching on her flashlight, she aimed the beam into the cave and took a tentative step inside. She sucked in a deep breath. J.T. turned on his flashlight and doubled the illumination inside the cave as he urged her to venture farther.

Together they explored the small cavern. Able to walk upright less than twelve feet inside, they stopped when the sandstone ceiling had gradually lowered from a good eight feet to less than five. From there, the cave decreased to a crawl space.

"Is this what I think it is?" Joanna asked.

"I believe so," J.T. said.

"How did you know about this place?"

"I discovered this cave when I was about eleven. I used to ride all over, exploring. I knew someone had used this place as a refuge of some sort, but not until I read part of Annabelle's diary did I put two and two together."

Joanna ran the flashlight's beam over the floor, where an animal skin of some sort still lay. Had Annabelle and Benjamin made love, their bodies entwined, on that fur rug? A shimmering glow of light reflected off the shattered pieces of a kerosene lamp, the bottom portion broken into only two pieces.

"I found this cave when Cliff and I were out riding," J.T. said. "His father was ranch foreman and he and I grew up together. We're the ones who accidentally broke that lamp."

"This is Annabelle and Benjamin's special place." Joanna's mouth felt dry, her throat tight. She bit down on her bottom lip. Her nerves zinged with excitement.

"Yeah, I think it probably was." J.T. placed his hand in the small of her back. "It would have been fairly close to camp and yet far enough away to have been private. And you've got to admit, the place is pretty isolated."

"The way she wrote about their special place in her diary, I pictured it cosy and warm and inviting." Joanna continued visually exploring the cave, waving her flashlight back and forth in slow motion.

"In reality it's a dark hole in the side of the mountain. Hard, rugged and very unromantic."

"But it was their special place." Joanna glanced down at the ratty old fur rug. "The only place on earth they could truly be together, where they could be lovers."

"Kind of sad, isn't it? But remember, things looked a lot different seventy years ago. The fur rug was undoubtedly new and clean, not rotted with age. And the kerosene lamp probably cast warm shadows on the wall." He set his flashlight on its base, allowing the light to shine straight up and create pale shadows.

Joanna set her flashlight down beside his, increasing the muted glow and doubling the sense of cosy warmth. "From what Annabelle wrote, the happiest moments of her life were spent here, because she was with the man she loved."

"There's something I want to show you. I think it'll pretty well confirm that this was our great-grandparents' trysting place." J.T. turned her to face him. "You stay right here. It's in my saddlebag."

When he started to walk away, she grabbed his arm. "What is it?"

"Just let me get it and show it to you."

She nodded agreement and waited in the cave for his return. The eerie silence crept up her spine. She shivered. Somewhere off in the distance she heard the sound of drums. She listened, thinking she was imagining the rhythmic beat.

No, the sound was real, even if it existed only in her heart, as surely as it had existed in Annabelle's heart long ago. A magical drumbeat, summoning lovers together, speaking without words of a love that was meant to be.

"Here it is." J.T. came back into the cave, a blanket over his arm and a tattered book in his hands. "I found this ragged old book in the cave when I was up here exploring by myself one day. I was always collecting stuff, taking it home and adding it to my treasure trove. But it's not so much the book itself I wanted to show you, but something pressed between the pages."

He held the book out to Joanna. Her hands trembled as she reached out for it. The binding had been broken and numerous pages had fallen out, probably years ago. She opened the book to the first page. J.T. spread the blanket on the ground, lifted one of the flashlights and slid his hand under Joanna's elbow.

"Come on, honey, sit down."

He eased her down on the blanket, then sat beside her and held the flashlight on the thin volume of verse. "Go ahead and read it."

The inscription read, "To Benjamin. Forever and only yours, A."

"It's a stupid book of poetry," J.T. said. "Why an eleven-year-old boy ever kept such a thing, I'll never know. I suppose at that age, I considered it some sort of treasure. I stuck it in a bottom desk drawer in my room, where I kept a lot of the junk I collected."

"Christina Rossetti's poems," Joanna said. "This book

must have belonged to Annabelle. There're references to Christina Rossetti's poems in her diary. One in particular.''

"Look about halfway into the book," J.T. told her, then watched as she carefully turned the brittle, yellowed pages.

There, lying atop the poem entitled "Echo," was a four-inch braid of hair—strands of jet-black hair and fiery red hair blended together and tied with a faded yellow ribbon. Joanna gasped. Moisture stung her eyes. She swallowed her tears.

Closing the book with reverence, she laid it beside her on the blanket, then looked at J.T. "You think it's all a bunch of stupid, sentimental hogwash, don't you? You can't understand why they would have cut strands of their hair and braided them together as a keepsake for Benjamin, can you? Or why she would have given him a book of poems by her favorite poet?''

"Hey, seventy years ago, people were different than they are today. Maybe everybody was more romantic." J.T. rubbed his hand up and down Joanna's back. "I think we both know Annabelle Beaumont had a romantic streak in her a mile wide. So if Benjamin really loved her, then he would have catered to her romantic nature, don't you think?''

"Well, I'll say one thing for you, J.T. Blackwood, you certainly know how to get a woman's mind off her troubles." She tried to smile, but the effort failed. Instead, she caressed his cheek with her fingertips. "That's why you chose today to show me this cave and the book with the hair braid. You wanted me to forget about Claire's disappearance and Lenny Plott's threats.''

"Obviously it didn't work."

"Yes, it did. I'd much rather think about and talk about our great-grandparents than about living in fear of what Lenny Plott will do next.''

"I thought you'd like to keep the book," J.T. said. "I figured it'd mean a lot more to you than it ever could to me.''

"Thank you." She caressed his cheek again. He covered her hand with his, trapping it against his face.

"What are the odds that you and I would ever meet, let alone become lovers?" he asked.

"You don't believe in destiny, but I do. You and I were destined to meet and become lovers, just as Benjamin and Annabelle were."

"Now, Jo, don't start comparing us to—"

"I'm not! I know very well that you and I aren't our great-grandparents, and we aren't destined to relive their tragic love affair. We're very different people than our ancestors were, and our affair is different from theirs." She pulled her hand from his.

"I'm glad you see it that way. I don't want you to think just because I showed you this cave and gave you that book—" he pointed to the volume of poetry "—I'm buying into any of this romantic nonsense. I'll go so far as to admit that I believe Annabelle and Benjamin probably cared deeply for each other, but I think this tragic, eternal love between them is something your great-grandmother concocted in her fantasies. Benjamin had to have gone on with his life and married someone else and spent his life with her. After all, he did have a child—my mother's father."

"You don't know anything about your family history, do you? Your grandfather Blackwood really did cut all your ties to the Navajo, didn't he?"

"Yeah, you're right. I don't know anything about my mother's family, but I don't see what my ignorance concerning my Navajo heritage has to do with—"

"Benjamin Greymountain was a young widower with a four-year-old son when he met Annabelle. His wife had died in childbirth, and he never remarried. When I asked Elena about Benjamin, she told me that her mother said he died of tuberculosis at the age of thirty-eight."

J.T. grunted, then blew out a huffing breath. "I give up. Benjamin went to his grave pining for Annabelle, and she loved him and no other as long as she lived. Now, are you satisfied?"

Joanna grinned. "You don't really believe it. You're just saying that to pacify me." Lifting her arms, she circled his neck. "In your own gruff, moody way, you're very sweet, you know."

"I've been called a lot of things, honey, but never sweet. There's no reason for you to read more into what I say and do than—"

"I know. I know. You can't give me anything, aren't offering me anything, except your protection and a temporary love affair."

She realized that he had no idea he was catering to her romantic nature. Just as, perhaps, Benjamin had catered to Annabelle's romantic nature. When a man cared deeply for a woman, he made concessions. Was that what J.T. was doing? Did his feelings for her run far deeper than he wanted to admit? She could only guess at J.T.'s true feelings. It was possible, even probable, that he didn't know himself. Long ago, as a young boy, he had sealed off his emotions, protecting himself from being hurt. He had been stolen from the only love he'd known—his mother's. And he'd been raised by a bitter old man who obviously hadn't known the first thing about love; only about controlling and possessing.

"Exactly what did you have in mind when you brought me up here to this cave?" Joanna leaned closer, hugging J.T., pressing her breasts against his chest. "Considering how intrigued I am by Annabelle and Benjamin, you might have thought I'd want to make love here, in their special place."

Clearing his throat, J.T. shuffled his hips on the blanket. "I don't want you to think I brought you up here with the intention of—"

Joanna covered his lips with her index finger. "Why did you bring along a blanket?"

"Now, Jo, you're doing exactly what I told you not to do. You're reading something into my actions that—"

She silenced him with a tongue-thrusting demanding kiss, then toppled him down on the blanket, knocking off his

Stetson. Covering his body with hers, she ended the kiss and smiled at him.

"If I promise not to misinterpret your actions and start thinking there's something magical happening between us the way it did between our great-grandparents, will you make love to me here... in this cave... now?"

J.T. cupped her buttocks in his big hands, lifting and positioning her so that her softness settled directly over his hardness. "Honey, I'll make love to you... anywhere... anytime."

She had dreamed of this moment, but she didn't dare tell J.T. Since the first time she'd read her great-grandmother's diary, she had fantasized about meeting her own passionate lover, here, in this special place where Annabelle and Benjamin had consummated their love. Perhaps she was just a foolish romantic, a woman for whom reality had become cruel and bitter. But Annabelle had been a romantic fortunate enough to find a lover who had fulfilled her fantasies.

Joanna kissed J.T.'s leather brown neck, then laid her head on his shoulder as she draped her body over his. "I'm glad I waited for you. It wouldn't have been the same with anyone else. It wouldn't have been so absolutely right."

He rolled her over onto her back, leaned down and unbuttoned her shirt. She shivered when his fingers touched her bare skin. "Are you sure this is what you want?"

"Yes, I'm very sure." Reaching up, she unsnapped his shirt and stretched her hands out over his chest. When he sucked in his breath, she smiled. "You make me want to learn all there is to know about making love. You make me want to trust you completely, to give myself over to you and believe you'd never hurt me."

He undid the front opening of her bra, lifted her just a fraction off the blanket and removed her shirt and bra. He gazed down at her breasts—round, full and tempting. Covering them with his hands, he slid one leg between her thighs. Lifting his knee, he massaged her intimately.

"I want you to trust me completely," he said. "To know that what happens between us now is a mutual loving. We both give and we both take." Clasping her hand in his, he carried it to his belt buckle. "I take you. You take me. And when you lose control, I lose control."

With a precision of familiarity, as if they had undressed each other numerous times, Joanna and J.T. divested themselves of their clothing. When they lay naked, side by side on the blanket, J.T. took her in his arms and turned her to face him. "Will I frighten you if I'm not gentle this time?"

He fondled her, testing her readiness. She clung to him, her answer a gasping sigh against his lips. "No, you don't have to worry. I don't feel very gentle myself. Not here. Not now." Not when the passion within her had been ignited by the chance to fulfill a dream, to capture for herself some small portion of the magic Annabelle had known.

His kiss devoured her, as hers did him. He rolled her on her back and cupped her behind, lifting her. She clutched his back, biting into his flesh with her fingernails, bucking up to meet him. Wrapping her legs around his hips, she issued him an invitation into the sheathing warmth of her body. He thrust into her forcefully. Moaning with pleasure, she kneaded his tight buttocks.

Heat poured into her body as if a searing liquid fire had entered her bloodstream. Her breasts ached, her nipples beaded into tight buds. As he moved in and out of her, his hard chest grazed her sensitive nipples, the sensation shooting pinpricks of pain and pleasure to the very core of her femininity.

Her breathing quickened. She gasped for air as the tumult within her built, stronger and stronger with each powerful stab. What he gave her was too much, and yet at the same time, not nearly enough. She wanted him to end this torment, but she wanted the loving to go on forever.

He increased the depth and pace of his lunges. Erotic words, spoken harshly and urgently, told her of his needs and intentions. Joanna trembled as the first warning signs of fulfillment rippled through her.

J.T. didn't know if he could hold on much longer; the tight clutching of her body brought him to the very edge. The moment he felt her shatter into paroxysms of release, he hammered into her repeatedly, his own release coming hard and fast. He cried out, the sound one of a triumphant male animal. Pure masculine completion controlled his body.

His jackhammer thrusts created anew the climactic spasms within her. Her moans of pleasure grew louder and louder. In the final moments, he uttered Navajo words to her, words neither of them understood. *"Ayóí óosh'ni."* But in her secret heart of hearts, Joanna believed she knew what J.T. had said to her, even if he did not. His words were Benjamin Greymountain's words—his proclamation of love to Annabelle.

J.T. wrapped his arms around Joanna, their bodies resting spoon-fashion. He lay there, holding her, listening to the soft, sweet sound of her breathing as she slept peacefully, sated and safe. Somehow he'd allowed this beautiful, loving woman to get under his skin, to get past the protective armor he'd kept securely around his emotions. He was a fool for getting personally involved with her, but heaven help him, he had never wanted or needed a woman so much.

He had promised her that he'd never hurt her, but he had lied. He had lied as much to himself as he had to her. Oh, he'd never hurt her physically, but he knew that sooner or later he'd break her heart. And for a woman like Joanna, his precious romantic Joanna, breaking her heart would be far more devastating.

She believed in things he didn't, and wanted more from him than he had to give. He almost wished he could be the man she wanted. But he couldn't. She wanted him to be the reincarnation of Benjamin Greymountain; to come to her with a Navajo soul, to love her with a mindless passion. Joanna wanted the two of them to capture the spirit of their ancestors and bring to life the love Annabelle and Benjamin had taken to their graves.

When Joanna awoke, they made love again. Sweet, slow love, each learning the other's body by touch and taste and sight. The burning sun melted into the late-afternoon sky, splaying the earth with golden light. They dressed unhurriedly, taking time to savor their last moments alone in this special place. Joanna clasped Annabelle's book of poetry to her breast. A shadowy sense of sadness settled on her heart. Would this be the only day she and J.T. would make love here? Was there no future for them?

J.T. helped her mount Playtime, then took the book from her and put it in her saddlebag. "Time to go back to the ranch. Elena and Alex should be home by now, even if Elena did a lot of shopping while they were in Santa Fe."

Joanna nodded. Yes, it was time to go back to the ranch, back to reality, back to the threat on her life.

Joanna and J.T. returned Washington and Playtime to the stables, taking time to give their horses a rubdown themselves, instead of handing them over to a stable hand.

"After we shower, how about my grilling steaks tonight?" J.T. said. "We can call Alex and Elena and see if they want to join us."

"Sounds like a great idea." She tiptoed her fingers up J.T.'s arm. "Especially the part about taking a shower."

"Are you suggesting we shower together?" He slipped his arm around her waist and drew her to his side.

"I've never taken a shower with anybody. It would be another new experience for me."

J.T. eased his hand down, spreading it out over her behind. "I'm glad I'm the one who's getting to share all these new experiences with you."

Joanna unlocked the front door and walked into her house, with J.T. following her, his hand still on her rear end. She gasped when she saw the state of her living room. She rushed inside, then stopped dead still. J.T. cursed.

"The place is a total wreck," she said. "What could have— Oh, my God, no!"

J.T. came up behind her, draped his arm around her middle and rested his chin against her temple. "Take it easy, honey."

"The room's been ransacked," she said.

Sofa and chair cushions lay haphazardly about the floor. Lamps had been shattered and pictures ripped from the walls. Someone had done a thorough job of plundering, turning neatness and order into total disarray. Pulling away from J.T., Joanna crossed the room to the easel that held Elena's portrait.

"Dammit!" she cried when she saw the defaced painting. "He destroyed Elena's picture."

J.T. read the message that had been written in red paint across the surface of his sister's portrait. "I'll be back." He gripped Joanna by the shoulders, then closed his eyes for a moment, a burning black rage searing him.

"He's been here." Joanna trembled in J.T.'s arms. "He's been inside my home. How did this happen? Why didn't someone see him and stop him?"

"I don't know." J.T. tightened his hold on her, silently cursing Lenny Plott, damning his soul to everlasting hell. The man was a slippery, slimy, conniving polecat. Somehow he had slid past Dane Carmichael and Hal Landers when he'd come through Trinidad. But what if he hadn't come through Trinidad? It was possible that he'd gone southwest, then north and had doubled back in the opposite direction.

J.T. knew from having read reports on him that Leonard Plott III was a sick, evil man, but he was nobody's fool. In his own way, the man was a genius, having raped dozens of women and eluded the police in Virginia for several years. If his last rape victim's boyfriend hadn't returned home unexpectedly, Plott might never have been caught.

Not only was Plott smart, he was rich. And with his kind of money, he could buy just about anything he needed—even certain people's help and other people's silence.

Leonard Plott was a dangerous animal. Sooner or later, someone was going to have to bring him down. J.T. wanted to be the one to do it.

"It's not safe here, is it?" Joanna turned in J.T.'s arms. He hugged her fiercely. "I'm not safe anywhere from that monster."

"You're safe with me," J.T. told her. "Right this minute, you're safe. Here. In my arms. And I'm going to keep you safe."

"What are we going to do? He'll be back. He won't stop until he's—"

"Don't say it, honey. Don't even think it. If you don't feel safe here on the ranch, we'll find another place."

"Someplace where he can't find me?" Joanna asked. "Dear God, J.T., I don't think such a place exists."

Chapter 11

"We're going to catch this guy," Dane Carmichael said. "It's only a matter of time."

"Time isn't on our side." J.T. glanced across the room at his old FBI friend and Special Agent Landers, the two men seated side by side on the leather sofa in J.T.'s study. "Plott has already kidnapped and killed one woman, and possibly a second. And today, he came onto my ranch, right under our noses, and ransacked Joanna's home. No one saw him. Not one person on this ranch had any idea an intruder was anywhere around. That should tell us all something about Plott, shouldn't it?"

"It tells me what I've known all along. That we're dealing with a highly intelligent and very dangerous criminal." Uncrossing his legs, Dane eased to the edge of the sofa. "His access to an unlimited amount of money makes our job more difficult and his revenge scheme easier for him to achieve."

J.T. cut his gaze toward Joanna, who sat in the swivel chair behind his desk. He had asked her to let him speak privately with Carmichael and Landers, but she'd insisted on being present. He understood her need to be involved with the investigation; after all, it was her life on the line. She was one of Plott's prey, possibly his next intended victim. She looked up at J.T. and nodded, silently telling him that she was all right.

"It doesn't help that Plott has somehow changed his appearance," Agent Landers said. "He didn't have time to get any kind of plastic surgery done, so whatever changes he's made have to be superficial. Dyed his hair, maybe. Possibly got contacts. There's no way to know."

"We've been running checks in Richmond, passing out Plott's photograph to see if anyone anywhere recognizes him. We're desperate for a lead of some sort." Dane stretched his long lean frame up and off the sofa. "But a man with Plott's money can pay people off, get whatever help he needs and make sure nobody talks."

"His mother insists she hasn't seen him or talked to him," Landers said. "But Lieutenant George has told us that the old woman would do anything to protect her son."

"Has the FBI sent more agents to Texas to protect Libby?" Joanna asked. "I know that she can't afford private security any more than Claire could have."

"We're taking every precaution where Ms. Felton is concerned," Dane assured Joanna. "In Shelby, where Ms. Felton lives, we've brought the local authorities in on the case, just as we're doing here in Trinidad."

"You understand that resources and manpower are limited, Ms. Beaumont," Landers said. "We're doing all that we can. And I can assure you that we're going to get Lenny Plott."

"Before or after he kills all four of the women who testified against him?" Although she quivered inside, Joanna's voice was strong and steady.

J.T. noticed that her tight little fists rested in her lap. Lifting himself up from where he'd had his hip propped against the edge of the desk, J.T. walked around behind the desk and gripped the back of the swivel chair.

"I'm taking Joanna away," J.T. said. "First thing in the morning, we're leaving the ranch."

"There's no need to do that, Mr. Blackwood." Agent Landers jumped up off the sofa. "Dane's bringing in more agents, and we've got the local police department and county sheriff's office to back us up."

"Where do you think you can take her where she'll be safer than she is here?" Dane asked.

J.T. glanced at Dane, then over at Landers. "To the Navajo reservation. My sister is making arrangements with members of our mother's family. Elena and Alex will know how to reach us."

"See here, Blackwood, are you saying you plan to take Ms. Beaumont to some sort of hideaway on the Indian reservation?" Landers asked. "I don't recommend this move, and if you insist on—"

"I insist." J.T. glared at Landers.

Landers's face reddened. He cleared his throat. "In that case, I'll have to insist on our knowing your exact whereabouts. Perhaps you can have your sister draw a map and give us telephone numbers where we can locate you."

"Dane has my cellular phone number," J.T. said. "And the tribal police will know our whereabouts."

"I don't understand your reasoning." Landers marched across the room, stopping in front of the huge oak desk. "You've got the FBI here, as well as local authorities as a backup, and you're taking Ms. Beaumont out in the middle of nowhere and expect the tribal police to protect her."

"You've said too much," Dane told his subordinate.

Snapping his head around, Landers glowered at Dane, who was watching J.T. Landers looked at J.T., then swallowed hard. "I didn't mean—"

"I'll protect Ms. Beaumont," J.T. said. "I expect the FBI to do their job and find Lenny Plott."

Landers wisely kept his mouth shut when Dane Carmichael asked J.T. to walk them outside. Dane said goodbye to Joanna, then motioned for Landers to follow him into the hallway.

J.T. slipped his hands down the back of the chair, grasped Joanna's shoulders and squeezed. "I'll be back in a few minutes and we'll talk to Elena and Alex."

She laid both of her hands atop his, patting him reassuringly. "Try not to kill Agent Landers before he leaves the ranch."

J.T. chuckled. "It'll be an effort to keep from strangling him, but I'll do my best."

Joanna watched J.T. follow the FBI agents. Leaning over, she rested her elbows on the desk, then lowered her chin, cupping it in her hands.

In such a short period of time, her whole life had changed. She had found peace and contentment in Trinidad, and her career as an artist had excelled beyond her wildest dreams. And after waiting for so many years to find a special man to love, J.T. Blackwood had ridden his Appaloosa stallion into her life.

But as he had done once before, Lenny Plott threatened to destroy her happiness.

"Are you all right?" Elena's question interrupted Joanna's thoughts.

Joanna gasped, then looked up to see Elena standing in the doorway. "I'm fine. Come on in. J.T. will be right back. He's seeing the FBI agents to their car."

Elena nodded, then walked across the room and lifted herself up on the desk. Dangling her legs off the side, she faced Joanna. "I just got off the phone with my cousin Kate and she's going to go out tonight and tidy up Mama's house. No one has lived there since she died, but Kate and Ed keep an eye on the place and Kate airs it out and cleans it a couple of times a year."

"I remember you telling me about your home on the reservation," Joanna said. "I had planned to have Kate take me out there to see it the next time I visited her."

"Now, you'll be living there with J.T." Elena bent over, leaning closer to Joanna. "He's been back to the reservation only three times since he was a child. Once when Mama was dying, and again a few days later for her funeral. Then the last time, to get me and bring me back to the ranch."

"Maybe our stay in your mother's home will help J.T. as much as taking refuge there might keep me safe from Lenny Plott." Joanna clasped Elena's hands. "I'm in love with your brother, you know. I didn't mean for it to happen, but it did. He hasn't made me any promises—other than to guard and protect me."

"J.T.'s afraid to love anyone," Elena said. "I know he cares about me, but . . . well, I think maybe Mama was the only person he ever loved. You know, when he was a little boy. After he was taken from the reservation, he was told Mama had given him away because she didn't want him anymore. That cruel grandfather of his taught him to hate Mama and everything Navajo. Old John Thomas Blackwood saw to it that J.T. grew up hard and cold and cynical, just like him."

"I think J.T. needs to come to terms with his mixed heritage." Releasing Elena's hands, Joanna rose from the chair and walked over to the window, looking out at her converted bunkhouse. "If only he would allow himself to be the man he is. Half white. Half Navajo."

"He told me once that the reason he didn't stay in New Mexico is because out here he isn't either. Not white and not Native American. He doesn't feel accepted by either people, doesn't feel a part of either world. But in the marines and then in the Secret Service, he was just J.T. Blackwood. A soldier. An agent. His past didn't matter. He had a job to do and he did it."

"But he has no personal life. No real home, despite having inherited this ranch from his grandfather," Joanna said. "And although, as you say, he cares about you, he won't let himself be part of a family."

"You've gotten to know J.T. very well in a short period of time, haven't you?" Elena smiled. "I knew you and J.T. would be good for each other, if I ever got you together."

"I don't know about that. Sometimes I think maybe J.T. and I are very bad for each other. I've fallen in love with him and I trust him with my life, but... Well, there's still a part of me that doesn't completely trust anyone. I love J.T., but I don't trust him with that love. He can't make a commitment to me, can't promise me a future. And I don't trust what there is between us enough to believe we have a chance together.''

''Be patient with him. Try to have faith in his ability to change.'' Elena walked over and placed her hand on Joanna's shoulder. ''If you can learn to trust him and trust what you feel for him completely, then maybe he can learn how to love you.''

''Maybe I'm the wrong woman for him.'' Joanna stepped away from Elena. Stretching her shoulders, she clasped the back of her neck with both hands and tilted her head. She took a deep breath, relaxed and dropped her arms to her sides. ''After what happened to me...the rape...maybe I'll never be enough woman for a man like J.T. He's so...so...''

''All man,'' Elena said. ''Yeah, my big brother is primitive macho masculinity personified, isn't he? But I'll tell you what I think. I think that if J.T. can't love you, he can't love anybody.''

''Where's J.T.?'' Alex walked into the study.

''Seeing the FBI men off,'' Elena told him. ''Did you tell Benito that J.T. wants to take Washington and Playtime with him when he leaves in the morning?''

''Yes, I told Benito. He'll have them in a trailer and have it hitched to J.T.'s Jeep by eight in the morning,'' Alex said. ''J.T.'s already told me that he wants to get an early start.''

''I'll have to go back over to my house to pack.'' Joanna dreaded walking into her living room again, although she knew J.T. had asked Benito's wife, Rita, who worked as a part-time maid for Elena, to clean and straighten the mess Lenny Plott had created. ''I want to take some supplies and try to do some work while I'm gone. We have no idea how long we'll be away. It could be days or even weeks.''

''There's an old hogan close to Mama's house,'' Elena said. ''My great-grandparents lived there. You might want to do some sketches.''

"Are you saying this hogan belonged to Benjamin Grey-mountain?" Joanna asked.

Elena nodded. "While you have J.T. on the reservation, see if you can get him to open himself up to our heritage and become acquainted with our relatives. You know our mother's family far better than J.T. does."

"I'll try," Joanna said.

Returning to his study, J.T. found Alex and Elena with Joanna. Taking Joanna to the reservation had been Elena's idea, but after giving it some thought, J.T. had agreed with her. There was no way to predict what Lenny Plott's next move would be or when he would act. One thing for sure, he knew exactly where Joanna lived and how to get to her. Taking her away was the wisest move. Of course, even on the reservation, hidden away from the world, there was no guarantee that Plott wouldn't figure out a way to find her.

If and when Plott showed up, J.T. would handle him. A part of J.T.—that primeval, protective, possessive male part of him—actually looked forward to a confrontation with Plott. Although J.T. had killed before, in the line of duty, he took no pleasure in it. But if he had to kill Plott, he would, and have no regrets.

"Well, did you get in touch with your cousins?" J.T. asked Elena as he walked into the study.

"*Our* cousins," Elena corrected him. "And they have names. Kate and Ed Whitehorn. Kate's mother and our mother were sisters."

"Fine. Did you get in touch with this Kate and make arrangements for me?"

"Yes, I did. She'll clean up Mama's house and have it ready by the time you and Joanna get there tomorrow," Elena said. "I explained the situation to her and—"

"How much did you tell her?" J.T. asked.

"Everything! We can trust our family completely, J.T. You are a member of that family, you know. And a member of our clan. They would never betray you." Planting her hands on her hips, Elena glared at her brother. "Besides, Kate and Ed are very fond of Joanna. She has stayed with them several times when she's gone to the reservation to work on her sketches and paintings."

"Calm down, little sister, I didn't mean to rile you. I'm sure your cousins—our cousins—are fine, trustworthy people," J.T. said. "It's just that the fewer people who know exactly where Joanna and I are, the better."

"Kate and Ed raise sheep, but Ed works at the NFPI sawmill," Elena said. "Their house is pretty isolated, but neighbors will see you and Joanna as you travel the road to Kate's house, so Kate has asked her brother to speak to these neighbors, most of them friends and family, and caution them to tell no one of your presence on the reservation."

"I appreciate all you've done to help us." Joanna hugged Elena. "Maybe the FBI will capture Lenny Plott soon and this nightmare will be over for all of us."

"J.T. will keep you safe." Elena glanced at her brother and smiled. "And he will have Ed nearby, as well as Joseph, who is very handy with a gun. And we both know that Joseph would do anything for you, Jo."

"Speaking of Joseph reminds me that I promised to do a sketch of him as well as one of the children next time I came to visit," Joanna said.

"Who's this Joseph?" J.T. frowned.

"Joseph is Kate's younger brother." Elena ran her fingers through her long dark hair, pulling the flyaway strands off her face. "He's been sweet on Joanna since the first time they met."

"Elena!" Joanna's green eyes widened. Her cheeks flushed.

"Joseph is our cousin," Elena told J.T. "His mother and our mother were sisters, so that makes Joseph the great-grandson of Benjamin Greymountain, too."

"Is that right?" J.T. deliberately avoided eye contact with Joanna, knowing exactly what his sister was trying to do. She wanted to elicit his jealousy over another man's interest in Joanna. And not just any man, but another direct descendant of Annabelle Beaumont's one true love.

"Well, why don't you two finalize your plans for the trip." Elena grabbed Alex's arm. "I'll get one of the guest bedrooms ready for you for tonight, Jo." She pulled Alex toward the door, halting just before walking out into the hall. "Let me know if you want my help packing. I can run over to your house with you and J.T. before supper."

When Elena and Alex had left, Joanna turned to J.T. "I'm sorry about that. Elena wasn't very subtle, was she?"

"Subtlety isn't one of Elena's strong points." J.T. rubbed his chin. "Have you ever dated my cousin Joseph?"

"Have I ever . . . ?" Joanna smiled, bit down on her bottom lip and then covered her mouth, trying to suppress her laughter.

"Why do you find the question so amusing? All I asked was whether or not you'd ever dated Benjamin Greymountain's other great-grandson."

"Yes, Joseph and I have *dated* a few times," Joanna said. "I've dated several men since I moved to New Mexico. Cliff Lansdell for one, and Joseph for another. I like Joseph a lot, I just don't like him in *that* way."

"He's a full-blooded Navajo just like Benjamin Greymountain," J.T. said. "If you've been looking for a lover like the one your great-grandmother had, what was wrong with Joseph? Is he ugly or stupid or a jerk or—"

Joanna kissed J.T. on the mouth very quickly, then tilted her head just a fraction and looked directly at him. "Joseph Ornelas is a handsome, intelligent, sweet man and I think of him as a friend, but there is no magic between us. Not the way there is between . . ." Joanna shut her eyes, escaping the hard look on J.T.'s face.

J.T. pulled her into his arms. "Not the way there is between you and me." His kiss proclaimed his barely contained jealousy as well as his need to brand her as his own.

Joanna gave herself over to his possession, accepting his momentary domination, realizing that he had no idea how revealing his actions were. Did she dare hope that at the very core of his protective, possessive desire, the seeds of love had taken root?

* * *

Joanna flung back the covers and jumped out of bed. There was no use trying to sleep; she had tried for over two hours. Sleep wouldn't come. She couldn't stop thinking, couldn't stop worrying, couldn't stop wishing tonight was last night, when she had become J.T. Blackwood's woman in every sense of the word.

Not bothering to turn on a lamp or put on her robe, Joanna walked across the room and slumped down in the chair beside the windows. Tucking her bare feet up under her, she sighed, leaned back and stretched.

If only there was a switch inside her brain that could be flipped on and off; she'd flip it off right this minute and put an end to her thoughts. Her mind kept running the gamut from the night Lenny Plott had raped her to today when she and J.T. had made love in Annabelle and Benjamin's special place. She had struggled diligently to put the past behind her, to come to terms with the brutal violation that had forever changed her life. But with Lenny Plott free and bent on revenge, she couldn't help reliving that horrible night when she had come home to her apartment after working late at the museum.

Don't think about it! Don't remember! It happened nearly five years ago. Put it in the past where it belongs. Don't allow Lenny Plott's threats to force you to relive what he did to you. That's what he wants—for you to recall the terror and the pain and the humiliation. He wants you to think about how it could happen again.

But it wouldn't happen again. She wouldn't let it happen again! And J.T. would never allow anyone to hurt her. He'd made her a solemn promise to protect her. She had to trust him, had to believe in him and his ability to keep her safe.

J.T. J.T. J.T. She had put her life in his hands. She had given him her heart. And yet she could not bring herself to trust him fully, completely, to have faith in their future together, when he had made no lasting commitment to her.

Would hiding away on the Navajo reservation keep her hidden from Lenny Plott, or would he find her regardless of where J.T. took her? And what would happen if Plott came after her, if he confronted J.T.? J.T. might have to kill him.

Joanna shuddered. Pulling her knees up against her, she wrapped her arms around her legs. Unless the FBI apprehended Lenny Plott before he found her, a showdown between J.T. and him was inevitable. On some purely primitive level, she gloried in the fact that her mate was a brave warrior who would defend her to the death. And yet there was a part of her that personally wanted to rip out Lenny Plott's heart and feed it to the buzzards.

How did such creatures as Leonard Plott III come into being? What malevolent twist of fate turned a man into an inhuman monster capable of physically, sexually and emotionally brutalizing woman after woman and deriving immense pleasure from subjugating them to his cruelties?

Joanna's stomach churned. Bitterness coated her tongue. Her body quivered. Tears gathered in her eyes.

The door to the guest bedroom slowly opened. Joanna snapped her head around, staring at the silhouette in the doorway. Biting down on her bottom lip, she tried not to cry aloud.

Moonlight filtered through the sheer curtains, spreading a soft, muted glow over the room. J.T. glanced at the bed, saw that it was empty, and visually searched the room.

"Jo?" he whispered, then saw her huddled in the chair by the windows.

Swallowing her tears, she tried to answer him, but couldn't. He closed the door behind him, walked over to the chair and knelt beside her.

"What's wrong, honey?"

Cupping her chin in his hand, he lifted her face. She pulled away from him. Her long, fiery hair covered her features when she lowered her head. Slipping his hands under her neck, he swept up her hair, then let it fall through his fingers and down onto her shoulders.

"I couldn't sleep, either," he said. "I kept thinking about how much I wanted to be with you. Wanted to hold you in my arms."

Placing his arms around her stiff body, he pulled her toward him. "Talk to me, Jo. Let me help you. You don't have to be alone, unless you want to be. Just tell me, do you want me to stay or go?"

Joanna grabbed J.T., clinging to him fiercely. Wrapping herself around him, she allowed him to slide his big body into the chair as he lifted her onto his lap. She gasped for air, then laid her head on his shoulder and wept.

"Stay...please...stay." She cried softly, quietly, but with heartbreaking force.

J.T. stroked her back, kissed the side of her face and whispered comforting words, telling her it was all right to cry, to be angry, to be afraid.

Holding her, he encouraged her to vent her feelings, and when she was spent and lay exhausted in his arms, he lifted her and carried her to bed. He laid her in the middle of the huge oak bed, then sat down beside her, pulling her upward to rest again in his arms.

"Would it help to talk to me, to tell me about it?" he asked.

"I thought I'd put it behind me," she said, cuddling against him. "I had to tell the police, the rape counselor, the district attorney, my own therapist and...worst of all, I had to sit there in a courtroom with Lenny Plott watching me and tell the jury what he'd done to me."

"You were very brave," J.T. told her. "It took more courage than most people have."

"I wanted him dead!" Joanna clung to J.T., pressing against him, seeking and finding comfort.

J.T. couldn't hold her close enough. He wanted to weld her to him, to encompass her completely and make her a part of him. "Plott deserves to die."

"I testified against him for the same reasons Melody and Claire and Libby did. We wanted him punished and we wanted to make sure he could never hurt another woman. And now Melody is dead and Claire is missing."

"It isn't fair," J.T. said. "Sometimes there's just no rhyme or reason to life."

"The FBI have to find him and stop him before he ... before he—"

J.T. placed his finger over her lips. "Hush, honey. Don't think about it. It isn't going to happen. They'll find Plott." J.T. slid his finger over her chin and down her neck.

"But if they don't—"

"Then I'll take care of Plott."

"I don't want you to have to kill him." Joanna jerked away from J.T. and sat up ramrod straight in the bed. Closing her eyes, she hugged herself, gripping her elbows in the palms of her hands. "If anyone should kill him, I should. But I'm not sure I could...that I'd have the guts to."

"The night he attacked you, would you have killed him, if you could have?"

"Yes. Yes. A thousand times, yes." Joanna covered her face with her hands.

J.T. touched her trembling back. Wiping the tears from her eyes, she turned around and looked at him.

"While he was beating me...touching me...I kept thinking that if only I had a gun...or if only I was strong enough to take his knife away from him. Yes, I would have killed him."

J.T. rubbed her back, but didn't try to pull her into his arms again. He waited, unsure what to say or do to comfort her. Tonight she had reverted to the past, to the most horrible night of her life, and only by allowing her to tell him about Plott's vicious attack, could J.T. truly help her. But, God in heaven, he wasn't sure he was strong enough to hear the details without completely losing control. Already, there was a part of him that wanted nothing more than to hunt Plott down and take him apart, piece by piece.

"I tried to fight him, you know," Joanna said. "He liked that, my fighting him. He beat me. God, how he beat me." She swallowed the tears, pushing back the emotions threatening to overcome her. "The first blow was to my stomach. I'd never been hit before. Not ever. It took me by surprise. And it hurt. Oh, how it hurt."

J.T. wanted to take her in his arms and beg her not to tell him anymore. He had read a copy of the police report, and that had been more than enough reality for him.

"And when I doubled over, he shoved me down on the floor and kicked me." With each word she spoke, her voice became calmer, her face more somber, her eyes glazed with an unemotional stare. "I fought him even harder when he tried to rip off my clothes. That's when he hit me in the face, over and over again. I—I think I passed out. All I remember is his tearing my clothes and pawing me. Squeezing. Biting. Hurting me." Joanna clutched her throat. "And cutting me."

J.T. clenched his teeth. The roar of his own pain rumbled inside him—an agonized, wounded bellow forced into silence.

"And when he...when he... I wanted to die. In that one moment, I prayed to God to let me die." Joanna clutched the bedcovers, wadding them up in her fists. "But when he crawled off me, I prayed to God to let me live, to let me live long enough to kill him!"

She had to stop talking! J.T. told himself. He couldn't bear to hear another word. But, dear God, if just listening to her tell about what Plott had done to her hurt J.T. more than anything ever had, how must Joanna feel? What indescribable suffering she must have endured, and must still, at this very moment, be enduring!

Slowly, cautiously and with the utmost gentleness, J.T. eased his arms around Joanna. A loose, tentative hold. One from which she could readily escape. He kissed the side of her face over and over again, soft, delicate touches along her forehead, down her cheek and to her jaw. "Will you let me hold you?" he asked, strengthening his precarious clasp about her waist. "Will you let me lie here in this bed and hold you in my arms all night? I want to show you that you can trust me. That you're safe with me. That I'll never let anyone hurt you ever again."

Joanna gave herself over to J.T.'s kindness, knowing in her heart that he meant every word he'd said. He could give her his comfort and his promise of protection. He could guard her against the threat of Plott's murderous scheme. He could hold her in his arms and make her feel cherished and desired. But he could not give her his love, when he had none to give. She could be J.T. Blackwood's woman on a temporary basis in the same way Annabelle had been Benjamin Greymountain's woman. And Joanna knew that she, as her ancestress had done, would go to her grave still in love with a man who could never be truly hers.

Chapter 12

J.T. had returned to the Navajo reservation only three times since old John Thomas had taken him away when he was five. Once when his mother was dying. Then for her funeral. And a final trip to get Elena. Now, after all these years, here he was, back on the land where he'd been born, back among his mother's people. Elena's suggestion to bring Joanna here for sakekeeping had made perfect sense to J.T., but he'd known that his sister's plan included more than keeping her best friend safe. Elena was hoping a stay on the reservation would open his mind and his heart to a part of his heritage he had been taught to shun.

Following Joanna's instructions, J.T. drove along the endless stretch of road leading to Kate and Ed Whitehorn's place. Finally he saw their mobile home, the metal gleaming brightly in the hot morning sun. He pulled the Jeep up in front of the corrals where Ed kept his sheep and cattle when they weren't grazing. A small dark-eyed boy sat on the fence, cradling a baby lamb in his arms. Jumping down, he ran toward the Jeep, calling out a greeting to Joanna.

"That's Eddie, Kate and Ed's oldest child," Joanna said. "He helps Ed with the sheep and cattle."

"He seems awfully young for that kind of responsibility." J.T. opened the door, rounded the hood and assisted Joanna out of the Jeep.

Little Eddie ran up to Joanna, skidding to a halt before running right into her. "Mama said you were coming back for a visit, and you and Elena's brother will be staying at Aunt Mary's house." Eddie stared up at J.T., his dark eyes sparkling with interest. "Are you my cousin? Mama says you are, that you're of our clan. If you're Elena's brother, why haven't I ever seen you before?"

Eddie wore faded jeans and a white cotton T-shirt. A strip of light-colored cloth wrapped around his forehead kept his chin-length black hair off his full face. When J.T. looked at the boy, he saw himself as a child and couldn't help wondering what his own fate would have been, had his grandfather not taken him away from the reservation. Would he have helped tend the small herds of sheep and cattle that had to be moved often from pasture to pasture because of the sparse vegetation on this land? Would he have attended a contract school the way Elena had, where he could have learned to read and write in *Saad?* His mother's language. A language he had forgotten, except for a few words and phrases. Except for something he said to Joanna every time they made love.

"Yes, Eddie, this man is your cousin." Smiling at Eddie, Joanna stroked the lamb he held in his arms, then glared at J.T. "The reason you've never met him before is because he lives far away in Atlanta, Georgia, and is here in New Mexico only for a visit."

The front door of the mobile home swung open and a plump young woman carrying a toddler on her hip stepped out onto the lattice-trimmed porch. A little girl with huge brown eyes clung to her mother's leg.

"Joanna!" Kate Whitehorn called out as she walked down the front steps. "And J.T." She stared at her cousin, her smile fading from brightness to softness, a look of curiosity in her eyes. "I'm sure you do not remember me. We met very briefly at Aunt Mary's funeral. I was just a girl then."

J.T. held out his hand to Kate, noticing the strong family resemblance between her and Elena. The two could be sisters. "I appreciate everything you've done to help us. Elena said she explained the situation to you and your husband."

"Yes. Ed is at work, but you will meet him during your stay here." Kate shook hands with J.T., then rearranged the child on her hip and petted the top of her little girl's head. "You've met Eddie. He's our oldest. And this young lady hanging on to me is Summer. She's very shy and quiet, much like her father. And this—" Kate hugged her youngest to her side "—is Joey."

J.T. could not resist touching the plump bronze cherub in his cousin's arms. He cupped the child's face between his thumb and forefinger. A thicket of black hair covered Joey's round little head and his big dark eyes sparkled as he looked up at J.T. and laughed.

J.T. had never had a family—not until he had brought Elena to the ranch. But in many ways, he and Elena still were not truly family, and he knew the strain between them was his fault. He had been raised a loner, taught to neither need nor expect anything from anyone, to be totally self-sufficient. Needing others was a sign of weakness.

But as he grew older, J.T. realized that keeping others at a distance doomed a man to loneliness. As Elena was family, so were these people. This woman and her children were his cousins, from his mother's clan, people who had offered a sanctuary to Joanna and him.

"You will come inside and have lunch with us?" Kate asked.

"Thank you," J.T. said. "But I'd like to go on over to my mother's house and get settled in. Is there a corral there where we can put our horses?" He nodded at the horse trailer hitched to the Jeep.

Kate shook her head. "No, I'm sorry, there isn't. But we have a small corral. We once had several horses, but now only one. You are welcome to keep your animals there. Eddie can show you.''

"Thanks." J.T. glanced at Eddie, who grinned from ear to ear. "Oh, yeah, I was expecting someone from the tribal police to meet us here. Has anyone stopped by?"

"Yes, Joseph is here. He came early to visit with the children and me," Kate said. "That's his truck." She pointed to the dusty red pickup beside the house.

J.T. looked at the truck, noticing the feathers attached to the rearview mirror, and remembered Elena telling him something about feathers being attached to Navajo vehicles to ward off evil spirits. Undoubtedly this Navajo policeman still practiced old customs. "You said his name is Joseph?"

"Yes, my brother, Joseph. Didn't Joanna and Elena tell you that he is a tribal policeman? He is off duty right now. When he discovered Joanna was in trouble, he asked to help, to be your police contact here on the reservation."

"Joseph Ornelas?" J.T. asked. "No one told me anything about him being a tribal policeman."

"Did I hear someone mention my name?"

Joanna turned at the sound of the man's voice. J.T. watched her smile at Joseph Ornelas as he walked out on the porch. Slipping off a huge white apron, Joseph draped it over the porch railing and took several giant steps toward Joanna. He grasped her by the shoulders.

"It is good to see you again, Joanna." Joseph slid his hands down her arms and took her hands into his. "It's good that you've come to us. We'll do all that we can to keep you safe."

Clearing his throat, J.T. stepped forward and placed his hand on Joanna's shoulder. He glared at Joseph Ornelas, a tribal policeman, his relative, a Navajo and the great-grandson of Benjamin Greymountain. His cousin was several inches shorter than him, but the man's big, muscular body compensated for his lack of height.

The two men looked at each other, then J.T. glanced down at Joseph's and Joanna's clasped hands, and at that exact moment Joseph stared up at J.T.'s hand resting possessively on Joanna's shoulder. Joanna pulled her hand from Joseph's and laid her open palm over J.T.'s hand resting on her shoulder.

Joseph looked directly into Joanna's eyes, nodded his head and smiled. "You must stay for lunch. We've prepared a delicious mutton stew. Come. Stay."

"It's up to J.T.," Joanna said. "But I'd love to stay."

Joseph held out his hand to J.T. "Enjoy a meal with your cousins and give us the opportunity to become better acquainted."

J.T. shook hands with Joseph, and both men were careful not to exert too much strength, keeping the exchange nonthreatening. "Kate—" J.T. glanced at her "—mentioned that she and I had met at my mother's funeral. Were you there, too?"

"Yes," Joseph said. "I was only a teenager, just a few years older than Elena. I was attending the Navajo Community College in Tsaile when Aunt Mary died, but I came home for her funeral."

"I'm sorry I don't remember either of you." J.T. removed his Stetson, ran his fingers through his thick hair and replaced his hat. "I don't remember much of anything about that day." *Except how out of place I felt. I was an outsider.* Mary Greymountain Neboyia had been his mother, and yet she had been as much of a stranger to him as he had been to her. Until Elena had told him the truth, J.T. had thought his mother had willingly given him to old John Thomas. That was one of the many lies his grandfather had told him. But even now, the bitter little boy who had hated both his Navajo mother and his white grandfather lived in J.T.'s heart. Knowing the truth and accepting it on an emotional level were two entirely different things.

"Let the women go inside and I will help you with your horses," Joseph said. "Then we'll eat and talk before you take Joanna to Aunt Mary's house."

J.T. squeezed Joanna's shoulder. "All right?" he asked her.

She nodded, stepped away from J.T. and followed Kate up to the porch.

"Joanna?" Joseph called out to her.

"Yes?"

"While you're visiting here, I promise that I will make time to pose for you, but it will have to be on my next off day."

Joanna swallowed, forced a smile and refused to look at J.T. "Wonderful."

"I will take you out to Painted Canyon," Joseph said. "The scenery there is beautiful and would make a good background for the picture."

"Anywhere Joanna goes, I go," J.T. said.

"Of course, I understand." Joseph placed his big, broad hand on J.T.'s shoulder. "You are Joanna's bodyguard and must be with her at all times."

"Come on, let's set the table for our meal." Kate hurried Joanna into the trailer.

Putting Joey in his high chair, Kate picked up Summer, handed her a pot and spoon and set her down in the middle of the kitchen floor.

"You are J.T. Blackwood's woman, yes?" Kate asked.

Staring wide-eyed at her friend, Joanna gasped. "What?"

"I saw it and so did Joseph, that you are J.T. Blackwood's woman. My brother is deliberately trying to make our cousin jealous because he is not pleased that you chose J.T. over him."

"Kate, I'm very fond of Joseph—"

"But you love J.T., yes?"

"I'll talk to Joseph."

"And say what?" Kate asked. "That your heart belongs to another? That somehow, against your will, even against your better judgment, you have fallen in love with a man made of stone?"

"You've been talking to Elena," Joanna said.

"She has told me what a hard man her brother is, how unhappy he is, but that now you have come into his life, she has hope."

"Sometimes I wonder if there is any hope for J.T.," Joanna admitted. "He's never faced the truth about who he is, never come to terms with his feelings for his mother or his grandfather."

"Perhaps there is no love or forgiveness in him." Kate opened an upper cupboard door and removed a stack of soup bowls. "Although I hope my brother marries a Navajo girl, I would not have been terribly disappointed to have you for a sister-in-law. Joseph is a good man. He will make a good, loving husband and father. Can you say the same for J.T. Blackwood?"

"I don't know. But it doesn't matter." Joanna took the bowls from Kate and set them around on the table. "I can't change the fact that I love him."

"We can wash up out here." Joseph led J.T. from the corral to an outside faucet beside the house, unbuttoned his shirt, turned on the water and threw several handfuls into his sweaty face. Rivulets of water ran down his leather-brown throat and hard, muscular chest.

J.T. watched while this man—his cousin, another great-grandson of Benjamin Greymountain—cleaned himself. All elements of a civilized man seemed to vanish. J.T. followed suit, tossing his Stetson on a nearby rusty barrel and thrusting his hands beneath the running water. He wet his head and face, lifting the sweaty black patch that covered his blind eye.

"Elena told us that you lost the vision in that eye by taking a bullet meant for another," Joseph said. "You're a brave man."

"I was just doing my job." J.T. unbuttoned his own shirt, allowing the water to cool his heated skin. "Being a policeman, I'm sure you understand."

"You're very good at guarding people, in risking your own life to save others. You would die to protect Joanna, wouldn't you?"

"Yeah, I would, but that doesn't surprise you, does it? I get the idea you'd be willing to do the same thing."

"Our Joanna is a very special woman." Joseph wiped his wet face with his shirttail.

"*Our* Joanna?"

Joseph grinned. "We, Elena's family here on the reservation, have adopted Joanna. She has a love for this land and for our people that endears her to us."

"She told me that you two have gone out together." J.T. lifted his face to the sun, soaking in the drying warmth. "And she said there wasn't anything serious between you."

"Her choice, not mine." Bending over, Joseph shut off the water faucet, then rose and faced J.T. "Is there something serious between the two of you? Have you made a commitment to her? Is that what you are trying to tell me?"

J.T. stared at the other man who would have gladly become Joanna's lover. If all she had wanted in a fantasy lover was a Navajo, why had she rejected Joseph Ornelas? He was young, handsome and intelligent, and seemed to be a good man.

"I don't think my relationship with Joanna is any of your business." J.T. turned his back on Joseph, walked away and finished buttoning his shirt.

Following him, Joseph laid his hand on J.T.'s shoulder. "Wait."

J.T. halted, but did not turn around.

Joseph removed his hand from J.T.'s shoulder. "Since Joanna has no father or brother to question your intentions, then perhaps I do have a right." When J.T. made no reply, Joseph grunted. "Joanna deserves marriage and children and a man who is unafraid to love. Can you give her what she wants and needs?"

Every muscle in J.T.'s body tensed. "Joanna is my woman. That's all you need to know...cousin." J.T. walked across the yard, onto the porch and into the mobile home, not once looking back at Joseph.

Joanna knew something had happened between J.T. and Joseph, despite Joseph's efforts at pleasant conversation during lunch. J.T. had been silent and withdrawn, speaking only when spoken to, his replies always the one-syllable variety. And he hadn't said a word to her on the ride from Kate and Ed Whitehorn's place to Mary's old house. Joanna hadn't even tried to talk to him, uncertain and a little wary of what he might say if she prompted him to speak.

He parked the Jeep at the back of the small, frame house. Peeling paint clung to the wooden surface. Several floorboards on the south side of the back porch had rotted. Joanna knew that this house had stood here, unoccupied since Mary's death, because Elena could not bear to part with her mother's home.

J.T. got out, but made no attempt to assist Joanna. Ignoring him, she walked around to the back of the Jeep. When she opened the lift gate, J.T. grabbed her hand.

"Leave the luggage. I'll get it later." He slipped the house key out of his jeans, then pulled Joanna away from the Jeep, almost dragging her as he headed toward the house.

She balked, digging her heels into the ground. "What's going on with you? What's wrong?"

"Not a damned thing you can't fix, honey." He growled the words in a deep, dark whisper.

She glared at him, wondering just who this man was and if inside him still existed any small part of the J.T. Blackwood she loved. "I don't understand what this is all about, but—"

He jerked her into his arms, staring at her with such intensity that she sucked in her breath. With their gazes still locked, he lifted her up in his arms and carried her onto the small wooden stoop, unlocked the door and kicked it open. Despite having been recently cleaned, the house reeked with the mustiness of disuse and abandonment. The living room windows had no curtains, allowing the afternoon sunlight to flood the small area.

With the front door wide-open and the whole room bathed in golden sunshine, J.T. lowered Joanna to her feet. Slowly. Allowing her to feel every inch of his big, hard body. She had never seen him this way—on the verge of passionate rage.

"J.T.?"

"Shh. Don't talk. I need you, Jo. I need you now." He covered her mouth with his, taking her with ravenous hunger, consuming her with his desire.

She trembled, unable to control her body's compliance, realizing that there would be no gentleness in his lovemaking, no consideration for her. And yet she did not fear his possession, understanding, as if by instinct, that this time she must be the one to do the giving. Whatever was wrong with J.T., she and she alone could ease his suffering and make everything right for him.

In his haste to uncover her body, he popped two buttons from her blouse as he ripped it open. Burying his face against her lace-covered breasts, he undid her bra and pulled it and her blouse down her arms.

While he unsnapped and unzipped her jeans, she worked feverishly to do the same to his. Suddenly taking fire, her passion and need kindled by his, Joanna wanted nothing more than to be J.T.'s woman, to give him pleasure, to take him into her body and become one with him.

The minute he jerked her jeans and panties off, he drew her up against him and leaned back into the wall, bracing his body. Her breasts crushed into his hard chest. She cried out. Her nipples hardened into tight, throbbing points.

He cupped her buttocks, kneading her firm flesh, pressing her intimately, upward and against his arousal. She placed her arms around his neck. He kissed her, thrusting his tongue into the sweet warmth of her mouth.

"I love you, J.T." She lifted her lips from his and whispered against his throat. "Only you. Always you."

Freeing his sex from his briefs, he lifted Joanna, positioning her legs around his hips, and drove into her with jackhammer force. Clinging to his shoulders, she cried out with the sheer pleasure of their joining, feeling as she had never felt before in her life. This was part of heaven and part of hell. Pleasure and agony combined. Bliss and torment. The promise of fulfillment grew stronger and stronger, increasing the savage ache at the very center of her being.

Holding her hips in his hands, J.T. shoved her back and forth, taking her...taking her...taking her! And all the while she gave to him—all that was hers to give.

Passion to equal his raged inside her, threatening to consume her with its overwhelming power. She was a woman in all her glory. Ecstasy was hers to give or deny.

The desire within J.T. overflowed, spilling into her, drowning him in the hottest, wildest, most complete fulfillment he had ever known. His release washed over her, bathing her in its fiery flood, igniting spasms of pleasure inside her so intense, she thought she would die from the sheer joy of them.

Completely spent, sweat dripping from their bodies, J.T. and Joanna clung to each other, their lips seeking and finding one final sweet contact as the last ripples echoed through their bodies.

Lowering her to her feet, J.T. held her in his arms, caressing her naked back. "I'm sorry if—"

She kissed him quickly, passionately, silencing him, then drew away from him and smiled. "Did I give you what you needed?"

"You know you did, you little she-cat." He rubbed his cheek against hers. "You don't hate me, do you, honey, for taking you like that? I couldn't bear it if—"

"How could I hate you for needing me so desperately? Don't you think I figured out what this was all about?"

"Just what do you think this—" he rubbed himself against her "—was all about?"

"It was all about staking a claim," Joanna said. "I assume you let Joseph know that I was your private property—"

"Now, honey, don't go putting words in my mouth."

"As I was saying, you let Joseph know that I was your private property, but once that was done, you needed to make sure I knew just which man I belonged to."

"You make me sound like some jealous, outraged, rutting animal."

She cupped his cheek, caressing him with the tips of her fingers. "No, my love, you're just a man who doesn't want to share his woman."

Grabbing her by the shoulders, J.T. surveyed her from head to toe, taking in every delicious feminine inch of her lovely face and beautiful naked body. "Why me and not him? He's Benjamin Greymountain's great-grandson, too. And he's the kind of man who could offer you everything you want. Marriage. Kids. 'Forever after.' The whole works."

"Maybe a part of me wishes it could have been Joseph," she said, her voice a hushed whisper.

J.T.'s big fingers bit into her soft, womanly flesh. "Why not him? Tell me. Make me understand."

"How can I make you understand when I'm not sure I do? All I know is that Joseph doesn't make me feel the way you do. When he kissed me, it was nice, but that's all."

"He kissed you?" J.T. growled the question.

"From that first day, when I saw you astride Washington, I felt alive in a way I couldn't explain, not even to myself." She ran her hand down his neck and shoulder, gripping his tense, muscular arm. "And I heard the drums. The drums Annabelle heard when she was with Benjamin."

J.T. stared at her with disbelief in his eyes. "You didn't hear these drums when you were with Joseph?"

"No. Never." Breath-robbing love filled her heart as she looked at J.T., at that strong, manly face, and saw pure, undisguised satisfaction. "Don't you know that I tremble when you look at me? That I shatter into a million pieces every time you touch me? And when you make love to me, I die from the pure pleasure of having you inside me?"

"Honey, you shouldn't say things like that to a man. Just look what you've done to me."

She glanced down and saw that he was once again hard with desire. "How do I make you feel, J.T.?" She slid her hand down his chest, over his stomach and then circled his arousal.

He sucked in a deep breath. "You make me feel like a twenty-year-old." He covered her hand with his, tutoring her in the precise moves his body craved. Within minutes, he stilled her caressing strokes. "Too much, honey. I can't bear any more. Let's go find a bed before I take you standing up again."

He slammed the door shut, locked it, and lifted Joanna in his arms. Carrying her through the first door to the left, he found himself standing in a small, dark room. An old iron bed waited for them, the covers turned down. A fresh bouquet of wildflowers in a glazed pottery vase sat atop the chest of drawers.

J.T. laid Joanna down on the bed, divested himself of his clothes and gazed down at her. "Every time I look at you, I tremble inside from wanting you so much." He lowered himself to the bed, straddling her body, aligning himself to perfectly fit her. When his hardness touched her softness, she cried out. "And when we touch, I shatter into a million pieces." He spread her legs and entered her slowly, taking her with her full cooperation. "And when I'm inside you, making love to you—" he plunged in and then withdrew, only to delve deeper and harder "—I die from the pleasure of it."

Their second joining did not possess the raging hunger of the first, but the joy was even deeper and the after-effects longer lasting.

J.T. stood just outside his mother's house gazing into the distance at the ragged, monolith-type stone formations reaching upward into the crisp, blue, morning sky. His mother had been raised in a fairly traditional Navajo family, or so Elena had told him. Her love affair with the son of a white rancher had been heartbreaking for her parents.

He had no real memories of his grandparents, could not put faces to the names Elena had given him. He thought he remembered a voice singing to him when he was a small child. Elena said it must have been their grandmother; she had often sung to her.

Glancing back at the house, he wondered if Joanna had awakened yet or if, naked, warm, and with his scent still clinging to her skin, she lay sleeping peacefully. He had never lived with a woman; had never wanted that close a relationship. He kept his affairs brief and uncommitted. But Joanna was different. And she made him different. Gut-wrenching jealousy was something new to him. He hated that anyone had so much power over him, but he could not deny the fact that the mere thought of another man touching Joanna sent him into a rage.

Maybe the coffee he'd put on was ready. He sure could use a shot of caffeine. Rubbing his hand over his face, he decided he should shower and shave after he'd downed the first cup of coffee. The small two-bedroom house had one tiny bathroom, with a shower stall and no bathtub. He didn't mind the idea of sharing a shower with Joanna. He could go back inside, kiss her awake, make love to her again and carry her to the bathroom.

Just thinking about her aroused him. Hell, he was thirty-seven. He shouldn't be walking around in a state of partial arousal most of the time because of one sweet little red-head.

J.T. breathed deeply, taking fresh morning air into his lungs. Reaching upward, he stretched the muscles in his long arms, in his broad back and lean waist. The mud-roofed stone hogan about fifty yards from the house caught his attention. Elena had told him that their mother had been born in that hogan, which now, like her house, was unoccupied. Close by the hogan stood the remains of a ramada. Had his mother, like her mother before her, sat inside that brush arbor, shielded from the sun, weaving intricately designed rugs?

A cloud of dust a good half mile up the road alerted J.T. that a vehicle was approaching. Although he was reasonably sure their early-morning visitor had to be a family member, his gut instincts warned him not to take anything for granted. He unlocked the Jeep, lifted his rifle out of the back and turned to await their guest.

Joanna opened the front door and stepped outside. "J.T.?"

Snapping his head around, J.T. took in the sight of Joanna standing there wearing nothing but his unbuttoned shirt. "Go back inside, honey. And put on some clothes."

"Is something wrong?"

"Probably not, but you don't want to welcome our first guest that way, do you?"

Nodding agreement, she went back inside. J.T. watched and waited while the cloud of dust grew larger and thinner. Suddenly he recognized Joseph Ornelas's truck. Hell and damnation, what did that man want?

Joseph pulled his truck to a stop behind J.T.'s Jeep. Smiling, he got out and walked toward J.T., calling out the typical Navajo greeting.

"*Yá ' át ' ééh,*" Joseph said.

"You're out and about mighty early." J.T. glared at his handsome, younger cousin.

"I have some news—official news—for Joanna." Joseph glanced at the house. "Is she still asleep?"

"What sort of official news? Something about Plott?"

"In a way." Joseph looked up when he saw the front door open. "Ah, there you are, *nizhóní.* I have good news for you."

When J.T. saw Joanna, he sucked in his breath. His cousin had been right to call her beautiful. She'd brushed her hair back into a hastily tied ponytail. Tendrils of red hair curled around her makeup-free face. Her billowing striped caftan hid the luscious curves of her body, the body J.T. now knew so well.

J.T. clamped his hand down on Joseph's shoulder, leaned toward him and whispered, "Any news for Joanna, good or bad, goes through me first. Remember that. You have my cellular phone number. From now on, use it."

"What sort of good news?" Joanna rushed out to meet Joseph, stopping abruptly when she saw the look in J.T.'s glittering eye.

Stepping out of J.T.'s grasp, Joseph glanced back and forth from his bare-chested cousin to Joanna. "Claire Andrews has been found. Alive."

"Oh, thank God." Without thinking, Joanna threw her arms around Joseph and hugged him.

Returning her hug, Joseph looked over her shoulder at J.T., who glared back at him. Joanna withdrew from Joseph, grabbed J.T.'s hand and smiled at him. Reaching out, he tenderly wiped the happy tears from her cheeks.

"Come inside and tell us everything," Joanna said. "Have coffee with us."

Joseph hesitated until J.T. said, "Join us for breakfast, cousin."

Joseph followed them into his Aunt Mary's house, through the living room and into the small, neat kitchen.

"How did Claire escape from Lenny Plott?" Joanna asked as she set out earthenware mugs for the three of them.

"Plott never had her," Joseph said.

"What?" Joanna and J.T. said in unison.

"Seems she panicked and ran away without telling her boyfriend or anyone else. When she'd had a chance to calm down and think clearly, she realized what her parents, her boyfriend and everyone would think. She called her mother to let her know she's all right. Her mother told the FBI that Claire is in California, but she doesn't want anyone to know exactly where."

"But Lenny Plott will find her. She needs protection. Doesn't she realize that?" Joanna lifted the coffeepot and poured the hot black liquid into their mugs.

"If Plott can find her, the FBI can find her." J.T. ran the back of his hand across Joanna's cheek.

"Let's just hope that the FBI finds her first." Closing her eyes, Joanna pressed the side of her face against J.T.'s caressing hand.

He knew what she was thinking and wished he could erase the fear from her heart. But all he could do was guard her and wait. Wait for the FBI to apprehend Plott or for Plott to make a move on Joanna. Perhaps it would be easier on

Joanna if the FBI found Plott and returned him to prison, but on a very primitive level, J.T. longed for a confrontation with the monster who had brutalized her.

Chapter 13

J.T. came up behind Joanna, slipped his arms around her and drew her up against his chest. *"Ayoigo shil hózhǫ."*

Leaning backward, she tilted her head. He nuzzled her neck, then kissed her on the jaw. "What did you just say to me?" she whispered.

"I thought Eddie was giving us both *Saad* lessons. Haven't you been paying attention in class? I just told you that I'm happy." J.T. gazed down at the sleeping child resting in the baby bed. Joey Whitehorn's fat little thumb lay in the corner of his open mouth. A pang of something unfamiliar hit J.T. square in the stomach. He had never thought much about having children of his own, hadn't really wanted any. But recently, since getting to know Kate and Ed's children and seeing the way Joanna acted around them, J.T. had begun to think about a family of his own. What sort of father would he be? He'd had no example set for him, hadn't known his real father and despised the kind of parental figure his grandfather had been.

"While Eddie has been giving you daily Saad lessons, I've been painting, or had you forgotten?"

"How could I forget, when I'm the guy who's posing for the damned thing?"

Taking his hand, Joanna led him quietly from the room, closing the door only halfway behind them. Once in the living room, she slipped her arm around his waist.

"Joseph offered to pose for me," she said. "If you don't want to continue as my model, I can ask him."

"Forget it, honey." J.T. jerked her around and into his arms, smothering her face and neck with quick, warm kisses. "I'm going to be the only naked Navajo brave you ever paint."

"You're painting J.T. without his clothes on?" Eddie Whitehorn stood in the kitchen doorway, his wide-eyed sister at his side.

Little Eddie had been appalled when he'd learned J.T. couldn't speak *Saad* and had made a point of coming by every day for the past four days to give him a lesson. When Joanna had volunteered for them to spend the day at the Whitehorns' taking care of all three children so Ed and Kate could spend their Saturday alone in Gallup, J.T. had opposed the idea. When he had reminded her of exactly why they were hiding away on the reservation, she pointed out that it was highly unlikely that Lenny Plott could discover their whereabouts, at least not this soon. So, J.T. had reluctantly agreed to help baby-sit. After all, he had thought, how much trouble could three little kids be?

J.T. groaned. "I thought you two were outside playing."

"We were, but Summer got thirsty and I had to bring her in for a glass of water." Eddie led Summer into the living room, then stopped and stared up at J.T. "If Joanna gets to see you without your clothes on, do you get to see her without hers on?"

Joanna covered her mouth, smothering a laugh behind her hand. J.T. cleared his throat. He didn't know anything about kids, had never been around any until he brought Joanna to the reservation a few days ago. How was he supposed to reply to Eddie's question? He had no idea how to handle this situation.

"I'm an artist," Joanna said. "You already know that, don't you, Eddie?"

The child nodded his head. "So?"

"Well, I went to school, to a college in Virginia, and took classes in art. Sometimes all the art students drew pictures of models who didn't have on any clothes. That's the way we learned how to draw the human body."

"Yeah?" Eddie twisted his mouth into a frown, scratched his head and blew out a huffing breath. "If I go to the Navajo Community College in Tsaile and take art classes, will I get to see people naked?"

Smiling, J.T. looked at Joanna as if to say, "You started this, honey. Finish it."

The sound of Joey whimpering saved Joanna from thinking of an appropriate reply. "I'll go get him," she told J.T.

"I'm hungry," Summer whined. "When are we gonna eat supper?"

"Go get Joey," J.T. said. "I'll handle this."

"Could we have some ice cream?" Eddie asked. "Mama's got some in the freezer."

"Fruit," Joanna called out from the hallway. "One apple each, but no ice cream until after supper."

"Ah," both children groaned in unison.

After Joanna changed Joey's diaper, she brought him into the living room, sat down in the rocker near the window and began singing to him. His little eyelids fluttered, but every time he heard his older siblings' voices, his eyes opened wide and he tried to sit up.

Coming out of the kitchen, J.T. tossed Eddie and Summer an apple apiece, then motioned for them to follow him out onto the porch. When J.T. sat down on the steps, Summer crawled up in his lap and Eddie sat down beside him.

"Tell us a story, J.T.," Summer said, looking up at him with big brown eyes he found impossible to resist.

"I'm afraid I don't know any stories," J.T admitted. "What about you, Eddie, do you know a story you could tell Summer and me?"

"What do you mean you don't know any stories?" Eddie asked. "Surely you know about *Asdzá Na'adleehe* and her two sons?"

"Who was this *Asdzá*—?"

"Changing Woman, the mother-creator of our people. J.T. you don't know anything, do you? You can't speak our language and you never heard of Changing Woman."

"Why don't you tell me about her?"

Eddie eagerly recited the myth of Changing Woman, her husband, the sun, and their offspring—the story his parents had taught him since early childhood. J.T. listened with great interest, realizing that he truly wanted to know more about the Navajo legends. The truth of the matter was, deny it all he wanted, he *was* half Navajo; a part of his mother and a part of these people.

Hours later, after the sun had set and the two younger Whitehorn children were asleep, Eddie and J.T. checked on the animals before Eddie went to bed. Then, alone in the living room, J.T. and Joanna slumped down on the sofa and stared at each other.

"I don't remember the last time I've been this tired," J.T. said. "Kids can wear you out, can't they?"

"They certainly can," Joanna agreed. "I suppose that's why it's a good idea to have them while you're still young."

"I feel as if I've been playing twenty questions all day. They want the answers to everything immediately. How on earth do Kate and Ed cope?"

"I suppose they do what all parents have done since the beginning of time," Joanna said. "They do the best they can and pray their best is good enough."

Kicking off her shoes, Joanna scooted to one end of the sofa, lifted her feet and put them in J.T.'s lap. He massaged her insteps. She sighed.

"I want children of my own someday," she said.

"Do you?" He caressed her ankles.

"Uh—huh. Have you ever thought about it? About having children?"

"I'd probably make a lousy father."

"Why do you say—" The ringing telephone interrupted Joanna midsentence. Gasping, she shuddered.

"It's okay, honey. It's just my phone." He lifted her feet so he could stand, then rested them back down on the sofa.

He picked up his cellular phone from where he'd laid it on the knickknack shelf filled with Kate's pottery collection. "Blackwood. Yeah. When did it happen? Is she all right? What about Plott?"

Joanna jumped up from the sofa and rushed over to J.T. Tugging on his arm, she mouthed the words, "Who is it?"

"Hold on a minute," he told the person at the other end of the line. "It's Dane Carmichael," he said to Joanna.

J.T. slid his arm around her waist, drawing her to his side as he finished his brief conversation. He punched the Off button on his phone and laid it down on the shelf, then kissed Joanna on the forehead.

"What's wrong?" she asked.

"Plott found Libby Felton."

Joanna gasped. "No. Please, J.T., what happened? Did he—"

"She's all right, just badly shaken. Libby's husband and an FBI agent were both shot, but they saved Libby from Plott."

"Is Libby's husband dead? And the FBI agent?"

"No. They're both in the hospital. Libby's husband is in stable condition and the agent is in critical condition, but he's expected to live."

"When—when did all this happen?" Joanna asked.

"Before daybreak this morning."

"Plott escaped, didn't he?"

"Yeah, honey, he did."

"He won't go back to Texas after Libby anytime soon after what happened," Joanna said. "And it'll take him a while to find out where Claire is, so that means...that means he'll come to New Mexico. He'll go to the ranch."

"Only a handful of people know where we are and none of them are about to tell Plott."

"He'll find out. Somehow, he'll figure out a way to find out where I am and when he does, he'll come after me."

J.T. grabbed her by the shoulders. "Dane is calling in more agents. The FBI will be in full force in Trinidad. No way will Plott get past them."

"I hope you're right. Dear God, I hope you're right."

J.T. hoped so, too, but any doubts he had, he intended to keep to himself. While reassuring Joanna and keeping things as normal as possible for her, he planned to prepare himself for the worst.

Lenny Plott seemed to have vanished from the face of the earth since attempting to kidnap Libby. No one had any idea where he was or what he was plotting, but Joanna knew it was only a matter of time before he resurfaced.

Minutes had turned into hours and hours into days as Joanna and J.T. fell into a flexible routine. They went horseback riding every day, exploring the land nearby and becoming acquainted with the neighbors, all members of Mary's Bitter Water clan. And every day, Eddie gave J.T. a *Saad* lesson.

Joanna's portrait of J.T. had begun taking shape, but she had refused to let him look at it. She had no idea how he would react when he saw the way she had depicted him. All primitive naked male, as rugged and wild as the landscape surrounding him.

And they made love. In the mornings when they first awoke. In the middle of the day when they couldn't go another minute without touching each other. And at night after Joanna covered J.T.'s portrait and the ghosts of their great-grandparents hovered in the darkness.

Each night Joanna read to J.T. from Annabelle Beaumont's diary, and the more they shared their ancestors' love story, the more they became a part of Annabelle and Benjamin's doomed affair.

Tonight they sat on the threadbare sofa, as they did every night, Joanna nestled between J.T.'s legs, while she read to him. He wore nothing except his jeans, and she her striped caftan. The side of his face rested against hers, and from time to time, he kissed her temple.

"Benjamin's son is ill—not seriously, thank the dear Lord—but being a good father, he has traveled to his mother-in-law's home to visit the child. I find it strange that these people have such a matriarchal society, where although children are said to be born for their father's clan, they are born in their mother's clan. And in a case like Benjamin's, when a man loses his wife, he must give his child over to be raised by his mother-in-law.

"I have not seen Benjamin in four days and I am dying from the agony of being apart from him. How will I be able to endure living when the time comes for us to part forever? He has become as essential to me as the air I breathe. Had I known the extent of anguish true love could bring, I would have done all in my power to have escaped its cruel clutches. No. No, I lie. Knowing all I know now—the pain as well as the ecstasy—I would change nothing. To have lived and died and never to have known this pure joy would have been a tragedy indeed.

"He has promised, if his son's health has improved, that we will meet tomorrow in our special place. I have a gift for him—a book of my favorite poems by Christina Rossetti. And I plan to ask him to allow me to cut a lock of his long black hair. I will braid it with a lock of mine and give it to him as a keepsake. Something to remember me by when I am gone."

Joanna's shoulders quivered. J.T. reached around her, closed Annabelle's diary and lifted it out of her hands.

He couldn't bear to see her cry and yet her tender, romantic heart was part of what made her so special. He would change nothing about her. She was as close to perfect as he would ever want a woman to be.

He laid the diary on the end table and turned off the table lamp, leaving only the dim light from their bedroom casting a shadowy glow into the living room. Cradling her in his arms, he hugged her fiercely and kissed her neck.

"Why do you do this to yourself, honey? You've already read that diary from beginning to end more than once. I don't see why you want to read aloud from it every night."

Resting her head against his chest, she closed her eyes and sighed. "If I didn't read it to you, you'd never read all of it, and I want you to know Benjamin and Annabelle's story. I want you to feel about them the way I do."

"Honey, I've already admitted that I was wrong about them." J.T. lifted her clasped hands to his lips. "What happened to them was tragic, but nothing we say or do can change the past. Annabelle and Benjamin are dead and buried, and their great love with them."

How could she ever make J.T. understand the way she felt and what she believed? Yes, Annabelle and Benjamin were dead, but not their love. Didn't he realize that love never dies, especially the kind of love their great-grandparents had shared? Annabelle's and Benjamin's spirits were together, forever; their love was still alive. It was a part of J.T. A part of Joanna. And a part of what they felt for each other.

In her heart of hearts, Joanna believed that Annabelle had sent her to New Mexico, that her great-grandmother had opened her heart to the hope and dream of love at a time when she had thought there was nothing left worth living for. She had been destined to meet J.T., to love him and to heal his troubled soul. He belonged here in New Mexico, where both his mother's people and his father's had fought and died to claim this land. His birthright was here, and if he could ever embrace his mixed heritage, he could find peace in his soul. He could be both Navajo and Scotsman, both cowboy and Indian. Why couldn't he accept the fact that he did not have to choose, that indeed he couldn't choose between the two? He was a unique man, and she loved him as she would never love another. He was, as Benjamin had been to Annabelle, the other half of her.

"I wish we could go back to their special place," Joanna said. "Tonight . . . right this minute . . . and share the magic of what we feel with them."

"We don't need to go to Annabelle and Benjamin's special place," J.T. told her. "And just as their magic existed only between the two of them, ours exists only between the two of us. It can't be shared."

"It's going to end for us, just as it ended for them." Joanna pulled out of J.T.'s arms and jumped up from the sofa.

"Jo? Honey?" He reached for her, but she moved too quickly for him to grab her arm. He stood and watched her. She ran to the door, unlocked it and grasped the knob.

"When this is over and Lenny Plott is either dead or behind bars, you'll go back to Atlanta, back to your job and your life there. And I'll stay here in New Mexico, except when you come home to visit Elena. Then I'll have to go away because—" she swallowed the tears trapped in her throat "—it will be unbearable for me."

She flung open the door and ran outside into the cool, starry night. A full moon spread a soft creamy blush across the land. J.T. raced after Joanna, calling her name as she fled from him. Following her, he cursed himself for hurting her this way. He understood only too well the desperation she felt, knowing that what they shared couldn't last forever. She was right. It had to end. She wanted eternity, a love that lived beyond death, and all he could give her was the moment—because that's all he believed in.

"Jo, stop running," he called after her. "Please, honey. You're going to hurt yourself."

But she kept running until he chased her down and pulled her into his arms. She struggled to free herself, but he tumbled her onto the ground and pinned her arms over her head as he straddled her.

"I can't stand to see you hurting this way." He tried to kiss her, but she turned her face away. "Accept what there is between us. It's real. It's magical. It's passionate. Maybe it isn't what you want, but it's all I can give you."

Turning to face him, she stared up at him, the moonlight illuminating her features in gold-tinted shadows. "You could give me everything I want and need if you'd only let yourself," she said. "But you're afraid. So afraid to let yourself love me the way you really want to."

He pressed his arousal against her feminine mound. "Why can't this be enough for you? It's never been like this with anyone else. Never been this good . . . this right."

"Oh, J.T., I love you. I love you so." She arched her body up and into his.

He groaned, then took her mouth with savage hunger. Squirming beneath him, she thrust her tongue into his mouth, engaging it in a duel with his. Releasing his hold on her wrists, he caught the caftan zipper between his thumb and forefinger and whipped the garment apart. Shoving the caftan off her shoulders and down her arms, J.T. lifted her, removed the caftan and laid her naked body down on the flowing robe's silky softness.

She touched his chest with one hand and lifted the other to his head, threading her fingers through his hair. Rising up just enough to grab hold of his zipper, he opened his jeans, jerked them down his legs and kicked them into the dirt.

"This is the magic, Jo." He lifted her hips and plunged into her. "This is the ecstasy. It might not last forever, but it's more than some people ever know."

"Yes. Yes." This was the ecstasy, but what J.T. could not admit to himself was that the love they shared was what made it magical for them.

He rolled over, placing his body against the hard, dusty earth as he lifted her into the dominant position. They mated, there on the ground, beneath the stars; primitive man and woman, joined in nature's most basic, instinctive ritual. Each of them giving and taking in equal measure, sharing the earth-shattering pleasure when their climaxes claimed them.

Leaving their clothes lying on the ground, J.T. lifted Joanna in his arms and carried her back to the house and to the bed they shared in his mother's house. Neither of them said a word as he cradled her in his arms. They lay together in silence, listening to each other's heartbeats until they fell asleep.

Hours later, J.T woke, eased her from his arms and slipped out of bed. Quietly striding into the living room, he stood in the darkness for several minutes, then turned on a table lamp and walked over to the easel Joanna had placed in the corner. He lifted the cover slowly. Groaning, he closed his eyes, but he could not erase the portrait from his mind. In that one brief glance, he had seen himself as Joanna saw him, and if he had ever doubted that she loved him, he no longer did.

Opening his eyes, he stared at the beautiful, noble man Joanna had painted. Straight blue-black hair hanging to his shoulders. Glistening bronze skin stretched over taut, well-developed muscles. An ageless man. A man of yesterday and today and tomorrow. A perfect man, seen through the eyes of love.

He did not deserve Joanna's love. He was unworthy of such pure sweet devotion. How was it possible that she loved him so deeply and completely and saw in him the man he longed to be? Did he have the courage to accept what she was offering, and the strength to become the man she wanted and needed?

He knew that if he didn't find that strength and that courage, he would doom them to a fate as tragic as the one that had befallen their great-grandparents.

Chapter 14

Rita Gonzales grumbled to herself when she heard the door chimes. "No company. We are not at home. Go away."

Leaning the mop against the kitchen counter, she wiped her pudgy, damp hands on her apron and waddled into the hallway. The chimes rang again.

"Who would be bothering people so early in the morning?" She peered through the peephole in the solid wooden door. A tall, dark-haired man with a thick mustache stood on the front porch. She didn't recognize the man, but then she didn't know all of Elena and Alex's friends and business acquaintances. Rita unlocked and opened the door enough to take a better look at the stranger.

When he saw Rita, he smiled and nodded. She liked his smile, and although she was unaccustomed to seeing men in suits and ties, she liked his neat appearance.

"Morning, ma'am. Sorry to bother you so early, but I'm here on official business. I'd like to see Mr. and Mrs. Gregory." He reached inside his coat pocket and pulled out his identification to show Rita. "I'm Eugene Willis, one of the FBI agents working with Dane Carmichael in Trinidad."

"Agent Carmichael has been here on the ranch several times," Rita said, then shook her head. "I'm sorry but Elena and Alex are not here. They went to Santa Fe on business yesterday."

"Oh, that's too bad. I have some news for them and needed their help in contacting Joanna Beaumont."

"Your Mr. Carmichael knows how to reach Joanna and J.T." Rita eyed the man suspiciously.

"Yes, we've been trying to call them, but can't get through. We thought perhaps the Gregorys would have another number where they could be reached."

"Something must be wrong with J.T.'s little phone—"

"His cellular phone? Yes, that's what we think."

"If Mr. Carmichael can't reach J.T., why hasn't he called the tribal police? Since J.T.'s cousin, Joseph Ornelas, is a policeman, he would gladly take the message to them himself."

"I'm sure Dane will have thought of calling the tribal police by the time I check in with him," Eugene said. "It's just that we're all so pleased about the good news we have for Ms. Beaumont that we wanted to reach her as quickly as possible."

"What good news?" Rita opened the door fully and stepped out onto the front porch.

"We've apprehended Lenny Plott. Caught him in Trinidad before daylight this morning."

"Oh, my, this is good news." Rita stuck her fat finger in Eugene's face. "You make sure that man is put back in a thick cell with many locks so he can never escape again."

Eugene grinned. "Yes, ma'am, that's just what we intend to do."

"You tell Mr. Carmichael to keep trying to call J.T. on his little telephone and if there is no answer, call the tribal police and ask for Joseph Ornelas." Rita snapped her fingers. "Perhaps Elena's cousin, Kate Whitehorn, would know how to contact J.T. and Joanna. Joanna has visited the Whitehorns many times when she goes to the reservation to paint."

"Kate Whitehorn. Yes, ma'am. Thank you. And please, give Mr. and Mrs. Gregory the good news when they return from Santa Fe."

"Yes, I'll do that." Rita stood on the porch and watched Eugene Willis get in his gray sedan and drive away.

Moments later, Cliff Lansdell drove in from the opposite direction, slowed his four-wheel drive in front of the ranch house and stopped.

"Who was that, Rita?" he asked, watching the car drive away.

"An FBI agent named Willis," Rita said. "He came here to talk to Elena and Alex. They've caught that man, that Lenny Plott, who wanted to kill Joanna. But they can't get J.T. to answer his little telephone to give them the good news. I told him I didn't understand why they didn't just call the tribal police."

Cliff flung open the door, jumped out and ran up onto the porch. "Rita, did you see that man's identification?"

"What?"

"Did he show you proof that he was an FBI agent?"

"Do you think I'm a stupid old woman?"

"No, I do not think you're old or stupid."

"He showed me his badge, showed me his picture. It was him. Big black mustache and all. And his name was Willis. Eugene Willis."

Cliff let out a deep breath. "Good. Good."

"I wouldn't talk to nobody who wasn't the police." Rita placed her hands on her wide hips. "Anyway, I didn't tell him anything he didn't already know. The FBI knows that Joanna is on the Navajo reservation."

"But no one off the reservation, except Elena and Alex, knows exactly where J.T. took Joanna," Cliff said. "Not even the FBI."

"I'm glad this whole thing is over and that awful man will be put back in prison," Rita said. "Now, Joanna can come home and not have to be afraid anymore."

* * *

Joanna slipped her sketch pad and pens into the saddle-bag and closed it. "I'm glad it isn't hot today. Maybe we can stay out longer than we did yesterday and I can finish these sketches."

"Too bad you need sunlight to sketch," J.T. said. "If you could learn to draw in the dark, we could go out at night when it's cool."

"Ha, ha. Very funny." Joanna adjusted her hat, tightening the drawstring under her chin.

J.T. dropped his Glock into his saddlebag, then slid his Remington into its sheath attached to his saddle. Patting his shirt pocket, he double-checked to make sure he had his cellular phone, then he mounted Washington.

"Kate's planning that get-together this weekend," Joanna said. "We really need to give her an answer today. It's important to her that we be there. She wants you to meet other members of your mother's family."

"I've met more relatives than I can count already." J.T. motioned Washington into a slow trot. "Half the Bitter Water clan seem to live in this area and I think we count relatives down to tenth cousins."

Joanna laughed. "Hey, we Southerners do the same thing." She wondered if J.T. realized that he had said "we" when he had spoken of the Navajo. Probably not. But Joanna had noticed that he was beginning to relate to his mother's people and seemed to enjoy not only the *Saad* lessons Eddie gave him, but the history lessons, too.

She urged Playtime into a trot alongside Washington. "We need to let Kate know something by tonight."

"Hey, we didn't come to the reservation so I could socialize with my relatives," J.T. said. "I brought you here to keep you out of harm's way until the FBI catch up with Plott."

"There's no reason that while we're here we can't socialize. No one is going to talk to a stranger and give away our hiding place. Joseph told you that he's spoken to everyone in this area, cautioning them to contact him if anyone they don't know comes around asking questions.''

"You're as determined as Elena that I accept my Navajo heritage, aren't you?''

"I want you to be happy, and I don't think you can be until you resolve all the hang-ups you have about being part Native American and part Scotch-Irish."

"You're beginning to sound like a psychiatrist."

"I suppose it comes from having gone through months of therapy after the rape," Joanna said. "I'm not sure how long it would have taken me to break away from Mother's domination if I hadn't reached a point in my therapy where I admitted that she had always run my life, that I had never made one decision on my own."

The afternoon sun warmed them as they traveled several miles from Mary's house. The land was dotted with yuccas, creosote bushes and mesquite. And the colors were sharp and pure; the earth itself was alive with vibrant hues.

When they reached Painted Canyon, J.T. searched for the spot Joanna had chosen several days ago when they'd first ridden out this way. He saw the huge rock where she liked to sit and look down over the plateau. He recognized the area because a scattering of cottonwood trees grew nearby.

He helped her dismount and retrieve her supplies, then spread a blanket down for her to sit on. "I'm going to walk around awhile. I won't go far and I'll keep you in sight every minute."

"I know this must be boring for you," she said.

Leaning over, he took her face in his hands, drew her to him and kissed her soundly. "I'm never bored when I'm with you. But if I stay too close, I might distract you."

Smiling, she rubbed his nose with hers. "You just might." He released her. "Go on off and explore."

J.T. climbed higher up the canyon, feeling as if when he reached the summit, he'd be able to touch the sky. He glanced down at Joanna, who was busy sketching.

"Help! Somebody, please help us!''

J.T. heard the loud cry. His heart raced. He recognized that voice. Eddie. Eddie Whitehorn.

"Eddie?"

"Help! Help!"

"Where are you, Eddie?"

"Down here!"

"Where?"

"J.T., is that you?"

"Yes, Eddie, just keep talking and I'll find you."

Within minutes, J.T. had located his young cousin. The boy sat at the bottom of a ravine, wedged between two steep sandstone formations. Eddie held a lamb in his arms.

"Good God, boy, how did you get down there?" J.T. guessed the boy was a good eighteen to twenty feet down.

"I came looking for a couple of the little lambs that got lost yesterday," Eddie said. "Don't tell Mama I got in trouble. She told me I couldn't come out here by myself looking for them."

"How'd you get down there?" J.T. asked.

"I climbed down here when I saw the lamb, but now, I can't climb back up and carry the lamb with me. And...and I think...well, I hurt my leg. I think I sort of sprained it."

"Stay put," J.T. said. "I've got to go tell Joanna. She can call your mother. I'm sure Kate is worried sick about you."

"No, J.T., don't tell Mama."

J.T. called out to Joanna, who turned sharply and stared up at him. He waved at her, motioning for her to come to him. She laid down her sketch pad and pen, then stood and climbed up the hill.

"Is something wrong?" she asked.

"Eddie's down in that ravine over there," J.T. told her. "He came out looking for a couple of lost lambs and found one, but he's hurt his leg and can't climb back up."

"Oh, my goodness. Kate will be terribly worried."

"Here." J.T. pulled his cellular phone from his pocket and handed it to Joanna. "Give Kate a call and let her know Eddie's all right and we'll bring him home in a little while." J.T. grasped Joanna's wrist. "I've got to climb down the ravine and get him and the lamb. After you call Kate, go get my rifle and keep it with you until I come back up.''

"Go get your... Surely you don't think anything could happen to me in the few minutes it'll take you to rescue Eddie.'' Joanna caressed his cheek. ''We're out in the middle of nowhere, and Lenny Plott has no idea we're on the Navajo reservation.''

"I don't believe in taking chances. Get the rifle. Pacify me, honey.''

"Okay. I'll call Kate and then I'll get your rifle.''

Dane Carmichael finished off the last bite of his ham-and-cheese sandwich, then washed it down with the strong coffee they served at the Trinidad Café. He wished to hell they could wrap up this case. He hadn't had a decent night's sleep in over a week. Sooner or later Lenny Plott was going to come back to Trinidad, and Dane's guess was it would be very soon. Since his attempt to kidnap Libby Felton had failed, and it would take him time to track down Claire Andrews again, his next likely target was Joanna Beaumont.

Between his agents and the local and state authorities, they pretty much had Trinidad sealed off. He doubted a fly could sneak by without being caught in their trap.

Just as Dane reached for his bill, one of his agents, Jim Travis, slipped into the booth across from him. "I need to talk to you, and I'd like what I tell you to be off the record, at least temporarily.''

"What's wrong?'' Dane asked.

"It's about Eugene Willis.''

"Yeah, what about Willis?''

"He met a girl the first day we got in town and he's been messing around with her. You know Willis. He's a ladies' man. He can't leave 'em alone and they can't leave him alone.''

"The damned fool!'' Dane wadded his bill in his fist. "Look, I don't know why Willis hasn't been dismissed before now, but if he messes up while under my command, he won't get a second chance.''

"Yeah, well, I tried to tell him that you weren't anybody to mess around with, but... Hell, the guy went out to get us some breakfast this morning and he hasn't come back. I figure he's off somewhere with that girl, since he had—"

"What time this morning?"

"Around six-thirty."

Dane glanced at his wristwatch. "It's twelve-thirty."

"Yeah, I've been trying to track him down, hoping I could find him before—"

"I don't want any explanations. You're off this case, and so is Willis. As a matter of fact, both of you are history in the agency as far as I'm concerned."

Joanna closed J.T.'s cellular phone and slipped it into her shirt pocket, then walked over and removed J.T.'s Remington from its scabbard on Washington's saddle. Although she was a fairly good shot with a handgun, she wasn't accustomed to the feel of a rifle.

She climbed back up the side of the canyon, looked down into the ravine and saw J.T. slowly, cautiously making his way toward Eddie.

"I called Kate. She was half out of her mind with worry," Joanna told J.T. "She'd already called several family members to have them search for Eddie."

"Did you get my rifle?" J.T. asked.

She held up the Remington so he could see it. "I told Kate we'd bring Eddie right home."

J.T. chose his steps carefully, knowing how dangerous these steep ravines could be. Eddie was damned lucky that he hadn't slipped and injured himself badly. A sprained ankle would mend soon enough.

J.T. heard a distinct rattling. His heartbeat accelerated. Without moving or saying a word, he visually searched all around him, looking for the poisonous snake whose bite could prove deadly. And then he saw the rattler slithering across the tip of Eddie's boot. The boy saw the snake, too; his face paled.

"J.T.?"

"Hush," he warned. "Don't talk. Don't move." J.T. slid his hand into his pocket, feeling around for his knife. Slipping the knife out of his pocket, he continued watching the snake as it curled around Eddie's leg.

Eddie swallowed. "J.T.!"

"Shh." He opened the knife.

The lamb in Eddie's arms nuzzled his nose against the boy's side. Overhead an eagle soared. The snake crawled up Eddie's leg and onto his arm.

"What's wrong?" Joanna called out as she hovered near the edge of the steep embankment. "What's taking so long?"

Tears welled up in Eddie's brown eyes. J.T. gauged the distance. He was an expert shot, but his skills with a knife were rusty. If he missed, he could wind up stabbing Eddie.

The rattler coiled to strike. Eddie cried out. J.T. hurled the knife through the air. The blade sliced through the snake. Eddie dropped the lamb and clutched his arm. J.T. ran over, lifted the snake by the knife handle and flung its limp body against the canyon wall.

"Did it bite you?" J.T. jerked Eddie's hand away from his arm. "Damn!"

"Am I going to die?" Eddie's bottom lip quivered. Tears trickled down his dusty cheeks.

"No, you aren't going to die," J.T. said. "But we'll have to move fast and get you a shot to counteract the snake's venom. We'll have to leave the lamb down here, but I'll get someone to come back and get him."

"You promise."

J.T. nodded. "Come on, Eddie—" J.T. squatted "—crawl on my back."

Eddie obeyed J.T.'s command.

"Joanna!" J.T. called out to her.

"What's wrong?"

"A rattlesnake bit Eddie. Get on the phone and call Kate, tell her to contact the clinic and have them send out some antivenom for a rattlesnake bite, then go get our horses ready!"

Joanna stuck the rifle under her arm, the barrel pointed to the ground. She pulled the cellular phone from her pocket. Her hands trembled so badly when she tried to dial the phone that she dropped it on the ground. When she bent over to pick it up, she heard the sound of an approaching vehicle. Standing, she gazed off into the distance and saw a cloud of red dust rising in the air, then clearing as a gray sedan came to a screeching halt a few yards away from where they'd tethered the horses. Playtime whinnied. When a tall dark-haired man in a suit got out of the car, Washington rose on his hind legs, then lowered his front hooves and pawed the ground.

"J.T.!" Joanna cried. "Somebody's here. A man with a black mustache, driving a gray car."

"Keep the rifle on him until I get up there," J.T. told her.

The man waved at Joanna. She slipped the phone back in her pocket and pointed the rifle at him.

"Don't shoot, ma'am, I'm an FBI agent. My name's Eugene Willis." He kept walking toward Joanna. "If you'll let me, I can show you my identification."

"Who sent you?" Joanna asked.

"Dane Carmichael. You are Joanna Beaumont, aren't you?"

"I might be."

"Well, if you are, I've got some good news for you."

"Don't come any closer. Just get out your ID, and do it very slowly."

"Yes, ma'am." Willis very cautiously pulled out his ID and held it up for Joanna to see, then took several more steps in her direction.

The sun glinted off the agent's ID. Joanna blinked. "What sort of news do you have?"

"We've apprehended Lenny Plott. He was taken into custody earlier today and Carmichael sent me out here personally to tell you."

Joanna let out a deep breath. "Thank God. Look Mr.—"

"Willis, ma'am. Eugene Willis."

"Mr. Willis, we have a young boy down in a ravine over there. He's been bitten by a rattlesnake."

"I'll do what I can to help. We can use my car."

"Thank you." She turned sideways and called out to J.T. "The FBI have captured Lenny Plott. This man's an agent named Eugene Willis. He can drive us back to Kate's." Joanna lowered the rifle, resting it against her hip, as she pulled the phone out of her shirt pocket and began dialing Kate's number with her thumb.

Willis jerked the rifle away from Joanna, whirled her around and slid the barrel under her neck as he dragged her back up against his chest.

"Drop the phone," he told her, "or I'll break your neck."

Dane Carmichael stormed into the Trinidad police station. "What's so damned urgent it couldn't wait?"

"A city worker found a body in one of the Dumpster trash containers about an hour ago," Police Chief Mc-Millian said.

"Don't keep me in suspense," Dane said. "I take it the identity of this body will have some significance to me."

"Yeah, if he's who we think he is. He didn't have any type of identification on him. His wallet was missing. But we did find a motel key."

"A motel key?"

"Yeah. And since Trinidad only has two motels, it wasn't hard to trace the key. Seems the key is from the Tumbleweed and the room was registered to one of your agents."

"Let me guess. Eugene Willis?"

"Yep."

"You need me to identify the body?" Dane asked.

"Yep."

Chapter 15

"Tell Blackwood that you're all right." The man pressed the rifle harder against her throat. "If you don't, I'll shoot him and the boy the minute they're in sight."

He brought the rifle outward, a half inch from her neck. Joanna gasped for air. Her throat ached. She licked her lips. Dammit! How could she have been so stupid?

"Joanna!" J.T. bellowed from below. "What the hell's going on?"

"Don't do anything you'll regret," her captor warned. "I really don't want to hurt any innocent people. I came for you, not your protector or that child."

"Nothing's wrong." Joanna's voice quivered. "I'm just overcome with...with the news about Plott."

"Good girl," the man whispered in her ear. "Now, you and I are going to leave and take a ride. If we hurry, we won't have to involve Blackwood and the little boy."

Joanna nodded agreement, not resisting, not putting up a fight of any kind. When J.T. surfaced with Eddie, he would be unarmed. He and Eddie would be sitting ducks.

Lenny Plott, disguised as an FBI agent! And she hadn't recognized him. Not with black hair, a thick mustache and sunglasses shading his eyes. Not when she hadn't been expecting him. She'd thought she was safe, hidden away on the reservation. How how Plott found them? Who had given away their location?

The cellular phone Joanna clutched in her hand rang. Plott braced the rifle under his arm, grabbed the phone away from her, then clasped her wrist, jerking her up against him. The two of them stared at the ringing telephone.

Plott flipped open the telephone. "Yeah?" He placed it to Joanna's ear.

"J.T.?" Joseph Ornelas said. "Listen, Plott killed an FBI agent and assumed his identity. Eugene Willis. Plott's wearing a black wig and mustache and he knows Joanna is on the reservation. Don't let her out of your sight. Dane Carmichael is taking a helicopter from Trinidad, and I'm on my way."

Lenny jerked the phone away from Joanna's ear, punched the Off button and then the Power button. "We'd better get going."

He dragged her to the car, opened the door and shoved her inside. "Stay put if you want to live just a little longer, and if you don't want anyone else to get hurt."

She heard J.T. frantically calling her name. He knew something wasn't right. By the time he brought Eddie up out of the ravine, J.T. would be half out of his mind with worry. And when he discovered that she and the "FBI agent" were gone, he would know what had happened.

Plott unlocked the trunk, tossed J.T.'s rifle and phone inside and then removed Eugene Willis's 9-mm from the shoulder holster. Opening the driver's-side door, Plott got in the car and started the engine.

"I didn't think it would be this easy." He backed the car up, turned and headed away from Painted Canyon. "I figured I'd have to kill Blackwood to get to you or maybe kill you both from a distance. But that wouldn't have been any fun for us, would it, baby doll?"

The sound of the endearment on his lips chilled her. The night Plott had raped her, he'd called her "baby doll" over and over again. Her stomach churned. Salty bile rose in her throat. Holding her hands in her lap, she knotted them into tight fists. She had to go with him. She had to protect J.T. and Eddie. But no matter where he took her or what he tried to do to her, she was not going to let him win. Even if he killed her, she was going to put up the fight of her life.

And all the while Plott drove her farther and farther away from Painted Canyon, she kept praying that J.T. would save Eddie and then come after her—and find her before it was too late.

As J.T. brought Eddie up from the ravine, fear ate away at his gut. Joanna wasn't answering him, and he'd heard a car engine roar to life. Cautiously, J.T. peered upward, scanning the area before showing himself. In the distance a cloud of thick dust swirled in the air. He swallowed hard. Whoever had approached Joanna, wasn't an FBI agent.

"Where's Joanna?" Eddie asked. "Did she call my mama?"

"No, Eddie, I don't think she got a chance to call Kate."

"Where'd she go?"

"She went with the . . . the FBI agent."

What the hell was he going to do? He had a dying child in his arms. If Eddie didn't get an antivenom injection soon, he wouldn't make it. But if J.T. allowed Plott much of a head start, he knew he might not get to Joanna in time to save her.

J.T. carried Eddie to the horses, mounted Washington, and pulled his young cousin around to sit in front of him. When J.T. motioned the big Appaloosa into a full gallop, Playtime followed. The sun burned hot and bright in the western sky. Dust swirled about the horses' legs.

He could not—would not—let himself think about what was happening to Joanna or how she must be feeling. If he thought about it, he'd go crazy. He knew what he had to do—what Joanna would expect him to do.

While riding as if the demons of hell were on his heels, J.T. bargained with the Almighty. *Keep her safe until I can find her, and I'll do everything I can to be the man she wants and needs. Don't let anything happen to her. Please. I haven't even told her that I love her.*

He was lost! Dammit to hell, this godforsaken country had tricked him. Everything looked the same. Every damn little dirt road. Every mesa. Every canyon. Every stupid shrub and bush.

Wide-open space. Never-ending sky. And a car with less than a quarter of a tank of gas. He had to take Joanna somewhere undercover and finish her off before finding his way out of this Indian hellhole. If he wasted too much more time trying to find the road he'd come in on, he'd run out of gas and Blackwood would have gathered his forces and come after him.

Lenny took the road to the left, slowing the car as he turned. Joanna grabbed the door handle and swung open the door. He reached for her, but she jumped out just as he clutched a handful of her shirt. The soft cotton material ripped right off her back.

Joanna fell onto the ground, knocking off her hat and momentarily stunning her as she rolled over and over. Breathless, she rose to her knees.

Plott slammed on the brakes. "Son of a bitch," he muttered. He flung open the car door and stomped around the hood. He lifted the black wig off his head and hurled it to the ground, revealing the thin, matted strands of his silver-blond hair.

Joanna lifted herself up from her knees and ran.

"Where the hell do you think you're going, baby doll? You can't get away from me. If you keep running, I'm just going to have to hurt you when I catch you." Plott scratched his head.

Joanna kept running and Plott chased her. Sweat seeped through his shirt—Eugene Willis's shirt. Plott cursed under his breath. When he caught her, he'd make her sorry she'd ever run from him.

She didn't look back. Not once. She stumbled, but didn't fall. Plott ran faster. When he got closer, he reached out for her, calling her name. His hand just missed grasping her long red hair.

Panting, sweat drenching her body, loose tendrils of hair plastered to her face, Joanna ran and ran. Lenny Plott reached out again. This time he caught a handful of her hair. She screamed. He jerked her backward. She whirled around, prepared to fight. He yanked on her hair, pulling her forward. Ramming into her with the full force of his body, he knocked her to the ground and trapped her beneath him.

"You women are so stupid." Lenny smiled at her. "When will you ever learn?"

Less than two miles from Painted Canyon, J.T. saw dust clouds in the distance and heard the rumble of vehicles. Within minutes, a truck, a Bronco and a patrol car surrounded him. Joseph Ornelas jumped out of the patrol car and ran toward J.T. Several men climbed down off the truck bed and stood watching. Kate Whitehorn flung open the door of her neighbor Peter Yazzi's Bronco and followed Joseph.

"Plott's taken Joanna," J.T. said. "He's got a head start. We're going to have to track them." J.T. slid off Washington and lifted Eddie down into his arms. "Eddie's been bitten by a rattler. He needs to be taken to the clinic as fast as possible."

Opening her arms, Kate ran to J.T., who handed over her son. Peter Yazzi walked up behind Kate. "We will take care of Eddie. You go and save your woman."

"Peter," Joseph called out to the older man. "I'll radio ahead to the clinic and have them meet you with the antivenom serum." He turned to J.T. "Get in the patrol car. I'll send Agent Carmichael word on our general location." Joseph turned to one of the men near the truck. "Donnie, take care of these horses for us. The rest of you can follow, but you're to stay behind us and don't make a move without my orders. Understand?''

J.T. removed his 9-mm Glock and holster from his saddlebag, strapped the gun on and walked toward the patrol car.

The youth named Donnie ran over, mounted Washington and trotted off, Playtime following. J.T. jerked open the passenger door of the patrol car and slid onto the seat. Joseph got in, started the engine and turned to J.T.

"Painted Canyon," J.T. said. "He was heading west."

Lenny pressed his body onto Joanna's. She tried to wriggle, but the harder she tried to move, the harder he pressed. She struggled to slip one of her arms free.

Plott grabbed her face in both hands and squeezed, squishing her cheeks inward, compressing her lips into a fish mouth. Lifting her head, he held it for a second, then slammed it down against the ground. Joanna gasped. He repeated the head-slamming three times. She cried out, the pain momentarily blinding her.

Releasing her face, he loosened his tie, unknotted it and slipped it off his neck. Joanna slid her arm, freeing half of it, but her hand remained trapped under Plott's chest.

The minute Joanna slid one arm completely free, Lenny shoved himself up, straddled her hips and grabbed her wrists. She tried to lift her knee. He sat down on her, knocking the breath out of her.

He bound her hands together with Eugene Willis's silk tie, stood and yanked her to her feet. "Come on, baby doll, it's too hot out here and not nearly private enough for what I have in mind."

Joanna kicked Plott. He slapped her across the face. "You stupid girl. The more you fight, the more I'm going to hurt you." Leering at her, he grabbed both of her breasts. She kicked him again and again. He tightened his hold on her breasts, squeezing until she screamed. Then he kicked her in the stomach with his knee. Doubling over, she fell to the ground. Plott grabbed the ends of the silk tie, jerked her onto her belly and dragged her for several yards. Stopping abruptly, he pulled her to her feet, lifted her and slung her over his shoulder.

He slammed her up against the side of the car, ripped her ragged shirt off her and tore it into a long strip. Giving her a hard shove, he pushed her into the car, leaned down and grabbed her feet. He bound her feet with the tattered material of her shirt, then locked and closed the door.

When he got inside the car he sat there for several minutes, staring at her. She was scared to death. He could see the fear in her eyes. Green eyes. Hot green eyes. He could smell her fear, too, and the smell was delicious. No matter how brave they tried to act, sooner or later, they all succumbed to their fears. The ones who had testified against him and sent him to prison knew what it meant to fear him. Joanna Beaumont knew. He had given her the sweetest kind of pain, the kind she'd never be able to forget. And he would give it to her again before he killed her.

But he had to find a hiding place before Blackwood found them. Surely there was a safe place somewhere out here in this damned desert.

"We'll find them," Joseph said. "It's obvious Plott doesn't have any idea where he's going."

"Yeah, well, I'm not sure that's a comforting thought." J.T. wanted to rent the air with his fury, yell at the top of his lungs from the highest peak on the reservation. He wanted to lash out and smash something—anything. If he had to contain his anger and fear much longer, he'd lose his mind. "If Plott's lost, then he's probably upset and taking his frustration out on Joanna."

"Stop thinking about it, okay?" Joseph gripped the steering wheel with white-knuckled ferocity.

"How the hell do I stop thinking about it? I promised to protect her. Vowed to her that I'd never let Plott get anywhere near her, and look what I let happen."

"You didn't let this happen. Quit beating yourself up. What were you supposed to do? Leave Eddie down in that ravine, or let him die from the snakebite once you brought him up? Besides, how do you think you'd have caught up with them on horseback?"

J.T. hadn't cried since he was five years old—not since he'd been ripped from his mother's arms. A real man didn't cry, didn't show emotion. Hell, old John Thomas had taught him that a real man didn't even feel any emotion.

The tears lodged in J.T.'s throat. *Dear God, please. Please.*

"Look, over there," Joseph said. "Thank God, the fool isn't trying to cover his tracks. See, it looks as if he's turned off on the trail leading up to the old mine."

Joseph stopped the car, got out and walked around, taking note of the tire tracks. J.T. got out when the truck filled with half-a-dozen relatives and neighbors pulled up behind the patrol car.

"There's been a car turn here recently," Joseph said. "If Plott took this road, then we've got him trapped. There's only one way out and that's the way he came in."

J.T. looked around, wondering how long ago Plott and Joanna had come this way. Long enough for him to have hurt her? Long enough for him to have raped her? Killed her?

J.T. spotted a wad of black fur lying on the ground. He walked over, picked it up and examined it. "Damn! Look at this. It's a black wig."

"Plott's wig." Joseph lifted the hairpiece from J.T.'s hand, then waved to the men in the truck. "He's gone toward the old uranium mine. Stay behind us and don't take any action on your own."

"Once he's figured out he can't get out of this alive, he'll kill Joanna." J.T. followed Joseph back to the patrol car and got inside. "We shouldn't go storming in there."

"Man, start thinking with your brain instead of your heart." Joseph tossed the wig into the back seat, then slid under the wheel. "He's planning on killing her, regardless.

If he knows we have him trapped, he might be willing to bargain for his life.''

J.T. didn't want to admit that he wasn't thinking straight, that at this moment he was far more lover than protector. Gritting his teeth, he shook his head. ''How far is this mine?''

''Not far. About two miles up into those hills.'' Joseph turned on the ignition and shifted gears. ''The place was abandoned years ago. Radioactive contamination to the workers caused a lot of our people to die from cancer.''

''He'll take her inside the mine,'' J.T. said, but he wasn't actually talking to Joseph, just thinking aloud. Before he could close out the thoughts, he pictured Joanna's face, her terrified green eyes, and a surge of sour bile rose from his stomach to his throat.

He was going to rip Plott apart, piece by piece. And if Plott had harmed Joanna, he was going to take his sweet time killing the man.

When they reached the old mine, they saw a parked car with both front doors standing wide-open. The late-afternoon sunshine glinted off the windshield of Eugene Willis's dust-coated gray sedan. Joseph slammed on the brakes of his patrol car, flung open the door and jumped out. J.T. swallowed the bitter juice coating his mouth and got out on the passenger side, then looked up toward the old, abandoned mine.

''Is there another way out of there?'' J.T. asked.

''Yeah, around on the back side.''

''Then it's possible Plott could try to escape that way.''

''He won't know about the back entrance, and it could take him hours, maybe days to find it,'' Joseph said. ''Besides, where's he going to go? I told you, there's only one way out of this canyon, unless the guy can climb better than a mountain goat.''

''We'll need some sort of light.'' J.T. checked his gun.

Joseph stared at his cousin. ''I've got a couple of flashlights and I'm sure they—'' he nodded toward the men getting out of the truck "—will have one or two if we need them."

"I want you to show me the way into the back of the mine. I'm going in alone. Understand?" J.T. waited for a reply, but Joseph only nodded agreement. "If you can keep him distracted from this side, I should have a good chance of sneaking up on him."

J.T. knew that this could be their only hope of getting Joanna away from Plott—alive!

Chapter 16

Joanna's eyes had become accustomed to the partial darkness and the eerie silence inside the old mine. Thankfully, Plott hadn't taken them very far inside. She could still see glimmers of sunlight toward the entrance. She lay quietly on the ground where Plott had tossed her, humming softly to herself.

If she thought she had a chance of escaping, she would try to crawl. But she'd never make it past Plott to get to the entrance, and if she tried to go in the opposite direction, she would be lost in total darkness.

Plott gazed around, turning his head from side to side. "Isn't this an appropriate place to die? Almost like being in a grave already, isn't it?"

Joanna shuddered at the thought. Was she really going to die like this? Wasn't there anything she could do to save herself?

Plott shone Eugene Willis's flashlight up, down and around, then dropped to his knees beside Joanna. She didn't move a muscle, didn't even breathe for several seconds. He laid the flashlight on the ground, within arm's reach.

"I'm going to untie you, baby doll, so we can have a little fun before I decide exactly how I'm going to kill you."

When he reached for her, Joanna scooted away from him. He threw back his head and laughed, then grabbed her by the feet and hauled her up and under him, straddling her hips.

"I want you to be free to fight me the way you tried to do the last time we played. Remember?" Lifting himself off her, he pivoted around until he faced her feet. "I'll never forget how much fun I had that night at your apartment. I bet you won't ever forget, either. Not as long as you live." Reaching down, he began untying her ankles.

His diabolical laughter echoed off the rock walls. Joanna raised her arms, aimed her bound hands and pounded Plott on his head and back. Twisting his body around enough to knock her hands away from him, he leaned backward and slapped her across the face. Then, after kicking the loosened strands of her ripped blouse away from her feet, he rubbed his hands up and down her legs.

Joanna shuddered. She couldn't bear for him to touch her intimately that way. She would much rather he beat her. The physical abuse didn't hurt her nearly as much as his sexual caresses. But his caresses weren't truly sexual. She understood that, now better than ever before. Plott's every touch, whether he was beating her or caressing her, was a form of brutalizing manipulation. To him it was all a matter of power.

Plott stood, removed Eugene Willis's suit coat and tossed it on the ground. Joanna glared up at him, seeing only his dark, shadowy outline as he loosened the shoulder holster, took it off and laid it down beside the flashlight. Joanna's eyes focused on the gun. She swallowed. If there was some way she could get hold of that gun...

Unbuckling his belt, Plott lowered himself back down, straddling Joanna's hips again. When he touched her cheek, she spat on him. He laughed, and the sound made her want to scream.

"So much to do," he said, "and so little time to truly enjoy ourselves."

He unbuttoned her jeans. She bucked upward, trying to throw him off, then lifted her arms and brought them down against his chest. Grabbing her wrists, he flung her arms over her head and spread himself out on top of her. He insinuated one hand between their bodies and slid it between her thighs.

"Just think, baby doll, your last moments are going to be spent with me on top of you. My face is the last one you'll see. What I've done to you will be the last thing you remember."

"No!" she screamed. Her adamant denial echoed in the empty caverns of the abandoned mine.

J.T. heard her scream at the same moment he saw the beam of light. A flashlight lying on the ground! All he wanted to do was go flying toward the sound of her terrified voice, but he stopped dead still and listened to his gut instincts and to his years of professional training. He checked his gun.

He had to take Plott unaware. It was the only way. Suddenly J.T. heard the rumble of men's voices. What the hell? Then he realized the sound wasn't people talking, but a distinct, synchronized chanting in a language with which he had recently become reacquainted. Why were they chanting? What purpose did it serve other than to alert Plott of their presence?

The rhythmic thumping of what sounded like a drum blended with the voices. A picture of men painted and ready for battle sprang into his mind.

Realization dawned on J.T. Damn, but Joseph Ornelas was a wily fox. The chanting and drumming would not only draw Plott's attention, they just might spook him. This was J.T.'s chance to strike. He had to act quickly and silently.

Listening, Lenny Plott lifted his head, turned left, right and left again. "Do you hear that?"

Joanna heard the chanting and the drumbeat. "They've found us. J.T. isn't alone. You'll never get away, now."

"Shut up! I need to think."

"Do you have any idea what they're going to do to you if you kill me?" Joanna wanted to cry out, to tell J.T. to come for her now, that she couldn't bear being trapped like this another minute. But she would not allow herself to panic.

"I said shut up!" Lenny grabbed her by the wrist, jumped to his feet and jerked her up beside him. "We'll go deeper into the mine. If they try to come after us, I'll be able to kill a few of them before they get me."

He bent over, clutched the 9-mm in one hand and picked up the flashlight with the other. Joanna jumped on top of his back, the sudden impact knocking him flat on his face. Even with her wrists bound, she tried to grab the gun out of his hand. Before she could reach it, Lenny threw her off him and moved a couple of feet away from her.

"You just don't know when to quit, do you, baby doll?" Standing, he aimed the gun at her and grinned. "Maybe I'll use all my bullets on you before those savages come in here and rip me apart. I can make your dying a slow, painful ordeal."

Joanna simultaneously heard the feral growl and saw the huge shadowy form of a man behind Lenny Plott. She sucked in her breath. J.T.! She bit down on her bottom lip to keep from crying out to him.

With the 9-mm in his hand, Plott spun around and faced J.T. The two men stared at each other for a split second in the semidarkness.

J.T. glanced down quickly at Joanna lying at Plott's side, directly below his hand that held the semiautomatic. Could he shoot Plott and put him out of commission before Plott could shoot Joanna?

Plott spread out his leg until his calf touched Joanna's shoulder. "Shooting me won't save her life." He pointed the gun squarely at Joanna's head, then smiled at J.T.

The moment Plott directed his attention on J.T., Joanna scooted slowly backward, inching her hips across the smooth rock surface. Plott glanced in her direction, then jerked around toward her. J.T. flung himself at Plott, knocking him over. The two rolled around on the ground, both men holding on to their weapons. Joanna scrambled to her feet and backed up out of the way. Lifting her bound wrists to her mouth, she bit into the silk material and began pulling on the tight knot.

She glanced up from her task and saw two forms rise to their feet. She heard fists striking flesh, grunts, groans and curses, then the rattle of metal hitting the rock wall, then another loud clank as something hit the ground. An ear-splitting gunshot echoed in the darkness.

Neither man slumped to the ground. She had no way of knowing whether one of them had been hit or whose gun had been fired.

She watched the two figures continuing their struggle, moving farther and farther back inside the tunnel and away from her. Giving a final tug on the silk knot, she managed to loosen the binding completely, and slipped her hands free.

Bending over, she picked up the flashlight Plott had brought into the mine with them. She pointed the beam inside the mine, but J.T. and Plott were almost out of sight. She shone the light all around over the ground, looking for one of the guns. When the light reflected off the barrel of J.T.'s 9-mm Glock, she ran over and picked it up, gripping it firmly in her hand.

Using the dim glow from the flashlight to guide her, Joanna headed back inside the mine. She saw J.T. throw Plott against a wooden support beam. If only she were closer, she could shoot.

A rumble drifted from inside the mine, then a loud crash. Joanna pointed the flashlight in the direction of the noise and saw Plott lift his fist, then suddenly stop and stare up above his head.

She shone the light toward the ceiling and screamed when she saw the heavy, rotted beams cracking. Huge, loose chunks of old timber fell, knocking both Lenny Plott and J.T. to the ground. Joanna ran toward J.T. He didn't move.

Dear God, please, don't let him die!

When she neared, she heard J.T. groan. She glanced over at Plott, who seemed to be unconscious. Kneeling over J.T., she wedged the flashlight between her breasts, sticking the handle inside her bra. Holding the gun, she laid her hand flat over it as she placed it on the ground.

"J.T.?" She turned him over on his side and saw several small rivulets of blood streaking his face.

He groaned. She wiped his sweaty, blood-smeared face with her palm and called his name again. His eyelids fluttered.

Pain shot up from her hand to her arm. She looked down at the big foot crushing her hand that held the Glock, then she glanced up at Lenny Plott who stood towering over her. She tried to hold on to the gun, but knew she had lost it the minute Plott bent over and lifted her hand. He picked up the gun. Joanna's heart beat frantically. J.T. moaned, then opened his eyes. Plott jerked Joanna up and shoved her in front of him. She clutched the flashlight that she'd stuck between her breasts.

What was Plott going to do? Would he shoot her and then J.T.? Was there any way she could stop him? What if she hit him in the head with the flashlight? She might not be able to strike, but even if she did, the blow probably wouldn't stun him.

"Let her go, Plott." J.T. struggled to lift his head.

"You're in no position to bargain," Lenny said.

A rifle shot hit the wall behind Plott's head, sending shattered pieces of rock crashing down onto the ground. "But I am." Joseph Ornelas's deep voice echoed in the stillness of the dark mine.

"I'll kill her!" Plott yelled. "Whoever the hell you are, stay back or I'll put a bullet in her head right this minute."

"Do what he says," J.T. shouted.

"Yeah, you'd better listen to your friend."

Using Joanna as a shield, Plott backed farther into the mine. Taking her one free hand, Joanna reached inside her bra, pulled out the flashlight and tossed it toward J.T. Plott cursed her, but didn't stop moving, backing farther and farther into the darkness.

J.T. rose to his knees, grabbed the flashlight and stumbled to his feet. He pointed the beam toward the mine entrance where Joseph Ornelas stood waiting. He motioned the other man to come on inside, then turned and followed Plott deeper into the mine.

Joanna knew she wasn't going to die without putting up a fight. Turning on her assailant in the darkness, she jerked out of his grasp and pelted him with her fists. He reached for her, but she escaped his grasp. He grabbed her arm. She cried out as his fingers bruised her flesh.

He jerked her toward him. She shoved against his chest, pushing him with every ounce of her strength, but he held on to her arm as he staggered backward. He screamed when the ground disappeared beneath his feet and continued screaming as he dropped straight down into an open shaft, dragging Joanna with him, but unable to keep his hold on her wrist.

When she realized what was happening, Joanna reached out, praying for something—anything—to grab on to to stop her deadly fall. She clutched a jutting piece of timber sticking out from the rock wall.

Plott's scream ended when his body hit the bottom of the deep shaft.

With her feet dangling over the precipice, Joanna struggled to hold on to the edge of the wooden beam with both hands. J.T. thrust the flashlight into Joseph's hand, fell to his knees and called out to Joanna.

Joseph flashed the light over the edge of the shaft. Joanna gazed up at J.T., her eyes wide, her mouth trembling. The tight emotion-formed knots in J.T.'s stomach constricted painfully. One wrong move on his part and Joanna would fall to her death.

"Hang on, honey. I'm going to pull you up."

Lying flat on his stomach, J.T. leaned over the shaft and stretched out one hand. Instantly he realized he couldn't reach her.

"You're going to have to give me your hand," he told her. "Just reach up to me with one hand."

"No! I can't! If—if I let go, I'll fall." Sweat dampened her palms. The wooden beam felt moist. What if her hands slipped off? What if she couldn't continue holding on?

"You won't fall, honey. I'm right here. See how close I am—" He wiggled the fingers of his right hand. "See how easy it'll be to just reach out to me."

What if she let go and lifted her hand to him and he still couldn't reach her? What if he caught her hand and couldn't hold on to her? "I can't, J.T. I can't. Please, think of something else. I just can't let go."

"She's scared," Joseph said. "She's not thinking straight."

"Joanna, hold on. I'll find a way to get you." J.T. looked up at Joseph. "I'm going to have to lean over farther to reach her. I need the light to see her, but I also need you to anchor me to keep me from falling into the shaft."

"No, J.T., don't risk your life," Joanna yelled. "Can't you go get a rope or—" The beam she clutched with all her might groaned, loosening just a fraction from the rock wall and sending a shower of granular sediment cascading down over her. "J.T.!"

"Give me your hand, Jo. Now!" He leaned into the shaft, stretching out his hand as far as he could. "Trust me. Believe that I can save you."

"I want to trust you, to believe."

"Lift your right hand and give it to me."

Joanna looked at his hand and saw Benjamin Greymountain's silver-and-turquoise ring on his finger. J.T. noticed the way she stared at the ring. "This was meant to be a wedding band," he told her. "Just like the one you're wearing. A symbol of a love to last a lifetime and beyond." He slammed the palm of his hand against the rock wall of the shaft. "You can't hang on much longer. If your hands slip, you're going to fall. Do you understand what I'm saying to you?"

"I know! I know!" Joanna panted, taking in short, choppy breaths. "Don't let me fall, don't let me die."

"Either give me your trust and lift your hand up to me, or I'm going to risk coming over the edge far enough to grab you."

"No! Don't! You could fall."

"Yeah, I know." He leaned over just a fraction farther.

"Don't do it," she pleaded.

"Honey, haven't you figured it out? If you don't come out of this alive, there's no reason for me to live. Either we both get out of this damned mine together or we die down there together. It's your choice."

J.T. held his breath. Joanna closed her eyes. She couldn't let J.T. risk his life any more than he already had. Her only chance to save him and maybe save herself, too, was to put her complete trust in him, to truly believe that he could save her.

She eased her right hand to the edge of the wooden beam, released it and shot her arm straight up. J.T. clasped her wrist, tugging her upward.

"That's it, honey."

Letting go of the beam completely, she gave herself over to J.T.'s strength as he lifted her up and out of the shaft. With both of them on their knees, J.T. hauled her up against him, hugging her fiercely. Weeping, she clung to him. Tears stung his eyes.

He lifted her to her feet, then swept her up into his arms. "It's over," he said. "And you're safe. Safe in my arms forever."

She laid her head on his shoulder and closed her eyes. "He's dead, isn't he? Really dead?"

"Yeah, he's about as dead as a man can get." Joseph shone the flashlight down into the shaft where Lenny Plott had fallen. "If you want to be sure, take a look," he said. "But I warn you, it's not a pretty sight."

"You don't have to look at him if you'd rather not," J.T. told her.

"I want to see," she said. "I need to see him dead."

Held securely in J.T.'s strong arms, she peered over the edge of the shaft. The flashlight illuminated just a fraction of the deep shaft, but enough for Joanna to see the lower half of Lenny Plott's lifeless body impaled on a sharp, jagged rock formation. She shuddered.

"My God!" Joanna gasped.

"Yeah." Joseph nodded. "I'd say the Great Spirit had a hand in Plott's demise."

"I'm getting you out of here," J.T. said. "The sooner we put all of this behind us, the better."

Joanna clung to J.T., rejoicing in their being alive, as he carried her out of the mine and into the light. Squinting against the glare of the late-afternoon sun, she stared at the Navajo men waiting in a straight line just outside the mine entrance.

J.T. carried her to the patrol car, opened the back door and slid inside, holding her in his arms. "After we get you thoroughly checked over at the clinic, we'll stay tonight on the reservation at my mother's house," J.T. said. "I'm sure the FBI will want to question all of us. But tomorrow, I'm going to take you home, back to my ranch. And as soon as you and Elena can do whatever you women do to plan a wedding, we're getting married."

"What?" Joanna gazed at him in disbelief.

He looked at her dirty, tear-streaked face and knew that no power on earth or in heaven would keep them apart. If Benjamin Greymountain had loved Annabelle as much as J.T. loved Joanna, the man would have found a way to keep her. Maybe their ancestors hadn't been able to fulfill the promise of their love, but J.T. intended to make sure he and Joanna reaped all the benefits from this once-in-a-lifetime love they shared.

"We're getting married as soon as possible," he said.

"Is that what you call a proposal?"

"It's all you'll get from me." With a shaky hand, he reached out and touched her beautiful face. "I'm not much of a romantic, honey, but you already know that. And I won't be much of a bargain as a husband, but I have a feeling you'll whip me into shape without too much trouble. Heck, by the time we have kids, I'll probably be downright domesticated.''

"J.T. Blackwood, you are without a doubt the most irritating, infuriating—''

"Should I take that to mean you'll marry me?''

Joseph pecked on the window. J.T. motioned him away. Joseph opened the car door, stuck his head in, propped his booted foot inside and held up his cellular phone.

"I just talked to my sister, and I thought you'd like to know that Eddie's going to be fine. Or at least he will be until Kate takes a switch to his skinny little legs.''

"I doubt she'll have the heart to whip him," Joanna said. "I know that if he were mine, I wouldn't.''

"Maybe this has taught him not to go off alone again.'' J.T. motioned with the side of his head, indicating for Joseph to get lost. Removing his foot, Joseph stepped back and closed the door. Smiling, he turned around to wait for the helicopter carrying Dane Carmichael to land.

"I can think of only one thing I'd rather have from you than a marriage proposal.'' Joanna kissed J.T.'s lips softly, her breath mingling with his.

"Name it and it's yours.''

"Don't agree too hastily," she told him. "This might be something you can't give me.''

"You'll never know until you ask.''

"All right.'' She lifted her head from his shoulder and looked directly at him. "More than anything, I'd like to have a declaration of love from you.''

"A what?''

"A declaration of—''

"Yeah, I heard you.'' Shaking his head, he grunted. "During the past few hours I've said it over and over again. 'I love Joanna. I love her more than anything on earth. I love her so much it hurts. I never thought it possible to love anyone the way I love her. If she dies, I don't want to live.' I've said it to myself so many times, I guess I just forgot that I hadn't told you.''

"I think you just did."

He lifted her right hand in his, interlocking their fingers. They both glanced down at their matching rings.

"Yeah, I guess I did." J.T. looked at her with longing. "*Ayóí óosh'ni,* Joanna." And this time he knew exactly what the words meant. *I love you.*

Cupping the back of her head in his hand, he covered her mouth with his, claiming her, possessing her, telling her more eloquently than words ever could what was in his heart.

Joanna thought she heard the sound of drums, way off in the distance. Just a faint echo, as if the sound had traveled a span of decades to reach this moment in time.

Epilogue

Richmond, Virginia
June 1965

I *shall soon join my beloved Benjamin. The years that have separated us will vanish. Not one day has passed that I have not thought of him, yearned for him, loved him beyond all reasoning. Although our time together was so brief, I would not give up one precious, stolen moment for a lifetime with any other man. I have lived my life in the only way I knew how. Benjamin understood that I could not desert my sons. And once the boys were grown, Benjamin was gone. If I have but one regret, it is that Benjamin and I did not have a child. A child would have made our love immortal.*

Joanna wiped the tears from her eyes. Glancing down at the last entry in Annabelle Beaumont's diary, she traced her great-grandmother's handwriting with the tips of her fingers. There, beneath the final entry, Annabelle had neatly penned a stanza from her favorite Christina Rossetti poem.

Yet come to me in dreams, that I may live
My very life again though cold in death:
Come back to me in dreams that I may give
Pulse for pulse, breath for breath:
Speak low, lean low,
As long ago, my love, how long ago?

Joanna closed the diary and placed it inside her desk, then, one by one, she turned out the lights in the living room of the new house she and J.T. had built shortly after their wedding seven years ago. Hesitating briefly in front of the fireplace, she looked up over the mantel at her most recently completed portrait—an oil painting of her three children, which she had hung between her prized portraits of her great-grandmother and J.T.'s great-grandfather.

These three strong, healthy offspring of hers and J.T.'s were the true legacy of love, one they knew in their hearts they shared with their ancestors.

Six-year-old John Thomas, with his black hair, green eyes and tall, sturdy body already taking on the long, lean proportions of his father's, was their firstborn. The twins, Annabelle and Benjamin, had just turned three last week, and still possessed chubby toddler forms. A riot of red curls circled their little brown faces, which possessed their father's strong Navajo features.

Joanna flipped off the last lamp, walked down the hallway and stopped by John Thomas's bedroom, peeping in on him. Her heart always caught in her throat whenever she looked at him. He was so beautiful, so absolutely perfect. She went on to the next door, stopped and walked into her twins' bedroom. In a few more years, they'd want separate rooms, but for now they were happy being together twenty-four hours a day.

Her precious little Annabelle and Benjamin. Born of a love that would live forever. She pulled up the blanket Annabelle had kicked to the foot of her bed. She'd been a restless sleeper since infancy. Occasionally, Joanna would find her completely turned around in her bed, with her feet resting on the headboard.

Joanna tiptoed out of the twins' room and down the hallway. Opening the door to the master suite, she deliberately ignored J.T., who lay stretched out naked in the middle of the bed. She slipped off her silk robe, letting it puddle around her feet, then reached out and picked up J.T.'s tan Stetson from the dresser where he'd placed it. She set it on her head, turned around and put her hands on her hips.

J.T. sat up in bed, bracing his back against the headboard and crossing his arms behind his head.

"Howdy, partner." Joanna swung her naked hips provocatively as she walked to the foot of the huge four-poster bed. "Want to play cowgirl and Indian?"

J.T. grinned. "I might, if I like the rules of the game."

"The rules are very simple," Joanna said, taking off the Stetson and holding it in her hand. "The first part of the game is ringtoss. If I can circle the object of my choice with this cowboy hat, I win a free ride."

"And if you lose?"

"Then you get to tie me to a stake and set me on fire."

J.T. blew out a deep breath, lifted his hips up off the bed and laughed. "What the hell are you waiting for, woman? Toss that hat!"

Joanna sized him up, taking note of every inch of his masculine beauty laid out before her in naked splendor. She swung the Stetson around and around on her finger, lifted it and whirled it through the air. It landed right on target, sitting up straight over his arousal.

"Looks like you win, honey." He held open his arms. "Come get your free ride."

Joanna crawled onto the bed, lifted the Stetson, tossed it to the floor and circled J.T. with her hand. He groaned deep in his throat.

"You'd think after seven years of riding, I'd have you broken in by now." She licked him intimately.

J.T. grabbed her by the shoulders and lifted her on top of him. Joanna giggled, then sighed when he placed her over his erection and eased himself into her body.

"Ride 'em, cowgirl," he said.

And she did.

* * * * *

▼INTIMATE MOMENTS®
™ Silhouette®

COMING NEXT MONTH

MILLION DOLLAR SWEEPSTAKES
AND EXTRA BONUS PRIZE DRAWING

As seen on TV!
Free Gift Offer

With a Free Gift proof-of-purchase from any Silhouette® book, you can receive a beautiful cubic zirconia pendant.

This gorgeous marquise-shaped stone is a genuine cubic zirconia—accented by an 18" gold tone necklace.

(Approximate retail value $19.95)

Send for yours today...
compliments of 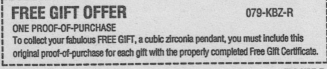 *Silhouette*®

To receive your free gift, a cubic zirconia pendant, send us one original proof-of-purchase, photocopies not accepted, from the back of any Silhouette Romance™, Silhouette Desire®, Silhouette Special Edition®, Silhouette Intimate Moments® or Silhouette Shadows™ title available in February, March or April at your favorite retail outlet, together with the Free Gift Certificate, plus a check or money order for $1.75 U.S./$2.25 CAN. (do not send cash) to cover postage and handling, payable to Silhouette Free Gift Offer. We will send you the specified gift. Allow 6 to 8 weeks for delivery. Offer good until April 30, 1996 or while quantities last. Offer valid in the U.S. and Canada only.

Free Gift Certificate

Name: _____

Address: _____

City: _____ State/Province: _____ Zip/Postal Code: _____

Mail this certificate, one proof-of-purchase and a check or money order for postage and handling to: SILHOUETTE FREE GIFT OFFER 1996. In the U.S.: 3010 Walden Avenue, P.O. Box 9057, Buffalo NY 14269-9057. In Canada: P.O. Box 622, Fort Erie,

---

FREE GIFT OFFER   079-KBZ-R
ONE PROOF-OF-PURCHASE
To collect your fabulous FREE GIFT, a cubic zirconia pendant, you must include this original proof-of-purchase for each gift with the properly completed Free Gift Certificate.

079-KBZ-R

is on its way
in April, May and June 1996!

Join us for the celebration of Desire's 1000th book! We'll have

- Book #1000, *Man of Ice* by Diana Palmer in May!
- Best-loved miniseries such as **Hawk's Way** by Joan Johnston, and **Daughters of Texas** by Annette Broadrick
- Fabulous new writers in our Debut author program, where you can collect <u>double</u> Pages and Privileges Proofs of Purchase

Plus you can enter our exciting Sweepstakes for a chance to win a beautiful piece of original Silhouette Desire cover art or one of many autographed Silhouette Desire books!

SILHOUETTE DESIRE'S CELEBRATION 1000
...because the best is yet to come!

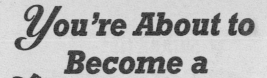

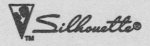